DISCOVER LOVE

SAINTS PROTECTION & INVESTIGATIONS SERIES

By

Maryann Jordan

Discover Love (Saints Protection & Investigation Series)
Copyright © 2017 Maryann Jordan
Print Edition

Cover Design by: Becky McGraw
Editor: Shannon Brandee Eversoll
Cover Photographer: Eric McKinney, 6:12 Photography

ISBN: 978-0-9975538-6-4

DEDICATION

For many young girls, it is very hard to be smart—there can still be a backlash against a woman using her brains. I raised two highly intelligent daughters, one now has a doctorate in veterinarian medicine and the other is an engineer. And I remember how difficult middle school, high school, and college could be at times for them. So this book is dedicated to the women who rise above the taunts that women should not use their brains. Ladies...go for it!

ACKNOWLEDGEMENTS

First and foremost, I have to thank my husband, Michael. Always believing in me and wanting me to pursue my dreams, this book would not be possible without his support. To my daughters, MaryBeth and Nicole, I taught you to follow your dreams and now it is time for me to take my own advice. You two are my inspiration.

My best friend, Tammie, who for twenty years has been with me through thick and thin. You've filled the role of confidant, supporter, and sister.

My dear friend, Myckel Anne, who keeps me on track, keeps me grounded, and most of all – keeps my secrets. Thank you for not only being my proofreader, but my friend.

Going from blogger to author has allowed me to have the friendship and advice of several wonderful authors who always answered my questions, helped me over rough spots, and cheered me on. To Kristine Raymond, you gave me the green light when I wondered if I was crazy and you never let me give up. MJ Nightingale and Andrea Michelle – you two have made a huge impact on my life. EJ Shorthall, Victoria Brock, Jen Andrews, Andrea Long, A.d. Ellis, ML Steinbrunn,

Sandee Love, thank you from the bottom of my heart.

My beta readers kept me sane, cheered me on, found all my silly errors, and often helped me understand my characters through their eyes.

Shannon Brandee Eversoll as my editor and Myckel Anne Phillips as my proofreader gave their time and talents to making Discover Love as well written as it can be.

My street team, Jordan's Jewels, you all are amazing! You volunteer your time to promote my books and I cannot thank you enough! I hope you will stay with me, because I have lots more stories inside, just waiting to be written!

My Personal Assistant Barbara Martoncik and Business Assistant Myckel Anne Phillips, are the two women keep me going when I feel overwhelmed and I am so grateful for not only their assistance, but their friendship.

Andrea Michelle of Artistry in Design has now created all of my covers and she is amazing at taking my vision and creating a reality. Eric McKinney, my photographer, and his wonderful models, grace my covers.

Most importantly, thank you readers. You allow me into your home for a few hours as you disappear into my characters and you support me as I follow my indie author dreams.

CHAPTER 1

N ERD. SMARTY PANTS. Teacher's pet. Brainy.

Twelve-year-old Luke Costas had heard them all before...and worse. And now, for every taunt, he kicked harder. Punched harder. Sweat poured off his lean, but muscular, body as he continued to pound his opponent.

He may be older than me...bigger than me...stronger than me...but I can take him. Just then Luke saw an opening and went for it, taking down Chris, his neighbor.

Chris jumped up, a huge grin on his face. "Way to go, Luke. Way to get in there!"

Feeling Chris clap him on the shoulder, he looked up and grinned. It was the first time the karate move worked on his neighbor...his mentor...his friend. Chris was as unlike his parents as he could be. Muscular. Rode a motorcycle. Owned a custom motorcycle shop. He even had cool tattoos, something Luke knew his dad would never have.

They continued to work out on the mat in Chris' garage for a while longer before Chris' wife, Tina, stepped out of the door leading into their kitchen, calling out, "Chris, honey, can you get the grill going?" Her eyes landed on Luke and she smiled, offering to let him stay for supper as well.

Ducking his head at first, he grinned shyly up at her, and said, "Thanks, Miss Tina, but I need to get home." As she went back into the house, he turned his attention to Chris as the two moved the mats to one side of the garage and stacked them. "I really appreciate your help," he said, hoping the desperate eagerness did not show in his voice.

Chris grinned as he appraised the boy-man in front of him. When he and his wife first moved into the neighborhood, they quickly became concerned about their neighbors, but eventually realized they were not neglectful parents. Just absentminded. And Luke desperately needed someone to teach him the things he would not learn at school or from his father. Stepping over, he resisted the urge to ruffle his hand through Luke's hair, knowing the young man was approaching the age where that gesture would not be appreciated. That thought led to the realization that he might be the one to teach Luke about women...how to appreciate them, care for them...love them. With a shake of his head, he just fist-bumped Luke and said, "See you tomorrow."

As Luke jogged across the yard to his house, passing his parents' old station wagon, he hoped his mother had been to the grocery store.

The family room sat empty as usual, the television gaining dust unless Luke wiped it off. Moving into the eat-in kitchen, he noticed it was deserted as well. Opening the pantry, he found the store-bought cookies that brought a smile to his lips. *Good. Mom must have made it to the grocery.*

Glancing into his parents' study, which had been a dining room with the former owners, he saw both parents hunkered over the open books on their desks. The room was littered with old documents, books, and papers that covered the shelves, desks, chairs, and even the floor. Corban and Phoebe Costas taught at the University, devoting their studies to ancient Greece—the language, the history, the lives of those from centuries ago.

"Hi, mom. Hi, dad," Luke called out, not expecting a response. When they were bent over the ancient texts, little penetrated—especially not when their heads were buried in their work.

His mother finally wandered out of her office and as soon as she laid eyes on her only child, her face brightened into a smile. Her short hair was swept back from her make-up free face and an ever-present pencil was tucked on her ear.

"Luke, I didn't hear you come in," she greeted, moving to the refrigerator. Opening the door, she stared inside for a long moment as though searching for the meaning of life.

"Mom, nothing's gonna jump out at you."

Glancing over her shoulder, she grinned. "Yes, well, I can always hope, can't I?" Turning back, she said, "Hot dogs with mac n' cheese?"

Hiding his sigh, Luke nodded. "Sure mom. That'll be great." He thought of the meals some of his friends boasted about...all home-cooked, including desserts. Still munching on his cookie, he hopped up on the stool at the kitchen counter.

"How was your day?" she asked, her gaze moving between his face and the study door.

"Luke!" his father greeted affectionately, walking into the room before immediately turning to his wife. "I think I've found the translation we need. I'm sure it's a combination of ancient Greek and Aramaic Hebrew."

His mother straightened at the refrigerator, the forgotten hot dog package still in her hands. "Are you sure?"

Pushing his thick glasses up on his nose, he pursed his lips. "Well, not for sure...but if you come see what I've discovered, I think we may have something before the next symposium. Want to take a look?"

The hot dog package landed on the counter as Phoebe rushed after her husband, back into the study.

Luke watched them leave, a sigh escaping as he moved toward the counter to fix the hot dogs. As he stood at the sink, he heard a noise from next door. Glancing out the window, he saw Chris at his grill. With a grin, he grabbed the hot dogs and ran outside.

"Chris!" he called out.

"Hey, Luke, you back so soon?" the friendly greeting met him. Looking down at the package in Luke's hands, he shook his head. "Your folks hard at work again?"

Stopping in front of Chris, Luke looked down at his shoes. "Yeah," he said dejectedly. "I thought you might like some hot dogs and I don't mind sharing if you don't mind them cooking on your grill."

Patting Luke's shoulder, Chris nodded. "No problem, buddy." Adding the hot dogs to his own fare, he jerked his head toward the lawn chairs. "Got some time to kill?"

Luke loved talking to his neighbor—he never felt judged even though Luke knew he was a nerd and Chris was definitely not. "Sure."

"So tell me about school," Chris said, after they settled into their seats.

Heaving a sigh, Luke twisted his face into a grimace. "I like school. I like learning. But I hate being called a nerd."

"Yeah, I used to hate being called that too," Chris acknowledged, earning a sharp glance from Luke. Chuckling, Chris continued, "I didn't always look like this. I was the skinny kid who always loved to read, but got made fun of a lot."

Eyes wide, Luke stared, unable to picture the massive man in front of him the way he described.

Leaning forward, his forearms on his knees, Chris pierced Luke with his gaze. "There's nothing wrong with being smart. Your parents are super smart—"

"Yeah, but they're boring—"

"No buts. Now you listen to me," Chris admonished. "Your parents are right for each other, even if you think they're boring. They're connected with their love of old books...and their love for you. Your parents are smart and even though they might be a little absentminded, they're good people, right?"

Nodding, Luke agreed, so Chris kept going. "I didn't have money to go to college, but I loved to work with my hands. So, I applied my brains to what I liked to do. Just 'cause your parents like ancient languages and history, doesn't mean you have to. But you need to discover what you like and then apply your intelligence to that. No matter what it is."

"I like math. I like computers, also," Luke said, his face scrunched in thought. "I'm really good in those." Then, huffing again, he said, "But I hate being called names." Grinning, he added, "That's why I'd like to learn what you're teaching me...so I can beat up on them!"

"Kids are rough on each other," Chris agreed, "but you gotta stay true to yourself. You know, the moves I'm teaching you aren't to be used lightly. You don't use your body to go after someone unless they're coming after you."

Shoulders dropping, Luke acknowledged, "Yeah, I know."

By now, Tina had joined them in the yard, plopping down in the other empty lawn chair. Smiling at the young man, she said, "Do you know anything about St. Luke?"

Luke's gaze jumped to the pretty woman and he rolled his eyes. "Oh, believe me, I've heard it all." Rotely reciting, he said, "St. Luke was Greek and was educated in languages and was a physician. He was an apostle and a historian as well as a writer of gospels, and some even consider him to have been an artist." He grimaced at his neighbors' expressions of mirth and added, "Yeah…I was named after an ancient nerd."

Chris threw his head back in laughter at Luke's description. Tina, unable to hide her smile, giggled as well.

"You know," she said, "St. Luke is also the patron saint of students. When I was in school, I attended St. Luke's High School and our principal always told us that we needed to be the best we could be…in whatever we chose to do." The smile slipping from her face, she leaned forward in her chair capturing Luke's gaze.

"You can be anything you want to be, Luke. You're smart, sweet, strong. Own that. Live up to that. And then continue to learn and discover all that you can.

Staring at the kind woman, he watched as she stood and, with a loving touch from her husband, moved back into the house. Chris jumped up to turn the meat on the grill, leaving Luke alone with his thoughts.

Later that night, as Luke lay in bed, he listened as his parents conversed in the other room, their voices warm as they discussed the upcoming symposium. *They discovered what they were good at...and found each other. Chris was right.*

He looked up as they came in to say goodnight and tuck him in. As pre-occupied as they were at times, they always remembered to come in at bedtime. After they kissed him goodnight, he thought back to Tina's words. *I'm smart, sweet, and strong. Be that. Own that. And live up to that.*

CHAPTER 2
(SEVENTEEN YEARS LATER)

THE ATMOSPHERE AT Chuck's Bar & Grille was boisterous; even more so than the typical Saturday night at the local watering hole. The Saints occupied their usual space near the back, although it now took several tables pushed together to make room for them all.

When Jack Bryant, a former Special Forces sergeant, retired he re-created one of his last assignments, where he worked with a diverse group of men on a mission in Afghanistan. Jack discovered that the group worked coherently and without egos, making the experience a life-changing one, as well as a successful mission. It took Jack over a year to build his compound underneath his massive, luxury house on over twenty acres at the base of the Blue Ridge Mountains. Jack had recruited men from the FBI, CIA, SEALs, Special Forces, ATF, police, and DEA to create his new business—Saints Protection & Investigations.

Luke, stepping in front of his boss' pregnant wife,

grabbed the edge of the old, worn, wooden table and shifted it next to another one. "Hold on, Bethany, let us move these around." She smiled up at the soft-spoken, tall, dark-haired man, moving out of his way while he and Jack replaced the chairs around the tables.

Finally, with enough room for them all, they took their seats. Luke slid his gaze around the gathering, a smile playing about his lips. What began as eight men now included two more men as well as eight wives and fiancés. Glancing to the side, he saw Marc doing the same thing. Now, it was only he and Marc without someone special.

That thought pierced him, realizing that he wanted what the others had. Not as social as his co-workers, he wondered if that were possible. He loved his work for the Saints, having left the CIA disgusted with the red tape and cumbersome political machine. The Saints offered a unique opportunity for his specialized computer engineering skill set, without the bureaucratic bullshit the CIA was mired in.

"Whoo-eee!" came the loud call from a tiny, powerhouse of a woman behind him, jerking Luke from his musings. She was sporting her usual attire—tight jeans, tight Chuck's t-shirt, and too-tall heels. Big bust, big hair, and big heart, she balanced a large tray on her shoulders, her blue eyes twinkling at the group.

Grinning, Luke turned around to see Chuck's iconic waitress, Trudi, walking up behind him, her gaze scanning the group. They had been coming to Chuck's for over a year and Trudi mother-henned the men as well as doted on the women.

She greeted each Saint, cooing over baby pictures from Cam and Miriam and Chad and Dani, while checking on the status of the other pregnant women or those soon to be married. As she made her way around the table, she finally ended with Luke and Marc. Lifting an eyebrow, she said, "So when are the last two of you big men going to fall? Looks to me like you're gettin' behind!"

Marc, the outdoorsman of the group, placed his hand over his heart and declared, "Trudi, until I can find a woman like you, I vow to be single!"

"Hell, darlin', they broke the mold with me!" Trudi cackled, slapping Marc on the back, before casting her gaze over to Luke.

Throwing his hands up in defense, Luke proclaimed, "Just gotta find the right one."

Leaning down, she said, "Well, you need to get out more. You stay stuck behind your computers all day and probably all night!"

The group laughed knowing she was right. Luke watched her walk away after she delivered the food and his heart squeezed once more. *I'm not like the others...I've got no idea what to talk about with women...and they sure as hell have no idea what to say to me.* For a second, his parents flashed through his mind. As unlikely as they were to find mates, their shared love of ancient texts brought them together and kept them connected over the years. *So where does a computer nerd like me find someone? Another computer nerd that's just as antisocial as I am? Yeah, right!*

As his eyes moved from Trudi heading back to the kitchen, he noticed a woman at the bar staring at him, a small smile curving her lips. He quickly glanced around at his fellow Saints, obviously all with women, except for Marc, but as he turned his gaze back to the woman, she was definitely not staring at Marc.

Cocking his head to the side, he blatantly observed her, his mind categorizing her traits the way he always analyzed things. Long, black hair, hanging in a sheet down her back. Dark, almost black eyes. Jeans encasing her crossed legs, and a light blue sweater falling off one shoulder. *Definitely nice. And definitely not the type that usually looks my way.*

Seeing their pitchers of beer almost empty, he excused himself as he headed to the bar to save Trudi a trip. *Okay...to be honest, I'd like to check out the interesting and interested lady at the same time.*

Sure enough, as he approached, setting the empty pitcher on Chuck's worn bar, the woman swiveled toward him, her smile now a little shaky. *Nervous...she looks nervous.* Dark bangs hung down almost to her eyelashes, making it difficult to ascertain what her eyes looked like, but her flawless complexion and soft smile was easy to appreciate.

Before he was able to speak, a man wearing an expensive suit leaned a long arm across the woman, placing his glass on the bar while simultaneously leering down at her breasts. Noting her wide-eyed expression of surprise, Luke stood up straight, walked over to her and threw his arm around her, saying, "Hey sweetie. Sorry, I'm late."

The man looked up hastily, grumbled, then snatched his glass back and moved down the bar.

Before Luke was able to step back, the woman smiled up at him.

"Thank you…I…well…thank you."

Distracted as she bit her bottom lip, he moved his arm from her shoulders and stepped back slightly. "Well, it seemed his attention wasn't what you wanted, so I thought perhaps—"

"Oh, yes," she rushed, a blush rising from her neck upward as she glanced around.

"I'm Luke. Luke Costas." He paused, but she simply smiled back, staring at his face, offering no name in return. "And you are?"

Startling, she jumped. "Oh, I'm uh—"

"Here's your beer," Chuck called out, drawing Luke's attention back to the bar. Nodding, he moved to pick it up before turning back to the woman. Seeing her slip from her barstool, he asked, "Would you…uh…like to join my friends?"

Her eyes jerked over to the loud, boisterous Saints before reluctantly shaking her head. "No, thank you. I'm not…well, that is…uh, I actually need to be leaving."

"Early night?"

Her blush darkened as she nodded. "Yeah, something like that—"

A shout of cursing came from the pool tables as one drunken man slugged another. Before anyone could intervene a melee broke out amongst several of the patrons in the back of the bar. Luke's gaze darted to the table of Saints as they all jumped up to create a barrier between the brawl and their women.

Luke instinctively moved toward the Saints since their table was close to the back pool area. As the three largest, Bart, Cam, and Blaise, hustled to break up the fight, Luke placed himself in front of their wives. With his arms out wide, he began to herd them toward the safety of the bar.

At the same time, his gaze searched toward the bar only to witness the dark-haired beauty once more being accosted by the man in the suit. *Fuck!* Chuck, no longer guarding the bar, had leaped over with a baseball bat to subdue the miscreants in the back. Luke attempted to hurry Miriam and Faith forward while maneuvering toward the woman at the bar.

A flash of movement caught his eye as she grabbed the suited man by the hand and, with a whirl, pinned him against the bar with his arm held painfully behind him. Luke, as stunned as the man must have been, watched as she continued to push the larger man to the floor using his weight against him. With a quick glance around, she disappeared through the crowd, her wide-eyed expression full of fear.

Luke watched as she slipped through the front door. Rubbing his chin, he realized he did not even get her name. The fight, now broken up, had Chuck clearing out the rabble with Trudi shouting curses and threats of bodily harm if they ever came back.

The Saints resumed their seats as Luke made his way back to the bar for the pitchers of beer. The suited man, now climbing up from the floor, glanced nervously around. *Guess getting your ass handed to you by a much smaller woman must be a real ball buster.* Grinning at the memory, he had to admit it was the sexiest thing he had ever seen.

Walking back, he set the pitchers down in the center of the table, taking his seat in between Marc and Faith, Bart's wife.

Marc chuckled, causing Luke to turn his way, his eyebrow lifted in question.

"You strike out with that beauty at the bar when the fight started?"

Ducking his head, Luke replied, "Yeah, I guess I did. Didn't even get her name before all hell broke loose."

Clapping Luke on the shoulder, Marc said, "No worries, man. Her loss."

Appreciating the gesture, Luke nodded. *Easy for you to say. You're the big, outdoorsy type the women ogle every time we go out.*

Feeling a close presence at his side, he turned and

looked down at Faith. Bart's beautiful wife was peering up at him, the intensity in her gaze overpowering.

"I feel…I'm not sure, Luke," she said, haltingly.

He watched her carefully, noting her struggle. Faith, while not a professed seer, had a special gift and occasionally her visions and intuition assisted the Saints.

"I saw her when you were over at the bar talking to her. I felt a danger with that woman. Uncertainty. Even fear."

Luke's gaze involuntarily jumped to the door where the woman had disappeared. Opening his mouth to speak, he hesitated, not knowing what to say. His eyes found hers again, hoping she had more to give him.

He leaned over as she lifted her head to whisper, "I sense…you will meet her again. She will need you." Cocking her head to the side, she added, "And you will need her."

Before Luke had a chance to ask Faith more, she leaned into Bart who pulled his wife in closely. The group of Saints and their women continued their party, laughs and tales abounding.

As the gathering disbanded, Luke said his goodbyes and walked with the others to the parking lot. His gaze moved around the large space, wondering if he would see the woman. *She left an hour ago. What the hell do I think she's doing? Hanging out here just to tell me her name?* With a mental shake, he gave the others a wave as he drove home. Alone. As usual.

CHARLIE SLIPPED INTO the old, tiny camper van after securing her Vespa onto the back. Keeping all lights off until she secured the door and made sure the few windows were closed tightly was her first order of business. Then, and only then, did she turn on the camper light sitting on the tiny table. Taking a thorough look around, she checked to make sure there had not been any intruders while she was gone. The few tricks she learned about the placement of items in the camper had been put to use and she was sure no one entered while she was gone.

Stepping into the minuscule bathroom that consisted of a toilet, sink, and a shower overhead, she looked into the mirror. Her black hair shone under the faint light as her dark eyes took in her appearance. With a sigh, she looked skyward as her fingers nimbly took out her contacts. Placing them in the contact case, filled with solution, she carefully shut the lid before replacing it in her makeup bag.

Sliding her hand upward over her forehead and under her bangs, she removed the wig. Holding it reverently, she gave the hairpiece a little shake. Stepping out of the bathroom, she placed the wig in a drawer, next to several others. Running her long fingers through her natural hair, she massaged her scalp. *Oh, that feels good.*

Next, she stepped out of her high-heeled boots, wiggling her toes in relief. *How do women wear these killer heels?* Sneakers had always been her footwear of choice...*well, the fact that I never learned how to walk with heels on probably had something to do with that!* Slipping off her jeans, she jerked her sweater over her head. Pulling on jersey pajama bottoms and a soft camisole, she washed off the unfamiliar makeup. Looking into the mirror again, she smiled. *Yeah...that looks like me. Whoever I am now.*

Turning around, she lit the small camper stove and heated the kettle full of water. In a few minutes, she placed a hot cup of steeping tea in the sink since there was no room on the twelve inches of counter. Hearing a noise outside, she held her breath until the car passed by. Releasing the deep breath in a sigh, she sat on the bench seat, opening her laptop.

Quickly checking emails, she ascertained there was nothing of importance. *No news is good news.* She worked for an hour for her latest client, creating a few fake profiles on social media and loading them with pictures and events.

Closing that file, her fingers hesitated over the keys, fighting the urge to see if *he* was on. Shutting her eyes for a moment, she relished the sight of him. Her mind slid back to the first time she had ever seen Luke Costas.

Freshman year at MIT and I rushed toward the Engineering building, hoping I was not going to be late for the meeting. All year long, my favorite professor spoke of the previous president of Tau Beta Pi, the Engineering society…Luke Costas…and even though he had graduated, he was coming back for the society's final meeting of the year. I'd seen his picture on the wall, along with all the former presidents, and every time I passed it, I had to force myself to not stop and stare. He was beautiful. Dark hair. Firm jaw. Dark brown eyes. Distinguished and oh, so handsome.

Glancing at my phone to check the time, I tripped, stumbling over my feet. I threw my hands out to keep from smashing my face on the concrete when my body suddenly stopped moving. Suspended over the step, I felt strong hands around my waist. Twisting around to see who my savior was, my mouth hung open in surprise. Luke Costas was bent over, holding me up, keeping me from disaster. Eyes wide, I just stared. He straightened, settling my feet back onto the sidewalk.

"You okay?" he asked, his warm eyes twinkling.

Unable to speak, I nodded, sure that my face must be as red as it felt.

Chuckling, he patted my shoulder. "Watch your step next time," he advised as he headed into the building. I have no idea how long I stood rooted to the ground before my feet caught up to my brain and I rushed to the meeting. Slipping into the back of the room, I watched as he delivered the end of year speech. I heard a slight catch in his voice and wondered if he were nervous.

At the end of the meeting, he stayed down front to greet some of the students, but I headed back to my dorm, daydreams full of the handsome grad. Once inside my room, I passed by the mirror and stopped short, taking *stock of myself. Messy hair. Baggy jeans and sweatshirt. Sighing, I knew there was no way a girl like me could ever be with someone like him.*

Pushing old memories from her mind, she sipped her tea, thinking about her newer memories of seeing him that night. *I did it...I finally got up the nerve to try to see him. And not only see him in person but to actually speak to him!*

Her skills of observation and simple research came in handy. She had never worn clothing for any other purpose than to be comfortable—and certainly not to gain attention. Her hair was usually pulled back in a ponytail to keep it out of her face. Watching makeup videos gave her the skills to apply just enough to play up her features. *And it worked! He noticed me!* Her shoulders slumped as the next thought slammed into her. *Then I chickened out and practically ran to the door after kicking the jackass who was bothering me.* Acting on instinct when she felt threatened, she now realized how that must have looked. *That must have left a horrible impression!* Just the sight of Luke in person had overwhelmed her.

Tall, muscular...not as bulky as some of the men at his table, but his lean muscles spoke of strength. His dark hair was neatly trimmed and a shadow of a dark beard covered his jawline. Shaking her head, she remembered how his brown, soulful eyes had stared right at her and, unlike the leers from the other man at the bar, his eyes had seemed...*kind. Understanding.* Giving a rude snort, she thought *Yeah, right. He's got no clue. Leaning her head back for a moment, she sighed heavily once more. If only*—

Just then her computer alert sounded, letting her know he was on, and her gaze jumped back to her monitor as a smile curved her lips.

CHAPTER 3

S LEEP DID NOT come. Tossing and turning did not help. Nor had the tried and true sleep inducer of running software codes in his mind. Finally, throwing back the covers, Luke swung his long legs out of bed and padded toward the kitchen. His house was small, one level, in an older neighborhood. Eschewing the large lots of wooded land that several of his friends had bought, he preferred the simplicity of the older house.

His neighborhood was filled with mostly retired couples, plus a few younger ones with small children. He fell in love with the location of his house at the end of the cul-de-sac. He enjoyed privacy, a large yard, and the three-bedroom house fit his lifestyle perfectly. One of the bedrooms was set up as an office. *Well, the office of a computer engineer.* It was filled with computer equipment, security equipment, and books. He spent most of his waking hours either at the Saints compound at his desk or in his study at home.

Looking at the clock on the microwave, he knew if he had any chance of getting to sleep he had to avoid making a cup of coffee. Sighing, he filled a glass with milk and set it in the microwave to heat. Glancing at his neglected, complicated coffee maker, banished to the corner of the counter, he longed for his younger days when he could work on little sleep and high-octane caffeine. *Damn ulcer. Well, the doc said my pain was the beginnings of an ulcer.* Rubbing his forehead, he pulled the heated milk out and moved to the living room to settle on the sofa with his laptop.

Jack had asked for some specific intelligence to be gathered for the meeting tomorrow—*well, now later today*—and Luke had already completed the task. Deciding to look it over, he fired up his secure system.

Glad to be out of the CIA's political quagmire, he relished the freedom he had with the Saints. And their friendship…even if a few of their women continued to hint that he and Marc needed to settle down.

Thinking of Marc, he chuckled out loud. *Mr. Out-doorsman probably has some woman off in a tent somewhere.* Slightly in awe of his friend, the comparison of Marc with his childhood neighbor, Chris, struck him. Smart, tenacious, and loved to work with their hands.

Without his contacts in, he grabbed his glasses off the end table to stare at his computer. A ping indicated an incoming message. Looking down, he smiled.

You're up late.

His mystery cyber-friend. He knew the moniker sounded dumb, but he had no other way to describe them. Old, young, male, female—he had no idea.

Months prior, investigating a complicated case, he had been contacted by someone with the ability to see what he was working on and had offered assistance. At first, furious that someone was hacking into what he considered to be an "unhackable" account, he realized the help they offered truly assisted them in solving the case. Since that time, they offered information on several occasions.

Never identifying themselves for security reasons, nonetheless, Luke considered them a friend...*albeit an anonymous, I'll-probably-never-meet-them-in-real-life kind of friend!* And he knew they were talented, if for no other reason than the untraceable account they messaged from.

Can't sleep. You? he typed.

After a pause, the reply came back. **I never sleep much. Too many things go through my mind.**

Same here, he answered.

Luke had no idea what the mystery friend worked on, but hoped it was legal. Mafia, drug cartels, and terrorists all recruited heavily from the computer geniuses graduating, targeting the ones with few friends, few social contacts, and who worked from home. These young computer analysts or engineers were often easy pickings for the unscrupulous underworld. *How is it possible that in only a couple of months of nothing but emails and messages, this person has become important to me?* After a long pause in which Luke began to think they were not going to send any more messages, another one came in.

I might need you soon.

Staring at the screen, his heart thumped audibly. His fingers hovered over the keys, unable to think of how to respond. In all the times his mystery friend contacted him, they never indicated needing anything.

Decision made, his fingers flew over the keyboard. **Anytime. Anything.**

Danger is all around. The ones I trusted may not be real. You may be the only real one I know.

Luke, drawn in, did not hesitate to respond. **You can trust me. I'm real.**

A long pause on the other end caused him to hold his breath. *Come on...answer.*

I know you are. I'll let you know if I need you.

Again—anytime, anything.

Thank you. Really...thank you.

With that, Luke knew the conversation was over. He did not bother to attempt to find where the location was of the mystery friend. *It's not necessary...they'll let me know if they want me.* Finishing his milk, Luke rinsed the glass, putting it in the dishwasher. Wondering if sleep was any closer, he flipped off the light and headed back to the bedroom.

As he lay in bed, his mind bounced between the beauty in the bar and his mystery friend as sleep finally claimed him. Dreams of the two of them melding together filled the night.

CHARLIE STOOD UP from the table and rinsed out her teacup. She left the clean cup in the sink to dry and moved to the bench seat on the side. With a quick flip, she slid it down creating a small bed once the back cushion was lowered as well. Grabbing the neatly folded sheets and blankets, she made the bed. Sliding under the light covers, she lay listening to the outside noises of the campground. It had been so easy to obtain her living transportation. Buying the camper van from an older couple no longer traveling, they were thrilled to get rid of it, and paying cash made them even more ecstatic. Now, she was not stuck trying to find temporary housing or staying in motels as she tried to hide.

A sigh escaped her lips as she thought about her nomadic life of the past six months. *How did I get into such a mess? Eli…what the hell were you doing?* As much as she hated to drag someone else into her situation, she knew she had approached the inevitable time…*I can't do this alone anymore.* Finally closing her eyes, she drifted off to sleep. Dreams of the dark haired rescuer intermingled with the constant nightmares.

THE TEN SAINTS sat around the conference table in the compound under Jack's large, luxury log house. The empty plates, previously filled with peach pie from Jack's wife, Bethany, were pushed to the side.

"I swear you must have married Bethany for her baking," Chad said, having eaten two pieces. Known as the gentle giant of the group, his tired face spoke of the little sleep gained with a newborn baby in the house.

Jack, his eyes twinkling as he rubbed his beard, smiled, pleased with the praise for his wife's culinary skills.

"Hell, we know that's why Monty married Angel," Bart laughed, looking over at the dapper Saint. "Her cupcakes alone would make any man rush home."

"As long as I can keep her baking and not trying to solve murders, I'm happy," Monty quipped.

"Tell me about it," Patrick said, referring to both his sister, Angel, and his fiancé, Evie.

Jude looked over at Chad and Cam and commented, "You two look like shit. How much sleep are you getting?"

"Not enough," both men replied at the same time.

"Hell, in the SEALs, we'd go for a long time with no sleep," Bart bragged. "Right, Jude?"

Before Jude could respond, Cam speared his friend with a glare. "As soon as Faith has your baby next month, we'll talk about how a baby crying all night stacks up against the mighty SEALs. Until then, shut the hell up."

The group laughed good-naturedly before Jack got down to business. "We've been contacted by the FBI to look into a situation that they've started investigating as well. Of course, we no longer have Mitch to work with."

This realization produced groans from around the

table. Mitch Evans had served as the Saints FBI contact and co-investigator for most of the past year, but recently had resigned and moved back to his small hometown to become the Chief of Police. And it was no secret that his assistance, and friendship, would be sorely missed.

Nodding his agreement, Jack continued. "It seems that a whistle-blower had contacted someone at the FBI about six months ago concerning unidentifiable problems."

Bart, not taking anything at face value, looked up sharply. "Unidentifiable?"

Jack confirmed, "That's what they said. The person I've been in contact with at the FBI is the agent in charge of the investigation...Lin Wang." Looking up, he pierced the group with his stare and said, "He's also requesting a meeting face to face. I told him I would send a contingency to the Bureau in D.C. Luke you're on point."

Luke, listening to the conversation while working on the computer program, jerked as he heard his name called. Looking up sheepishly, he said, "Sorry boss. What was that?"

Grinning, Jack repeated, "You're taking point on this assignment. You'll be heading up the team going to D.C."

Eyebrows lifted, Luke stared at Jack before sliding his eyes around to the rest of the group. "Me? Boss, I've always been a behind-the-scenes kind of guy."

"No shit," barked Jude, the outgoing ex-SEAL, joining the others in good-natured laughter. He often assisted Luke on computer investigating but preferred being in the field.

"This problem has something to do with computer codes," Jack explained before leaning back in his chair, pinning Luke with his gaze. "And, quite frankly, you've got more leadership in you than I've allowed you to show. So, tag, you're it."

Shaking his head while smiling, Luke nodded, his curiosity peaked. "So what do we know?"

"The Bureau was contacted by a man named Eli Frederick about six months ago. They had little information at the time, other than he said he needed to meet with an agent to discuss a situation he had become aware of. That was all he said. According to Lin, a meeting was set up, but Eli never showed. Last week, a body was discovered by some weekend fishermen in one of the small tributaries of the Potomac River. Decomposed, it was sent to the Virginia Department of Forensic Science for identification and finally a positive ID was made from dental records. It was Eli Frederick. And there was a bullet hole in his skull."

Several *fucks* resounded from the Saints as they looked up from their tablets.

"Executed?" Cam asked. His mind shot back to his youth spent in drug gangs, where a bullet to the head was a quick way to get rid of an unwanted enemy...or someone who had been a traitor.

"They're still investigating and not turning up much about him in recent years. Seems he graduated from MIT with a degree in software engineering about six years ago and has worked privately from home since then."

"And they think he came across something that was suspicious and got him killed?" Bart asked.

Nodding, Jack confirmed, "That's the assumption they're going on, but they'll cover that more when you meet with Lin." Before the group could jump to volunteer, he added, "Luke, I want Monty with you since he knows the ins and outs of the Bureau. Marc, I've got a few security flight assignments for you to take so I won't send you to D.C. Patrick, I'm sending you with Luke and Monty. This'll get you more experience in the mission planning stage. Once they get back with their information, we'll meet to see what we need to do to unravel the mystery of the whistle-blower Eli Frederick."

The other Saints rose from the table, making their way upstairs as Marc and Jack stayed behind to discuss the assignments coming his way.

CHAPTER 4

T HE WAXED, WHITE tile floors gleamed under the bright florescent lights as Luke, Monty, and Patrick followed the security escort to the conference room. Stepping inside, Luke noted the muted, darker colors, mostly from the navy patterned carpet. The heavy wooden table in the center of the room was surrounded by navy upholstered office chairs and the framed black and white pictures of Washington D.C. nightscapes on the wall gave the room a less institutional feel.

Monty, having been a former FBI agent, smirked, "Looks like they're giving us a nice room to chat in."

The others grinned as the three Saints sat around the table waiting to meet their new contact. Punctual, Lin Wang walked into the room, stunning the Saints. A petite Asian woman, her requisite Bureau-boring navy skirt and blazer paired with a white blouse, did nothing to take away from her beauty. Her silky black hair hung in a sheet to her shoulders. Her dark eyes appeared to be assessing them from the instant she entered the room.

Walking to the other side of the table, she leaned across, greeting each man as she offered her hand.

"Gentlemen, nice to meet you. I'm Lin Wang. Thank you for coming in to meet with me today."

Quickly recovering from his surprise, Luke introduced himself, Monty, and Patrick. As they took their seats, Lin opened a file in front of her, immediately getting down to business.

"I understand you have read the preliminary report sent to Jack Bryant, so some of this will be a bit repetitive," her voice clipped sharp and clear. "Approximately six months ago, the FBI was contacted by a man who did not identify himself but said he wanted to talk to someone about a possible crime. This is not unusual...the Bureau receives dozens of calls or emails daily and most turn out to be either something that a local police department would handle or they are from delusional persons with a penchant for conspiracy theories. There was little we could do since he would not give any details. About a month later, he contacted the Bureau again and this time gave a few more details about his concerns and said his name was Eli. No last name, just Eli. And before you ask, he was untraceable from his computer."

Luke's eyebrows lifted in surprise, knowing the Bureau would have the equipment to ascertain where a call or email was coming from unless it had been deeply encrypted. His interest, already piqued, shot up even more.

Lin pushed several papers over to the Saints and gave them a chance to peruse them before she continued. "He gave enough information that time so that his request to speak to an agent was granted. Eli insisted on the location and the time, which was agreed upon. When the agent went to the meeting, he never showed."

Luke's eyes skimmed the report, his mind immediately pulling together the information. *Eli. Worked for a private company. Crimes against humans. Has proof. Evidence. Will turn it over for protection. May have others that need protection as well.*

"Was any attempt made to find him?" Luke asked, earning a grimace from Lin.

"As I'm sure former Agent Lytton can tell you," she paused, nodding toward Monty, "the Bureau had enough evidence of a crime to open a case. When he was a no-show, we went to his house and discovered he was not there, although there was blood in the kitchen. It was investigated but, without a body, it wasn't considered a murder case...only a possible missing person's case."

"And now?" Monty asked, glancing through the report in front of him.

"A body was found over a month ago by some weekend fishermen on one of the tributaries of the Potomac River. It was greatly decomposed, but it was determined to be the body of a male, in his late twenties, and it appeared death had occurred within the last year. When compared to the missing person's reports meeting those parameters, dental records were examined and a positive identification was made. The body was that of Eli Frederick."

Luke and the other Saints continued to peruse the information in the file concerning Eli Frederick. Software Engineering graduate from MIT. *My Alma Mater, graduated three years after I did,* Luke noted. Worked independently, taking private contracts. Last known address…Baltimore, Maryland.

"When we went to his home in Baltimore," Lin explained, "it was mostly empty…and wiped clean. It was evident there had been blood on the floor but whoever cleaned the place had used bleach in an attempt to eradicate the crime scene. There were a few personal effects in the bedroom closet and bathroom, but no computers. None."

Luke's gaze traveled from the files in front of him back to Lin's face. Her tight-lipped expression showed she was not happy, but he was not sure of the cause. *She's pissed to call in a private investigation firm? She's pissed because the FBI missed out on a possible case by ignoring it to begin with? Feels guilty because a man, who obviously knew something about something, is now dead?* Stifling a sigh, Luke knew he was much more comfortable with the computer aspect of investigating. *Reading people was never my strong suit!*

Relying on Monty's experience with the Bureau, he watched as Monty peppered the agent with more questions and noticed as Lin's grimace became more pronounced.

"Gentlemen," she bit out, "I'll be honest. I had no desire to bring in an outside company to assist with the investigation, but I was overruled. And, quite frankly, we are taxed to the max right now. My part of this case is to try to solve the murder of Eli Frederick. My time is limited due to also being assigned to certain security details with the Chinese Embassy." Piercing them with a cold glare, she added, "There are few agents of Asian descent, and fewer who speak Chinese, so I have now been thrust into a role there. So while I'd prefer not to have to deal with an outside investigation business, we need to know what Eli wanted to meet about. That will be your part of the equation."

"You don't think the two are interrelated? His contact with the FBI and his murder?" Luke queried.

"I'm sure they are, but it's my understanding that you have the ability to dig into his situation more than I can right now."

Nodding, Luke agreed. As the meeting came to a close, the participants stood, shaking hands as they filed out of the room. The Saints did not speak until they were out of the building. Patrick took a nonchalant walk around the car, a small piece of equipment in his hand, before he gave an almost imperceptible nod to the others.

Once inside, he reported, "No bugs."

"Monty," Luke began, "you gotta tell me what you

thought, because working with Lin will be nothing like working with Mitch."

"Mitch was special," Monty agreed, thinking back to the efficient, but easy-to-work-with agent. "This lady's got an axe to grind and I don't know what it is yet. But I intend to find out."

"What does your gut tell you?" Patrick asked. "I thought she acted like a lot of women officers in the Army...where they have to be extra tough to make sure they survive."

Nodding, Monty agreed. "It's hard, sometimes, for a woman in a predominately man's field...and the Bureau can be brutal. Still very much an old-boys-network kind of workplace. And she is right, there are precious few Asian agents."

"So she has to present the right attitude?"

"Could be. Could just be that she doesn't like working with an outside group. Could be that she's getting pressure from above to close out the case. Could have been implied that she can't handle it. Who knows?"

An hour and a half later, as they drove back into Charlestown, Luke looked at the clock on the dashboard as he told Monty to drop him off at his house. Turning onto Luke's street, the SUV swerved as Monty cursed, "Damn Vespa! They shouldn't be out here on the roads!"

"College towns are full of bikes and Vespas," Patrick commented. "It was the same in California."

Luke looked into his side view mirror, seeing a lone figure riding a small Vespa. "Must be the best way to get around for a poor college student," he surmised before his attention re-focused on the case again as Monty pulled into his driveway.

As Luke stepped out of the SUV, he turned back and said, "I'll spend this afternoon digging into Eli Frederick. Chances are, I'll get a lot further than the FBI. We can meet tomorrow at Jack's and go over what I find."

With a wave, he watched as the two Saints threw their hands up in salute before turning to head into his house.

Once inside, Luke walked into his kitchen and opened the refrigerator. *Cold pizza. Leftover lasagna. And a container of...hmmm, not sure.* Closing the door with more force than necessary, he grabbed his keys and headed back out. Within a few minutes, he sat at the counter of a local diner, thankfully almost empty since the lunch crowd had thinned.

He was almost finished gulping his burger and fries as the bell jingled over the door. A woman walked in, a riot of red curls framing her face. As she turned toward him, she smiled as she strolled by. Purple glasses, along with her curls, partially hid her face making it difficult to get a clear look at her. Wearing fitted jeans that did not appear painted on, and a green short-sleeved sweater, she sat at the counter two seats from him and ordered a cup of coffee. He watched as she slowly turned toward him, smiling once more.

Two different women...two different places...both catching my attention. Luke had no idea what was going on, but after a long time of being with the Saints, when they were single, who gained female attention quicker than he did, he was not about to pass up a rare opportunity.

"That's all you're having?" he asked, secretly hoping his words did not sound cheesy as he wiped his hands on the wadded up napkin.

A slow smile spread across the woman's face as she offered a little shrug. "Not very hungry today, but thought a little caffeine would perk me up."

He nodded, unsure of what to say next. "The pie here is pretty good, but if you really want a treat sometime with your coffee, you should try Angel's Cupcake Heaven. The owner is the wife of a co-worker and believe me, they're special."

The conversation remained stilted but continued as she drank her coffee. He knew she would soon leave and his thoughts jumped back to the raven-haired woman from Chuck's. *I let that woman walk away. Am I going to do the same thing again?* Taking an unprecedented chance, he rushed, "My name's Luke. I'd love to take you to Angel's sometime...or meet there."

Her smile appeared genuine before she glanced down at her empty coffee cup, once more the red curls hiding her face. "I...uh...well, I..."

"Here," he continued, taking a napkin and scribbling his cell phone number down onto the thin scrap of tissue. As he pushed the paper over to her, he noted her smile was still on her face. Breathing a sigh of relief, he grinned. "I won't even ask for yours...just your name. And if you ever want to try a life-changing cupcake, you can call me first and I'll meet you there."

Tucking the scrap into her oversized purse, she slid down from the stool. Glancing up at him from behind the large glasses, she nodded. "I'm—"

Just then his phone rang and he knew it was Jack. *Damn timing!* "I'm sorry, but I've got to take this call. It's my boss."

Before he had a chance to speak again, she smiled as she turned, walking quickly to the door, disappearing into the parking lot to the side of the building.

Grinning ruefully, he thought, *Well fuck. I keep losing them before I get a name.* Smiling at the waitress, he tossed down his money and headed out into the sunshine taking his call. *Time to get to work and find out who the hell Eli Frederick was and what he wanted to tell the FBI so much that it got him killed.*

CHAPTER 5

CHARLIE WALKED AROUND to the side of the diner, making sure she was out of sight. Swinging her leg over the seat of her Vespa, she left through the alley behind the restaurant and then quickly turned in the opposite direction.

Driving toward the campground, she kept a vigilant eye out for anyone who might be following her. The roads became more rural and she felt the pressure of crowded roads lessen...an emotion that made her cautious. Turning into the wooded campground, she drove along the gravel path making her way around the one-way road. Having selected the perfect spot for her camper van, she smiled as it came into view. Tucked into the woods it was near the end of the road, making it easy to pull out and escape if needed.

As she drove into the space by her camper van, she secured the Vespa on the back as usual. *Always be ready for a quick getaway* had become her motto.

Walking to the side, her gaze swept the area and found nothing but woods, squirrels scampering amongst the trees, and the sounds of a few children playing in the distance. Slipping discretely around the camper, she checked her security measures. *Another useful skill I've learned.* The unobtrusive security cameras and trip-wires were all intact. Stepping into her camper, she repeated the same steps as the other evening. Slipping off the red-haired wig and taking off the large purple-framed glasses, she once again stared into the mirror.

"What are you doing? I'm such a stalker," she stated out loud, dropping her chin to her chest. After a moment of quiet self-reflection, she knew the answer and lifted her head.

I'm sick and tired of being alone. Fighting this alone. Trying to stay alive while figuring out everything by myself. And…I just wanted to see him again. He looks so trustworthy. So capable. Who am I kidding? He's so gorgeous. She thought of how her life had changed in the last five months. The fear. The horror. And then, in the midst of it all, like a flower growing from the asphalt, she stumbled into Luke. Even if it had only been through the cyber-waves, they had formed a friendship of sorts. At least, for her.

Stepping out of the minuscule bathroom, she pulled the Glock G26 from her purse and secured it in the drawer next to the fold-down bed. Sitting down at her computer she quickly worked for a couple of hours, continuing to build a fake identity for one of her ongoing clients.

Finally, she was able to ascertain Luke was on as

well. *If anyone can help me...and find out who killed Eli...it's got to be Luke.*

BEGINNING WITH THE most basic information, Luke delved into Eli Frederick. Not trusting the FBI report, he preferred to begin from square one and peel back the layers of Eli's life, while keeping the Bureau's file next to him when he needed it for the posthumous information. He slowly created the background to the young man whose life had ended so horrifically.

The beginnings were easy to decipher. Eli Frederick was an only child of two academic parents. His school records indicated a brilliant young man but his high school social media indicated a tendency to be bullied. Taking a fortifying breath, Luke recognized much of himself in Eli's upbringing, with the exception of having someone like Chris in his life.

Eli's parents moved several times due to different jobs at various universities and Luke began to see a pattern evolve. With each move, Eli had few new friends on social media and more problems with bullying. *He not only had to contend with being the smartest, but was always the new kid on the block as well.*

Methodical, thorough...Luke poured over the information he was gleaning. His stomach growled and, glancing at the clock, he realized he had worked straight through supper. Finding a few pieces of bread and a half full jar of peanut butter, he made a sandwich and grabbed a water bottle. Stepping out onto his back patio, he watched the sun slide over the trees. Leaning back at the waist, he cracked his neck a few times before bending over.

Grabbing a cup full of seed, he walked out into his yard and filled the birdfeeders before moving back to the patio. Stretching his stiff muscles, he toyed with the idea of going for a run, but the lure of the investigation called.

Finishing his meager supper, he walked back to his desk and continued for several more hours. Finally the yawns took over and he shut everything down. Securing his home and turning out the lights, he walked by his kitchen, knowing that in the recent past he would have cranked up his coffee maker and worked long into the night. *No more,* he lamented, acknowledging that his ulcer was so much better without his high-octane caffeine.

Climbing into bed, he checked his phone before placing it on the nightstand by his bed. He wondered if the woman from the diner would actually call or text sometime. Chuckling, he remembered how many times Bart or Cam would wink at a woman at Chucks and go home with them for the night. *Well, at least before Faith and Miriam entered their lives.*

Rolling over, he punched his pillow. *I've never been very interested in getting someone for a night…but finding someone for a relationship was proving to be much harder.*

THE PATIENT SMILED up at the surgeon, Dr. Cheung, whose face was hidden behind the scrub mask. Anesthesia created a blurry, happy world and the patient was more than willing to rest comfortably.

"The pain you've been having will be alleviated," Dr. Cheung promised, nodding to the head surgical nurse. "So close your eyes, count backward from one hundred, and it will all be over soon."

Truer words were never spoken, as the patient slipped into unconsciousness and Dr. Cheung began the operation of removing the kidneys. Both of them. And then the harvesting of other organs to be delivered across the nation to needy patients with enough money to fetch them. Keeping the patient alive long enough to complete the harvesting, Dr. Cheung worked swiftly before nodding to the assistant to turn off the machines.

Turning from the bloody operating table, he walked through the surgery doors, snapping off his gloves. Standing at the sink, he scrubbed his hands methodically. A shadow approached from his left but he did not startle, confident in his security measures.

The woman's voice bit out, "I told you to take it easy. To slow down. There are those that may start looking a little closer at your business here."

Drying his hands on the towel provided to him, he tossed it into the laundry bin before turning to face the angry woman. His eyes moved over her appreciatively. Sleek black hair bobbed to her shoulders. Her oval eyes expertly made up. Her boring clothes. The same boring, institutional clothes.

She caught his eyes roaming down her body before coming back to rest on her eyes. Placing her hands on her hips, she glared. "I'm telling you, once and for all, to chill the fuck out here. Until we know what your fuck up with the computer nerd is costing us, you need to keep up with your legitimate medical business!"

"My fuck up?" he said coldly. "I'm not the one who pulled the trigger. So you'd better keep working your magic to make sure I'm safe. Because, as the American saying goes, 'If I go down, you go down with me'." Leaning back, he smiled, long and slow. "But then, only one of us has diplomatic immunity."

THE SAINTS GATHERED around the table the next morning, listening and taking notes as Luke, Monty, and Patrick discussed their meeting with their contact. The others listened carefully, especially as Lin Wang was described.

As shoulders began to slump around the table, Jack said, "Well, as competent as she is, I definitely get the feeling that the special relationship we had with the Bureau is gone now that Mitch is no longer with them."

Luke nodded while Patrick grunted. "Yeah, boss, I'd have to agree. While she seems more than capable, I got the feeling she wasn't too happy to share the investigation with us."

"If she wasn't stretched so thin, she'd have fought her superiors more about bringing us in, I think," Monty concurred.

"Well, we play the cards we're dealt," Jack declared, leaning back in his seat, his eagle eyes on Luke. "So what have you discovered?"

Luke grinned as he sent his preliminary report to their tablets. "This guy is interesting, to say the least. Just when I think I've got him pegged, I find out something more. And I'll warn you, I've got a lot more digging to do on him. I'm only beginning to uncover the real Eli Frederick."

Taking a gulp of his caffeinated energy drink, he continued, "Eli Frederick was the only child of two academics. Now, while at first I thought of the similarities between him and me, I quickly realized that we had fundamental differences."

As he began to talk, weaving a few of his own experiences into the tale of Eli, the other Saints listened intently, realizing Luke was divulging more about himself than he had ever before.

"Eli's parents moved fairly often to different university cities. He was a brilliant student but, looking at notes from schools and social media, he was also bullied, had virtually no friends and I would bet he probably had rudimentary social skills. By the time he hit high school, he was already writing computer codes, in the math club...although not a leader, and, from what I can tell, was a loner with no friends."

With a self-deprecating shrug, he added, "With me, I was fortunate in that my parents didn't move around and we had a cool, kick-ass neighbor who took me under his wing. He taught me martial arts and how to stand up for myself. I used to talk to him and his wife all the time when my parents were buried in their ancient texts, so I learned conversational and social skills."

Luke's excitement was palatable and the other Saints shared smiles as they watched Luke's animation as he reported.

"Now, here's where it gets interesting, and I'm still digging so this is only preliminary. Eli went to MIT and was in their Engineering program. He was two years younger than me, but I started early so he was actually three years behind me in college. I never heard of him but, then, I was a senior by that time, so a freshman wouldn't have been in any of the same classes."

"Even as smart as he was?" Jude asked.

Luke smirked as he realized Jude was prodding him. "Hell, Engineering at MIT? Everyone was smart." Sobering, he said, "At a place like that, no one is a big fish anymore. Just all little fishes swimming in a great, big, fucking pond!"

The others laughed at Luke's college description before turning their attention back to his findings.

"At MIT he seemed to find his stride and, I've got

to tell you, a university can be a mecca for someone like Eli...hell, for someone like me."

The other Saints looked up and Luke sighed, rubbing his forehead. He battled how much to tell them...*how could they possibly understand?* But then he realized that the ten of them around the table had become a family, of sorts. As much as he knew about them, he also had to admit he had given them precious little of himself.

Leaning back in his chair, he pinned them with his stare. "Guys, I'm not going to insult you by assuming your childhood or young adulthood was easy...I know it wasn't for all of you. But as you stepped into manhood, it surely hasn't escaped your notice that most of you are big men, made even more powerful by your sports, exercise, or even former jobs. And this may sound weird coming from another guy, but not one of you is hard on the eyes and back before you found your special someone, our trips to Chuck's typically ended with the majority of you finding your evening spent with a hot girl on your lap and probably later in your bed."

At that, Bart, the most notorious, former chick-magnet of them all, had the good grace to blush. "Damn man, you know how to lay it on the line!"

"Just keeping it real, bro," Luke laughed. Sobering, he continued, "And you were probably that way in high school and college, if I had to guess. But in high school, for someone like Eli...and well, even me...whose social skills did not involve knowing how to converse with a girl, it was easier to throw myself in with the smart nerds. Now, college became a different thing for me. I was in the martial arts club sports and ran with the MIT running club as well as being an engineering student. Built the body up and finally managed to learn how to talk to girls. Sort of," he joked with a shrug.

"And you're saying that Eli didn't have anything else to fall back on?" Cam asked.

"Not from what I can tell. He threw himself into his classes, although he made a couple of friends. But even in that world of academia, he didn't step outside of his small group very much. He continued to be mostly a loner with just a few friends."

"And those friends?" Jack prompted.

"It appears he was closest to a group of three others. Tim Kelly, Hai Zhou, and Charlotte Trivett. From what I've been able to discover, those four met in a group project and remained friends. I've discerned that Tim Kelly is married with three kids, lives in Boston and works for an international accounting firm as a software designer. Hai Zhou went to California for about three years after graduating from MIT and then returned to China. I haven't had time to get a lock on Charlotte yet, but it looks like she lived in the northern part of Virginia, near the Maryland line."

"And Eli?"

"Eli took a job, similar to Tim's, in Baltimore and worked there for six months. Then he quit and, according to his tax records, he worked for himself. He never incorporated or set up his own business, but instead began to take private software design orders. From what I can tell, a company would contract him to work on a software project from home, he would design it, and then get paid. And paid well, I might add."

Monty's head jerked up. "You mean he just worked from home without any of the protections of having his own business? Why would he not set up an LLC or some business license?"

Shrugging, Luke answered, "From what I can tell from his bank and investment accounts, he was making serious bucks doing what he was doing, so it may have never entered his mind. Hell, he got paid and his bank account shows it."

Jack leaned back again, rubbing his hand over his face and asked, "Why do I get the feeling that you're going to tell us this guy left very little for us to go on?"

"One of his specialties was encryption and I'm having a devil of a time breaking it. So far, I can find out a few of the businesses that hired him and I'm not coming up with much in the way of who would want him dead."

"What about his friends?" Patrick asked, hoping for a chance to interview. The newest Saint had recently joined after his tour of duty with the US Army Corps of Engineers.

"From what I can tell...he doesn't have any." Seeing the incredulous looks shot his way, he threw up his hands in defense. "Guys, I'm telling you this man had almost no virtual footprint. His encryption is brilliant." Shaking his head, Luke sighed heavily. "If he wasn't dead, I'd be trying to find him just so I could see if I could get him to work for us!"

"So we've got nothing?" Jack clarified, his piercing gaze staying on Luke, never having seen his computer expert so frustrated.

"Well, here's what I can get my hands on," Luke continued. "I can find a few of his contracts, I can see what he worked on up until about nine months ago. I can tell that he maintained a bit of communication with Tim Kelly and Charlotte Trivett. Tim, we can talk to. Charlotte, I haven't checked into yet, but plan on doing so this afternoon. I know the intel is there, I just have to discover it."

The group, almost in unison, leaned back in their chairs, the information swirling in their minds.

"Okay," Jack began, "I want Luke to dig more on Charlotte and see if there's anything on Hai from the time he left MIT, including what he worked on in California before going back to China. Once he's got that we'll go to Boston to check with Tim."

Most of the other Saints filed out of the room, their own assignments to accomplish. Marc and Jack moved to the equipment room to check on their weapons and ammunition. Luke sighed as his eyes traveled to his special coffee maker sitting neglected on the counter.

Grimacing he rubbed his chest before turning back to his keyboard.

Time to get back to work and find out what the hell Eli Frederick was involved in...what he was hiding...and what his friends knew about him.

CHAPTER 6

S HOVING HIS CHAIR back in frustration, Luke stalked into his kitchen, his glower only pacified when he remembered his trip to the grocery store before he came home. Throwing a frozen pizza into the oven, he frowned at the timer on the stove as he watched the minutes slowly click by.

How the hell can anyone disappear? Luke had spent the past four hours attempting to find Charlotte, but could not connect her to anything recent. He knew Hai would be difficult so he saved him for last, but he assumed she would be easy to investigate.

Pulling the hot pizza out, steam rising from the melted cheese, he slid it onto a large plate and moved back to his computers. Plopping down, he stared at the notes he had taken. Charlotte Trivett was the only child of divorced parents. He determined her father left when she was only four and married another woman, having nothing to do with his ex-wife or daughter after that. Her mother worked in a grocery store during the day and as a waitress at night.

Charlotte's academic records revealed what he had

already assumed by her admission to MIT. She was brilliant, analytical, and appeared to be a loner. Her high school yearbook yielded no pictures of her, not even in the math or science clubs. She had attended a posh private school on an academic scholarship. *With her mom working as a waitress, I'll bet she was shunned by the little princesses there.* Her social media footprint was scant at best.

One year younger than Eli, she would have started after Luke graduated, so he knew their paths did not cross. Sighing as he continued to peruse his notes, he continued to find little about her other than school records. Just like high school, she was not in clubs or a sorority. She worked in the Engineering library for work-study to assist with costs. Her mother died during Charlotte's junior year of college, leaving her very much alone. Most of her education was financed with financial need and student loans, which she paid off within two years of graduating.

Where the hell did you get the money to pay back your loans? She would have graduated about the time that Eli began taking private jobs. *I wonder?* Quickly pulling up a comparison of both Eli and Charlotte's bank accounts, he discovered the connection he had been searching for. *Bingo!* They both made large deposits about the same time. Not every time, but almost sixty percent were on the same day.

So you were working privately also...and often on the same projects as Eli. Feeling as though he finally made a modicum of progress, he smiled as he leaned back in his seat. His grin left his face as he glanced to the side and viewed his cold pizza. Sighing heavily, he decided to forgo the microwave and chomped down on the congealed cheese sitting on top of the slice.

By midnight, his frustration reached an all-time high once more. Charlotte Trivett disappeared at the same time Eli Frederick went missing. She was gone. Completely and totally off the grid. Her email, social media, and phone had been disconnected and discontinued. Groaning, he began to fear the worst. *Did she die too? Is her body going to wash up on a shore?*

Deciding to call it a night, he shoved in the last piece of pizza and stood to take the plate back to the kitchen. Before he turned off his computer, it pinged with an incoming message.

Hard at work?

Attempting not to choke as he swallowed a large bite quickly, he sat up straight. **Starting a new case. How are you? Do you need my help?**

Not yet.

A pause settled in as Luke tried to decide what else to say. Before he had a chance to attempt wittiness, his friend commented.

Be careful what you seek. You may not like the answers.

Once more astonished that this person could tell what he was doing, he typed, **Why will I not like the answers?**

He waited, his heart pounding faster with each

passing second. His gaze never left his screen, as though staring would make the person respond quicker. Finally the ping sounded again.

You want to find someone but to do so may not give you the satisfaction you seek.

Luke's brow furrowed as he realized this person knew he was searching for Eli's friend Charlotte. Unable to decipher their intent he sat for a moment, his fingers twitching over the keys. **I really want to meet you. I want to know how you operate.**

Then I would lose my edge...it's what I have going for me. I'm like a shadow on the wall.

Grinning, Luke realized this was more than he normally received from his cyber friend. **I got a question.**

Sure you can ask...I might not answer.

Chuckling, his fingers poised over the keys wondering if he was about to mess up their unusual partnership. *Oh, hell, go for it!* **Any chance you will tell me your name?**

A long pause had Luke rethinking about asking. *Damn, I shouldn't have pushed.* Just as he was about to type an apology for asking, a response came back.

Charlie.

Stunned that he received an answer, Luke typed, **Promise me you will contact me when you need assistance.**

Luke waited impatiently to see if there was more coming. The silence became deafening as his computer sat blank...waiting. Suddenly another ping.

I promise.

Knowing no more was forthcoming, Luke took a swig of beer. As he sat pondering the case and the cyber friend, whose name offered no insight on whether they were male or female, he realized that with each of the friend's contacts with him, they had offered insight, assistance. But this time, they only offered a warning.

Bolting upright, nearly knocking over his beer, he realized, *they can see what I'm working on and are warning me away. That means I'm on the right track. Eli and Charlotte did work together and whatever frightened Eli into contacting the FBI, she must know about it also. And my cyber-friend, Charlie, must know about it as well. I wonder if Charlie is investigating Eli and Charlotte too?*

BY THE TIME Luke finished his diatribe with the Saints the next day, they understood his frustration.

"I don't know how anyone disappears," Chad acknowledged. "You'd think there'd be some-thing...anything to follow."

"Her money was moved to an offshore account and with the encryption she either knew or learned from Eli, she's hiding the use of any credit cards or bank withdrawals that I can find. No address. No social media. The last picture I've got of her is from her driver's license."

Flashing it on the screen, they all observed the elu-sive Charlotte Trivett. Dark brown hair, pulled back in a ponytail, wire-frame glasses, MIT t-shirt. Not smiling. Luke had stared at the picture on his computer screen the evening before for a long time, but until he saw it enlarged on the wall screen, he did not see anything familiar. Now something niggled his mind...as though he had seen her before.

"She...she looks..." he stammered, gathering the attention of the others around the table, then shook his head, a blush creeping up his face. "Never mind," he mumbled. Sitting up straighter, he confessed, "There's more. My mystery contact appears to know something about this case. They sent me a warning message."

"A warning?" Blaise asked, his large body leaning forward, pinning his gaze onto Luke. The other Saints mimicked Blaise's posture as they bristled at the idea of a warning.

Ignoring the others, Luke settled his gaze on Jack, and asked, "Boss, I'd like permission to pursue this person in hopes that they can lead us to information about Eli's death or Charlotte's whereabouts."

Rubbing his beard thoughtfully, Jack asked, "What do you think this person is up to?"

"I don't know. Up till now, I saw them as someone who was...well, to be honest, someone who was like what we know Eli was. A computer genius. Probably worked alone...possibly from home. Someone who stumbled across me and has lived a bit vicariously through us. They've never steered me wrong, nor given me incorrect information or direction." Leaning back, blowing out a frustrated breath, he added, "And I always hoped they were not involved in anything illegal."

"And now?" Bart prompted.

"Now? I don't know…but to warn me about my searches into Eli and his friends, makes me think that they already know something. And they finally gave me a name." He paused for a moment, then added, "Charlie."

Nodding, Jack agreed to Luke's request, but with a stipulation. "Pursue this guy, but I want you to meet with Tim Kelly this evening. Marc'll fly you and Patrick up to Boston. Monty, you take point with Lin Wang. We need her on our side to make our lives easier and, Monty, you've got the finesse and the Bureau know-how to try to make that happen."

"I'll try, boss, but she's a tough nut to crack. Not sure how successful I'll be."

Luke looked over to Marc and asked, "When do we leave?"

"You and Patrick can meet at my house in about two hours and I'll drive us to the Charlestown airport. I've got my Cessna there."

With that, the Saints dispersed, Luke's thoughts on finding out more about his cyber-contact instead of the upcoming meeting with Tim Kelly to determine, if Eli's former friend would have any information. As he walked up the stairs, he stumbled as the thought hit him…*Unless Tim also knows Charlie!*

FLYING WAS NOT his favorite way to travel. Luke's stomach bounced along with the tires of the small plane as Marc touched down in Boston. Trying to still his quivering stomach, he alighted from the aircraft, hoping his face was not as green as he felt. Jack had arranged the meeting and Tim surprised them when he suggested they meet at his house. Patrick drove the rental car into the suburbs of Boston, easily navigating the rush-hour traffic.

Arriving at a two-story, brick Colonial in an upscale, older neighborhood with stately trees in each yard, they stepped up to the bright red front door.

It swung open by a small child whose grin peeked up at them in curiosity. "Hi!" she squeaked. "Are you here for my daddy?"

Patrick, at ease with small children, immediately squatted down to be on her level. "We're here to see Tim Kelly. Is that your dad?"

Her smile widened, but before she could answer, a man stepped into view, his smile matching his daughter's. "Gentlemen, come in, come in. I'm Tim and this tyke is Sarah."

Luke noted the tasteful, expensive furniture and decorations as they made their way into the living room. He had investigated Tim and knew that he had secured a job with a large corporation after graduating from MIT and Tim's salary easily afforded him the luxuries Luke was eyeing.

A stately brunette walked into the living room,

greeting the Saints, and was introduced as Lisa, Tim's wife. She brought glasses of iced tea on a tray with cookies and set it on the coffee table. Smiling her goodbye, she shooed the little girl out of the room after reminding Tim that they were off to pick up the boys from soccer.

Luke watched as Tim's eyes followed his wife until she was out of sight. Giving himself a mental shake, he brought his mind back to the matter at hand.

"So," Tim began, taking a sip and then setting his glass down again. "I understand you want to talk about Eli Frederick." He smiled and said, "I haven't heard from Eli in a long time."

Luke's gaze shot up quickly to Tim before darting to Marc and Patrick. Clearing his throat, he said, "Um...Mr. Kelly, I'm sorry to be the one to tell you this, but we're investigating his...his murder."

At those words, Tim's eyes bugged, his Adam's apple moving up and down quickly as he choked on the cookie he had taken a bite from. "Murdered? What...I mean...I...what?"

"We assumed the FBI had informed you...but then...have you not been interviewed by the FBI?"

"FBI? No, why would I?" His friendly smile was now replaced with one of shock and irritation. "What's going on?"

"Eli Frederick had been missing for about five months and last month his body was found. The FBI is investigating but has asked us to assist in gathering background information on him." The partial truth slipped easily from Luke's lips as he watched Tim's reaction.

Tim sat silent, blinking rapidly several times. "I...I had no idea," he finally said, after a long minute of silence. Dropping his chin to his chest, he looked at his hands, now clasped in his lap. Sighing heavily, he said, "Jesus, Eli...hell, man."

Giving Tim a moment to grapple with the news, Marc asked, "What can you tell us about him?"

Leaning back, Tim gave a rueful grin. "Honestly, Eli and I haven't been in contact much since graduating five years ago. We shared occasional emails and the requisite holiday card, but," throwing his hands up slightly, "he was always an odd bird."

"Odd?" Luke prodded.

"You know the image that the outside world has of engineers? That we have no social skills, only knowing machines but not people? Well, that stereotype fit Eli to a T."

Luke appreciated what Tim was referring to. He felt at times as though he understood computers better than people but, because he was athletic, he forced himself away from his computers and interacted with others. *And, working for the CIA and then the Saints, certainly got me out of the house and around people.* He wondered, not for the first time, if he had stayed at home and worked free-lance for himself, if he would have been like Eli. Tim's reminiscing cut into Luke's thoughts, and he had to take a moment to catch up on what Tim was saying.

"We met sophomore year when we had a group project to work on. Everyone in the class quickly formed groups and there were just a handful of us losers who didn't know anyone else, so we got together." Chuckling, he added, "Turned out to be the best thing ever."

"How so?" Patrick queried.

"I got in with three of the smartest in the class," Tim grinned. "Eli Frederick was a genius software engineer. Hai's English was a little rough, but I quickly realized he was just as smart as Eli. And then Charlotte? She was only a freshman, but was allowed to take the class, and she was absolutely brilliant. We worked well together and created the most kick-ass project. Got an A and all four of us were offered teaching assistant positions. Eli and Hai didn't accept, but Charlotte and I did."

"And you maintained a friendship with the other three?"

"Yes. We four got along fine and actually liked each other. I played some sports and belonged to a small fraternity so I had friends outside that group, but I really liked their company. Hai was funny as hell without even trying. Charlotte was an enigma. I got the feeling that she hid behind the glasses and nerd-girl persona...as though she wasn't very comfortable around a lot of guys and that kept them at bay. And

Eli? His mind never shut down! He was constantly looking for a better way, a smarter way to do something."

"And after graduation?" Luke prompted. "What then? What can you tell us about the group?"

Tim's forehead scrunched in thought as he answered, "Hai got a job in California. I think he was with a Chinese based company that worked with hospitals...or something in the medical field. Then a few years later, he sent a group email saying he was moving back to China. Kind of a polite, kiss-off email. You know, an it-was-nice-to-meet-you email that was also essentially saying goodbye forever. And sure enough, I haven't heard from him since then."

"And Charlotte?"

Luke noticed a faraway smile light Tim's face and he wondered if a college romance had budded between the two.

"Charlotte was a year behind us, but she did a better job of staying connected. In college, she wasn't very social, but seemed to appreciate our group. She was brilliant, as I said, and really gave Eli a run for his money considering he truly thought he was the smartest. By the time she graduated, I have no doubt that she could have worked for any company and demanded good money, but Eli convinced her that she could live her dream by working from home."

Taking another large drink from his iced tea, Tim then explained, "You have to understand Eli to understand Charlotte."

Lifting his eyebrows in question, Luke did not need to prod to get more from Tim, who seemed to relish talking about his old college buddies.

"Eli truly hated being around people. He assumed they were not as smart as he was and, for the most part, he was right. His social skills were almost nil and his disdain for people in general was high. He tried having a job out of college, but he complained constantly. Then, after less than a year, he quit and became an independent, freelance software engineer. I tried to tell him to set up his own actual business with a license and tax breaks, but he refused to listen." Shaking his head, Tim added, "If Eli didn't understand something, especially if it didn't interest him, he would shun it. But what he was doing must have been working for him, 'cause he convinced Charlotte to do the same when she graduated." For the first time since speaking, Tim's voice held contempt.

"You disagreed about Charlotte working for herself?" Patrick asked.

Leaning forward, with his forearms on his knees, Tim focused intently on them, his lips pinched. "I liked Eli, but he could be a conceited prick at times. He touted the virtues of working in his sweatpants instead of a suit. He talked about how he could work a few hours a day and make more money than working for some company. He sang the praises of not having to work with people. I get it. For him, that was perfect.

But Charlotte? She was sweet, giving, smart. I got the feeling that in high school she'd been bullied for being uber smart so she learned to pull it all in and kind of hide. At MIT, at least with us, she became more at ease with herself. And I think it would've been good for her to have a job where her intelligence would be valued and she would be accepted in a group."

Settling back in his seat heavily, he said, "But Eli was very persuasive and she took his lead and worked freelance for herself...and from what I assume, quite lucratively."

"Have you had any contact with any of them in the last six months?"

Shaking his head slowly, Tim replied, "No...now that I think about, not at all." Blushing slightly, he admitted, "But then, to be honest, they're kind of like old friends that slowly fade away. My life now is my family, my kids and their activities, and my job. I'm embarrassed to say that I had no idea that Eli was missing...wow, and it's hard to wrap my head around the fact that he's dead." Holding Luke's gaze, he asked, "What can you tell me?"

"Eli approached the FBI with supposed information about a crime but wouldn't identify himself or the problem. Months later he approached them again and set up a meeting. He never made the meeting and the matter was closed. A month ago, his body was found."

"But, earlier, you said murder."

"Yes, it was determined he had been murdered."

Shaking his head, Tim said, "I'm afraid I can't help you there. I never had any idea what he worked on or who he had individual contracts with."

"And Charlotte?" Luke asked.

"I'm afraid I'm just as in the dark about what she was doing as well. I know for a couple of years, Eli would farm out some of his extra work to her, but as to what it was, I'm clueless. But, I've got her contact info for you to check with her." He was already pulling out his phone when Luke stopped him.

"Actually, it appears that she's missing also." These words gained a gasp from Tim and Luke tried to ascertain if he were truly surprised or perhaps was covering. *Shit! I can't tell. I hope to hell Marc or Patrick has a better read on him.* "We have no idea if she's in danger or not, but she is no longer at her previous residence and has discontinued any internet presence."

"Damn," Tim sighed.

"One last question," Luke said. "Did you know anyone named Charles or Charlie?"

"Charlie? No...I've never known a Charles...nor a Charlie."

Luke observed Tim's face carefully, but the other man gave no indication that he was lying.

"If I can be of any help, I'd like to be. These were my friends at one time. Will you please keep me up on anything you find out?" Tim asked. Gaining the Saints' assurance, he stood and walked them to the door, just as his wife was entering with four-year-old twin boys in tow.

As Patrick drove away, Luke turned to look back at the house, unable to see Tim on the phone with an angry expression on his face.

CHAPTER 7

L IN WANG SAT at the opulent dinner in the Chinese Embassy, her sharp eyes assessing everyone. Her dark, sleek bob was unadorned, swinging above her shoulders. Dressed in a modest evening gown of emerald green, she pretended to hang onto every word spoken by the boring man sitting next to her while attempting to scan the room.

Her eyes landed on Dr. Jian Cheung and her lips pinched together involuntarily. His eyes met hers and, much to her chagrin, he walked through the crowd toward her. Turning in her seat to face her table partner more fully, she hoped the doctor would ignore her, but her luck was not holding.

"Agent Wang, how nice to see you again," Dr. Cheung's voice purred from behind as she felt his fingertips slide across her shoulders. Sucking in a quick breath, she twisted around and gifted him with a tight smile.

"Doctor," she greeted in return, her voice barely a growl.

Just then the Chinese Ambassador's secretary, Yeng

Chow stepped into view, his eyes scanning the room before landing on Dr. Cheung and hustling over.

"Dr. Cheung," he said breathlessly in Chinese, "I've been looking for you."

Jian turned slowly, his smile never wavering, although Lin caught the irritation glistening in his eyes. "And now you have found me."

"The Ambassador has someone he wants you to meet," Yeng said, his eyes dropping to Lin's perceptive gaze.

"Anything I can assist with?" she asked, lifting an eyebrow, speaking in Chinese as well.

"No, no, my dear," Jian replied smoothly, his fingers digging ever so slightly into her shoulder. He turned and followed Yeng out of the room, Lin's eyes staying on them until they were out of sight.

"Hey, Agent Wang, you okay?"

Jumping, she turned to see her fellow FBI agent standing nearby. "Yes, I'm fine. Just trying to keep an eye on security as well as be a guest," she said, her voice brooking no doubt. She eyed the other agent as they nodded and moved away.

Sucking in a deep breath, she sometimes hated being Chinese-American in the Bureau. Her gaze landed on the door Dr. Cheung had left through and her lips curved into a small smile. *And then again...it gives me the perfect opportunity to blend in to keep an eye on things.*

CHARLIE WOKE SUDDENLY, unable to discern the sound that had jarred her from her sleep. With the fall chill penetrating the nights in the camper, she was already dressed in a long-sleeve black t-shirt and black leggings. Stealing noiselessly from the bed, she went to the security monitor screen mounted on the wall that showed her the images from the outside cameras.

Damn! One person slipped around the side of the camper toward her Vespa while another person stood at the end of the gravel campsite leading to the main road circling the campground. Biting her lip, she sucked in a deep breath before letting it out slowly, clearing her mind.

Watching the person in the back bend over her Vespa, she opened the specially oiled door without making a sound. Moving in the shadows, she slipped up behind the man, glad he was not overly large. With a quick karate move, she dropped him to the ground before he was aware of her presence. Slipping to the other side of the van, she waited until the lookout turned and approached her vehicle. Coming up behind him, she executed the same maneuver and dropped him as well. Staring down at the two men, she looked around in guilt. *What now? What do I do with them now?* Suddenly, she sprinted back inside her camper and rummaged through her toolbox. Grabbing the duct tape, she slipped back outside, holding her breath until she saw the two men still lying on the ground.

Bending down, she secured one man's hands behind his back with the tape and, with difficulty, dragged his body under a tree. *Thank goodness a wind is blowing through the trees creating a noise camouflage.* Within a couple of minutes, she had both unconscious men secured. Heart pounding, she stood for a moment, uncertain of what to do next. *If they found me...others will come.*

Checking her Vespa, she ascertained they had not placed a bug or monitoring device on it. Letting out her breath, she sighed audibly. *Good, they were only snooping.* She knew she should not have stayed in the campground for longer than a week or two at the most, but it had been so pleasant to not move, she allowed herself the luxury of staying in one place. *How the hell did they find me? Maybe they're just random thieves and not from...Well, it doesn't matter.*

Buckling into the driver's seat, she started the engine and pulled out of the campsite slowly, glancing into the side-view mirror, seeing the two slumbering intruders still reclined under the tree. With a grimace, she drove out of the campground, hesitating for a moment as to her next destination.

Time to do it, she vowed. *Time to let someone else in!*

LUKE'S EYES JERKED open from a sound sleep, instantly on alert. None of his security alarms were signaling, but something woke him up. Tossing the covers back, he sat on the edge of the bed for a moment, ears alert, waiting to see if he could discern anything. *Nothing.*

With over ten thousand dollars worth of computer equipment and programs, he was not willing to go back to sleep without checking first. Slipping a pair of sweatpants over his long legs, he grabbed his gun from his nightstand and stepped into the hall. Hearing nothing, he walked stealthily toward the living room in the front of the house.

Rounding the corner at the end of the hall, he jerked in surprise. The moonlight streaming through the window illuminated the outline of a woman standing in his living room. He kept his gun pointed at the intruder as he flipped the wall switch that turned on the lamp by the sofa, bathing them both in a soft glow. Luke's gaze traveled from the top of her head to her shoes and back again, landing on her eyes.

Long, rich brunette hair, braided and falling across one shoulder. Light brown...no...hazel eyes met and held his stare. At about five feet seven inches, her slim body belied a muscular strength underneath the tight, black t-shirt. Black leggings hugged her athletic frame and tucked into black tennis shoes.

As his gaze lifted to her face once more, he was struck by her beauty. Simple. Unadorned. Beauty. Then his mind came unglued as realization slammed into him. *Fuck me! Charlotte Trivett!*

She remained statue still except for her gaze, which dropped to the gun in his hand. "I'd appreciate it if you would lower your weapon." Her smooth voice shook with a slight tremor as her chest heaved with each breath.

Keeping his weapon trained on her, he replied, "And I'd appreciate it if you would tell me how the hell you got through my security and into my house."

Her tongue darted out, wetting her bottom lip, as she nodded slowly. "I notice you didn't ask who I was or what I was doing here."

"I've been staring at your picture for the past few days, from elementary school to your last driver's license. I must say the DMV photograph doesn't do you justice." He noticed the corners of her mouth lift ever so slightly.

Deciding to plunge in completely, she blurted, "I need help."

Watching the fear flash through her eyes, he lowered his weapon, but did not lay it down. *Not yet. I want answers and I damn well better get them.* "You're a hard person to find, Charlotte," he admitted.

"I know. I wanted to be."

"And yet..." he peered at her closely, his mind slowly churning through the possibilities. "You knew I was looking. You found out who I am. Where I live." As his gaze roved over her face, he noticed the slight dimple in her chin. Dimple. *I've seen that before...*

Another realization slammed into him and he rocked back on his heels. "You were the woman in the bar. With black hair." She did not need to respond, as he saw her pull her lips in, pressing them thin. Another thought jolted through him, causing him to lean forward slightly as he raked his eyes over her frame. "Holy shit. You're the woman from the diner." Tossing his gun onto the dining room table behind him, he whirled back around and growled, "Jesus, what the hell is your game?"

She took a step toward him then halted at the set of his jaw. Taking a shaky breath, she said, "No game. I promise. No game."

Letting out his breath, he ran his hand through his hair then crossed his arms over his muscular chest. Standing with his legs apart as he continued to stare her down, "You got any more surprise confessions before you tell me how you got in here?"

Her head jerked back, caught between a shake and a nod. Sucking in her lips again, she attempted an innocent look, but knew she failed when she saw the grimace on his face. "Can we at least sit down?" she asked, suddenly exhausted.

Her pale face beckoned to him and, immediately contrite, Luke apologized. "I'm sorry. I know you've been through something. Something that's made you run. Something that's made you go into hiding."

Following his outstretched arm, she walked over to the sofa and sat in the corner, curling her legs up under her. Staring at him, she waited, wondering what he was going to do. She did not have to wait long. He stepped over to re-alarm his house then stalked into the living room and stared at her for a moment before glancing around. Finally deciding to sit on the other end of the sofa, he twisted his body so that he was facing her.

Charlie realized she was seeing Luke up close for the first time...really seeing him. Not trying to keep her face away from his to hide her identity, but able to unabashedly stare at him. And just as she knew she would...she liked what she saw. His jaw was dark with stubble. His body was muscular and his arms bulged where they had been crossed. He looked like the runner he was. *And the karate expert. I've learned all I can about him in the past months, but never allowed myself to think that we would actually meet.* His dark, almost black, hair was trimmed neatly, but long enough that when he ran his hands through it, it would stand up on end. She longed to do just that. The realization hit her that she had not really touched another human in months. Not since being on the run.

As her gaze moved back to his face, she blushed as she saw that he was watching her appraise him. Dropping her gaze, suddenly unsure of herself, she wondered if she had made a mistake in coming to him.

"Charlotte," he said softly, drawing her eyes back to his. "Look, we got off on the wrong foot. I was startled, but to be honest, if you were able to get in, then I need to re-look at my security." Still facing her, he relaxed against the back of the sofa. "Let's begin again." He grinned as she lifted an eyebrow in confusion.

"Hello, I'm Luke. Luke Costas."

Unable to hold back her shy smile, she replied, "I'm

Charlotte Trivett. You already know that, but what you don't know…is that I go by the nickname my grandfather gave to me…Charlie."

She watched Luke's face during the millisecond it took for her confession to hit him. He jerked back, a gasp escaping from his lips. His mouth opened and closed, fishlike, before slamming tightly. Jumping up from the sofa, he paced to the other side of the room, staring wordlessly at the mantle before whirling around to pin her with a hard gaze.

"Charlie." His voice was only a whisper in the room, full of disbelief.

"Luke, I'm sorry. I know this is a shock, but I promised—"

"Promised?" he interrupted.

"Yes," she replied, curtly. "I promised I would let you know when I needed help. And this is me letting you know." She battled back the sting of tears that threatened the back of her eyes. "But you promised too." Swallowing deeply, she said, "You promised you would help me. Anytime."

Dropping his chin to his chest, Luke sighed. Long and hard. Lifting his eyes back to her, he saw the trickle of a single tear sliding down her cheek. Nodding slowly, he said, "You're right, Charlie. I did. This all just caught me by surprise."

Patting the sofa next to her, she begged, "Please come back. Please sit down and give me a chance to explain."

Walking the few steps over, he returned to the sofa, settling in once more. Holding her gaze, he said, "Okay. Tell me what the hell is going on. I know you as Charlie, someone who's been helping me for months, and as Charlotte, someone intrinsically involved in a case I'm investigating. Why the masquerade at the bar and the diner?"

Offering a little shrug, she said, "I needed to see you. To know if you were real."

"Real?" he asked, surprise leaking into his voice.

"Luke, you asked if I had any other confessions." Seeing distrust mask his face, she quickly continued. "Yes, I donned wigs to try to get close to you without anyone knowing who I was. Just like you said you'd been looking for me, well, others have too. But the truth of the matter is that you and I have become friends…well, online friends, for months, and I need you to trust that person."

"I want to, but…I don't even know what to call you," he admitted.

"Charlie. I go by Charlie. It was my granddad's nickname for me. In school, I didn't have a lot of friends, so Charlotte was what everyone knew me as. And in college, I never changed that. But ever since I needed to hide my identity, Charlie…well, it just fits."

"Okay, Charlie." Staring at the way she had her arms wrapped around her knees, he recognized the guarded posture. "Why don't you tell me what kind of trouble you're in? We'll start with that and then make our way to how the hell you got here." Before she could begin, he added, "But I'll warn you that you'll have to repeat all of this tomorrow with the rest of the men I work with."

His slight grin eased her anxiety and she smiled in return. Taking a deep breath, she nodded.

"I understand. I know that you've been investigating me, so I won't repeat all of my past, but I suppose I should start with Eli."

By the time she finished, the moon was high in the sky and her eyes were drooping. Luke placed a call to Jack, knowing the time of night did not matter. Setting up a meeting for the next day, *or, rather, in about six hours,* he thought ruefully, he disconnected. Turning back to Charlie, he saw that she had slumped down on the sofa, exhaustion finally claiming her. Repositioning her so that she was lying more comfortably, he twisted to grab a blanket off the chair near the fireplace. Covering her from her feet to her chin, he stood back watching her chest rise and fall in slumber. Dark hair spilled from her braid, some strands curling around her face. Long lashes rested on fatigue circles underneath her eyes.

It hit him that they never got to the part of her story where she explained how she hacked into what he was working on, nor how she had gotten into his house. Unable to hold back the grin, he thought the beauty on his sofa was the most intriguing woman he had ever met and a sudden rush of protectiveness overcame him.

As he thought back over her tale, he knew that finding out what Eli Frederick had wanted to talk to the FBI about was solved. But now...a new mission had begun.

CHAPTER 8

CHARLIE SAT ON the overstuffed sofa in Jack's living room, having been introduced to the nine men Luke worked with. Hating crowds, she fought the urge to pull her legs up under her to seek a less exposed position. *Geez, is every Saint huge?* Sucking in a deep breath, her eyes raked over them carefully, finding nothing but trust and intelligence in their expressions. Glancing to her side, where Luke sat protectively, she took in the comforting smile he offered.

The dark-bearded boss began, "Ms. Trivett, Luke's explained you have quite a story to tell. You need to understand that, while we're investigating with the FBI, we are a private investigation company. You are under no obligation to tell us anything."

"Thank you," she said, her soft voice strong and sure. "But I'm tired of running. Tired of hiding. And tired of trying to figure things out on my own."

With a nod, Jack leaned back in his chair and said, "Then we'll let you take it from here to explain your connection to Eli Frederick."

She had told most of the basic tale to Luke last

night but knew she needed to be more forthcoming today. *With everything.* With another deep breath, she began, "I met Eli my freshman year in college, when he and two others were sort of the last to get chosen for a group project. So the four of us worked together and, to my surprise, found that we got along." Her face softened as she thought of those early days.

"Tim Kelly had a natural leadership about him and took over that role. Hai's English was rough, but he was a hard worker and damn smart. Eli…Eli was actually funny. He had zero people skills and was an acquired taste, for sure. He was brilliant and had no problem letting others know he was so much smarter than them." She grinned again at the memory. "But with our group, he actually became more human.

"Tim couldn't wait to join a big company after graduation. Hai had family in California so I wasn't surprised when he moved there. And Eli? I was stunned when he took a company job and," she chuckled wryly, "not stunned when he quit six months later to work freelance." Shrugging as though in apology for him, she added, "He hated being in a cubicle world. I'm sure he thought he was much more intelligent than the others and, oh my God, if he had to work on large, group projects, that would have made him nuts."

Glancing over to Luke, unable to read his expression, she said, "I know I make him sound terrible. He wasn't. That was just Eli."

"Tell us about your continued involvement with

him," Luke prompted.

Nodding, Charlie said, "By the time I graduated, Eli was making a lot of money working freelance. Companies would hire him to write all or part of a program and he could do it in the ease of his own home. He'd bought an old two-story condo in Baltimore, near the waterfront, and since it was an end unit, he had windows overlooking part of the bay. I visited a couple of times. It wasn't a great place, but it seemed to suit him. Anyway," she continued, "he sold me on the idea of working freelance also. He said he had a ton of work he could send my way until I got enough clients coming in on my own."

"You didn't want to work for someone else? Someone with benefits?" Jude asked.

Looking around at the large group of men who all worked together, Charlie knew it would be hard for them to understand what it is like for someone who hated crowds. "I...well, Eli didn't like people very much. But for me, I...uh...well, big groups make me nervous. I seem to be okay if people are moving around, but when a lot of people are crowded in a room and I feel as though I can't get to the door, I get nervous...on the inside. Anxiety problems, so I've been told. It just seemed easier to do the same thing that Eli was doing."

"Are you okay in here, Charlie?" Luke asked, solicitously. He suddenly realized what an overwhelming crowd the Saints could be when piled into one room.

Nodding jerkily, she said, "Yeah. Um...I can see the door and, well, this room is huge so it feels safe." Looking at the two-story room with the stone fireplace along an outside wall with floor to ceiling windows overlooking the Blue Ridge Mountains on either side, she had to admit, "Actually, this room is really fabulous. It feels open and airy." Blushing, she said, "I guess that sounds silly."

"Not at all," Jack said, smiling at the description of his beloved home. He looked up as Bethany walked into the room, a tray filled with cold water bottles in her hands. He jumped up to take the heavy tray from her, stealing a quick kiss. Bethany gifted him with a glorious smile as she nodded toward Charlie and then left the room.

Charlie watched the exchange in interest. *If only,* she sighed. But men like the Saints did not go for computer nerds like her, she was sure. Glancing to the side at Luke, she could not help but wonder what type of woman he went for.

"So, more about Eli?" Cam asked, interrupting her musings.

Jerking back to the conversation she was supposed to be focused on, she blinked several times. *What's wrong with me? Maybe I have been alone too long!*

Clearing her throat, she continued, "It worked out well for the past several years. Eli sent some work my way and then I began to build up clients of my own. It was...well, nice for the most part. I worked from home.

On my own equipment. And I learned a lot. The money allowed me to pay off my student loans and then afford some expensive computers and programs. My clients included some government agencies where I would create false pasts for persons who would be going into hiding, or witness protection, or even just who needed to get *lost*."

At this, the other Saints gazed at her in a mixture of admiration and awe as she continued.

"I lost touch with Hai when he went back to China and Tim married and settled in Boston. But Eli and I would communicate weekly, if not more. I lived only about an hour from him, so it wasn't unusual for me to drive to his place to meet."

She watched as the men listened intently to her while taking notes on their tablets. *How odd to have all my words written down. To have been alone for so long and now to be in a room full of strangers who are delving into my business. But this is for you, Eli, and whatever the hell you got yourself into.*

"About two years ago, Eli contacted me and asked if I would help him work on some programming. He had a job that was taking a long time and the client was in a hurry. So I agreed. It was for a medical company that was creating databases to match up organ donors with recipients. I worked on part of the programing but Eli worked on most of it. It was actually his client and he got paid and then turned around and paid me from his money. And…" she pinned them with her hard stare, "that's probably why I'm still alive."

At this statement, Luke's gaze jumped to hers. He had listened to her story in the middle of the night but she was going into more detail now.

She rubbed her forehead, trying to focus on little sleep and lots of nerves. Feeling a hand on her shoulder, rubbing some of the tension away, she let out a sigh. *God, that feels good. Another time...another place...* Giving herself a mental shake, she shot Luke a smile.

"Almost eight months ago, Eli contacted me through a secure network we had established for sending sensitive materials back and forth to each other. He emphatically said he needed to talk to me but couldn't use his phone. We arranged to meet in a small town between Baltimore and where I lived. This was a pretty big deal for Eli, who hated leaving his area. When we met, I couldn't believe the change. Even working from home, Eli shaved, wore clean clothes, and generally had good hygiene. But this time, he looked haggard and I honestly wasn't sure the diner manager was going to serve us. Eli started rambling, peering around us as though someone was going to jump out, but I finally got him to talk to me."

Letting out a deep breath, Charlie continued, "He said that the contract we had worked on together was for something wrong. It was hard to understand, but he said that he did some digging into the contractees when he questioned some of the work they wanted him to re-do. They sent some work back to him and when he put my programs together with his, he saw a larger picture than just the part he had worked on himself. And he got suspicious, started digging, and found some-thing...horrible."

Luke watched as she twisted her hands together in her lap and he instinctively reached over to place his long fingers over hers, giving a comforting squeeze. The gesture was not ignored by the others in the room, but no one said anything.

Looking around at the faces focused on her, she shook her head slightly as her voice trembled. "All he would say that day was that he uncovered something illegal with the organ donor list. He wouldn't give me any details then, but wanted to know what he should do. Of course, I told him to call the police and he replied it was much bigger than the police. So then I told him to contact the FBI. He left soon after that but later he said he wanted to be sure. He told me about two months later that he had called the FBI, but was afraid to give them his name or any particulars." Shaking her head, she said, "He really had no clue what to do and since I didn't know what was going on, I couldn't help him."

"Did he ever share with you?" Bart asked. The large man gave an air of a laid-back surfer, but Charlie knew that belied his intensity as she noted his fierce blue-eyed gaze pinned on hers.

"Yes...or at least part of it." Licking her lips nerv-ously, she continued, "He said that it appeared that someone was...using questionable ways for getting organs for recipients." The reality of what she was saying –what she had known for six months—began crashing down on her. Throat constricting, she panted as she tried to continue to speak. "Eli thought they were just taking organs."

Luke watched as the blood drained from her face and planted his hand on the back of her head, forcing her head down between her knees. "Breathe, Charlie, breathe slow and deep."

His voice sounded far away, but calmed her nonetheless. Her vision blurred as she gulped in air. Hearing other sounds around her, she felt a cold cloth on the back of her neck. As she continued to breathe deeply she felt Luke's warm hand smoothing back and forth down her spine. After a few minutes her vision cleared and the sound of Luke's voice as he whispered in her ear was no longer far away. Pushing against his hand she raised up, embarrassed at having made such a spectacle of herself.

Blaise kneeled in front of her, his fingers on her wrist taking her pulse. After a moment, he released and nodded at Luke.

Charlie heard him say, "Heart rate is a little elevated," and she could only wonder about the world she suddenly found herself in. Bethany appeared in front of her, holding out a glass of orange juice, her hand on Charlie's shoulder. "Here, drink this. It'll help revive you."

"I'm so sorry—" Charlie began.

"Don't apologize," Luke said." It's all good. We know you've been through something traumatic, so take your time and just tell us what you know as best as you can."

Almost afraid to look around the room at the faces of the Saints, she took one last fortifying breath and lifted her head. Drinking deeply, she felt the tart juice jolt her system. She was pleasantly surprised to see nothing but concern etched on the faces of the others in the room. With this encouragement she continued her tale.

"When Eli told me what he feared, which was that a client was somehow taking organs from unwilling or unknowing patients, I understood his shock. He wouldn't give me specifics, so I have no idea who he was talking about. I told him that he had to talk to the FBI. He agreed and several days later told me that he had set up a meeting with an agent that he had spoken to there. The meeting was to take place two days after we talked but he called before the meeting to say he was going to send me all of his information just in case he needed a backup. So, using our secure communication network, he sent me some of his work, including what he had been investigating on his own."

Taking a sip of the juice, she shot Bethany an appreciative glance. "I knew the day that he was supposed to meet with them he might need moral support. So I decided to drive to Baltimore to be with him when he met with the FBI agent. And that was when I saw it happen."

"What? What did you see?" Jack queried.

"I saw Eli Fredrick…murdered."

At her proclamation the Saints sat motionless, the silence in the air hanging thickly over the group. Charlie stole a glance to the side at Luke, knowing he had only heard part of the story the evening before, but wondered what he thought now that he was hearing the whole thing. She did not have to wait long to find out.

"Fucking hell, Charlie," Luke said, his curse joined by the others resounding about the room.

Knowing she needed to continue, Charlie said, "I drove to his house a couple of hours before he was supposed to meet the agent. When I would visit I would walk around the side to the door that led into his kitchen. So I did the same as I always did. I parked on the street, walked around the side, but before I got to his backdoor I passed the first-floor window of the dining room that he used as his office. I normally wouldn't even look in, but I heard voices. Angry voices. Eli never had people over so, realizing he had company, I glanced into the window."

She shuddered as her mind went back to that day, remembering the details as sharply as if they were occurring in front of her right now. "He was sitting in a chair," her shaky voice barely able to be heard. "There were three people in the room. One man was holding Eli's arms behind him, another man was rummaging through Eli's computers and papers, and the third was a woman who turned around with a gun in her hand."

Luke looked over at Jack, wishing Charlie did not have to go over the story again, but knew there was no choice. His hand had not left her back and he slid it to her shoulder to pull her body against his slightly. His heart pounded as he remembered the many times the other Saints had their women sitting in this very room, telling their experiences. *But Charlie's not my woman. She's just a...well, a...hell, I don't know what she is! A friend?* Watching the beautiful, brilliant woman with a core of steel sitting next to him, he knew she was a friend and could easily be more. *But am I the type of man she would want?*

"Keep going, Charlie," he encouraged softly.

Her pale face with dark circles underneath her haunted eyes, turned toward him. She whispered the next part just to him, as though that would ease the telling.

"She fired...straight into Eli's head." She slumped against Luke, unable to hold herself rigid anymore.

Knowing she needed to recover, Luke signaled the other Saints and they began to move from the room. Hearing them leave, she jerked her head up. "No, no. Don't go. I need to finish this. It'll never get any easier so we might as well plunge on."

The Saints resumed their seats. "I'm so sorry to keep asking, Ms. Trivett," Jack apologized, "but what happened next?"

Her hazel gaze lifted to Jack as her chin quivered. "I ran."

Monty looked over at her and said, "There was no report filed about his murder. You didn't call the police? You didn't tell anyone?" Monty growled, unable to hide his irritation.

"No!" she shouted, her eyes now morphing from fear to anger. "And don't you dare judge me. You have no idea what my life has been like for the last five months!"

Luke's fingers flexed around her shoulder as the other Saints seemed to jerk back in unison at Charlie's vehement reaction. "No one's judging," he whispered.

Monty, immediately contrite, agreed, "I'm very sorry to have made you think I was judging, Ms. Trivett. It's my background. I used to work for the FBI."

"Why didn't you contact the authorities, Charlie?" Luke asked softly. "We just want to know what was happening. Honestly."

She held his eyes for a moment, then sucked in another shuddering breath before slowly moving her attention around the room to each of the other nine men, finally landing on Monty. "I didn't know who to trust," she explained, her voice now steadier. "The woman...holding the gun...on her belt...she had a badge."

CHAPTER 9

T HE SAINTS MILLED around the room for a while, allowing Bethany to show Charlie to the bathroom. Monty looked over at Luke and said, "I'm really sorry, man. I didn't mean to upset her earlier."

"It's not you," Luke acknowledged. "As soon as she told me the first part of her ordeal, I knew we needed to get her in here to go over everything."

Blaise asked, "So she's been on the run for all this time? That's a long time for someone to hide...especially someone who has no experience in staying covert."

"I agree," Luke agreed. "I have a feeling that she's been investigating as well, but we'll know more when she comes back in." His eyes continuously glanced to the hall where Bethany and Charlie had disappeared. As he looked around the living room, he noticed the watchful eyes of the other Saints as they focused on him. Lifting an eyebrow, he cocked his head, but before he could say anything, Jack spoke.

"Luke, we understand there's more she has to tell us and we also know she's been your unidentified cyber-contact for the last couple of months. I just gotta ask, since it looks like we'll be assisting her, is she someone special to you?"

"Honestly? I'm not sure," Luke answered, his arms lifted to his sides. "She's smart…special…and stronger than anyone I've met. I feel like I know her and yet she's an enigma to me. But one I'd like to spend more time with, seeing what might be there."

Nodding, Jack said, "Good enough. Then we'll make sure you're on her immediate protection detail."

With a jerk of his head in acknowledgment, Luke turned and walked down the hall to see if she was all right, missing the grins from the other Saints behind him.

Standing at the sink, Charlie ran cold water into her hand and splashed it on her face. The icy shock helped revive her and she patted her face dry with the decorative hand towel. *Jack doesn't seem like a decorative-hand-towel-sort-of-guy. But when he looks at his wife, I get the feeling he'd do anything for her. Even have fluffy, pretty hand towels.* A snort escaped as she looked up into the mirror. *God, I've just told them I witnessed a murder and I'm thinking of bath ornaments. I must have really lost my mind.*

Dreading going back out into the testosterone-filled room, she heaved a sigh before hearing a light knock at the door.

"Charlie?" Luke's voice called softly. "You okay?"

Opening the door, she leaned her head back to look

into his face. At five-feet-seven-inches, she was unused to having to lean so far back to look into someone's eyes. But Luke was tall. His lean, muscular body filled the doorway and she fought the desire to melt into his embrace. Shaking her head, she replied, "Yeah, I'm fine. Well, as fine as the witness to a murder who has now been on the run for almost five months can be."

Her attempt at a smile fell flat, but the corners of his mouth turned up slightly anyway. "Come on," he said, reaching his hand out to link his fingers with hers before gently pulling her out of the bathroom. He tried to ignore the tingle he felt all the way up his arm from their connected fingers, but almost stumbled as he drew her closer anyway. "Let's finish this, so we can figure out how to help you."

The feel of his fingers intertwined with hers sent warmth from her hand to her heart. She could not remember the last time someone had held her hand. Allowing him to take the lead, she followed him back into the large, airy room as everyone resettled into their seats.

"Are you all right for continuing?" Jack asked, his gruff voice softened by his kind eyes.

Nodding, she sucked in a fortifying breath and said, "Yes. I want to finish. I've held this in for so long…it feels…I don't know…kind of freeing."

Clearing her throat, she said, "I can't tell you specifically about the other people in the room other than the woman with the gun. It all happened so fast."

"What can you remember about her?" Luke prodded.

"I saw the gun first and was...stunned. My feet felt leaden and I couldn't even scream," she said, her eyes pleading with his for understanding.

He squeezed her fingers again, willing his strength to flow into her.

Her chest heaving with exertion, Charlie said, "Then she spoke Chinese and twisted around to face him. That was when I saw the badge clipped to her belt."

"Chinese?" Monty asked, keeping his tone neutral.

"I don't know Chinese, if that's what you mean, but it sounded just like Hai when he would slip back into his native language. She said a phrase I often heard him say." Seeing the raised eyebrows from the group, she explained. "Hai learned a few of our sayings, like, *Who knows,* when asked a question and he didn't know the answer. But he would generally slip back into Chinese and when Eli would ask why a computer program wasn't working, Hai would say *Shuí zhīdào.*" Looking back to Luke, she said, "The woman said those word to Eli before she shot him."

"Who knows..." Luke pondered out loud before looking at the others. "Was she asking who knew about what he was working on?"

"I'm not sure but, if so, that means the killers know that he may have shared the information with someone else," Patrick added, his focus landing on Charlie. His expression mirrored the others in the room—shock.

"What did she look like?" Monty prodded. "Was she Asian or Caucasian?"

"Asian," she answered definitively.

"Can you identify her?" Monty continued to ask, but frowned as Charlie shook her head.

Swallowing hard, she waded in again, "No...I just saw...she fired. I saw...I saw he was dead...and I ran. I made it back down the street to where I had parked and drove away." Pinning her gaze on them again, she said, "It's easy for you to sit here and think that I should have called the police. I should have done something. All I could see in my mind...besides Eli getting shot...was that badge on her belt. I made it back to my apartment, brainstorming the whole way. I knew he was supposed to meet with the FBI... what if that was them? What if one of them got to him first to keep him from talking? Or, if it was someone else, then the FBI would find him when he didn't show up."

Her face crumpled as she dropped her chin to her chest. "But they didn't look, did they?"

Fat tears slipped down her cheeks, spearing Luke's heart. Tucking her into his arms, he pulled her face into his chest. One hand slid around to cup the back of her head and the other banded around her waist. His eyes caught Jack's over the top of her head and he knew his expression gave off mixed signals. On the one hand, he wanted the interview to be over...to take her back to his home, let her sleep in a real bed. After she had confessed last night that she had moved around for months, his heart hurt for her. But he knew they could not stop. They had to know everything.

"Jack?" Bethany's quiet voice called out. He turned his admiring gaze toward her. "Why don't I fix some food? Maybe have some of the others come?" A quick smile and nod was his only answer, but the only one she needed. Turning, she left the room.

After a moment, Charlie lifted her face from Luke's neatly pressed shirt, realizing she had made a mess of it. "I'm sorry—"

He shushed her, giving her waist a squeeze. "Can you keep going a little more?"

Blushing as she looked around, she said, "Gentlemen, I really am sorry. I know you need this information. I'll try to be less emotional now." She appreciated their murmurs of accommodation and heaved a deep sigh once more before continuing. Wiping her eyes, she continued, "I got back to my apartment and immediately pulled up everything on my computers that he had sent. I was terrified and figured I'd better get out of there before someone used his computers to figure out who I was. But the file was incomplete. It was as though he was sending it to me when...when..." she gulped air again, shutting her eyes for a few seconds then shaking her head to clear her thoughts before continuing.

"I had a small, furnished apartment that I rented monthly as I tried to save money for a possible condo, so it was easy to move out. I loaded all my clothes, belongings, and computer equipment into my car and left. I lived in hotels for several weeks, never staying in one more than three nights in a row even though I was paying cash. Then I saw an ad where an older couple were selling a camper van, not much bigger than an old VW van. I paid cash and hit the road. I moved around to different states as I tried to figure out what to do and how to stay alive. Once, I rented a place for a month, just to throw off anyone who might be following me, but...well...that didn't work out so well." Her eyes darted around the room, hoping no one would question her about that, at least not now.

Cam leaned forward and asked, "Could you ever tell that someone was after you?"

"Yeah. I had ways to set up alerts on my bank account and once it was triggered, I pulled everything out and set up an overseas, off-shore bank account." With a wry smile, she said, "Eli was brilliant at encryption. He taught me a lot and then I taught myself even more. I had enough saved up to keep moving around and taking jobs as they came along. But I always had to be careful."

"And how did you find Luke?" Jack asked.

Inhaling sharply, she wondered if Luke was going to be angry. *We didn't get to this subject when we were at his house.* Glancing to the side, afraid of what his expression might hold, she let out her breath when she saw his curiosity.

"It's okay, Charlie. We need to know. I need to know."

"Eli had created a lot of security programs and never had them copyrighted. They were just out there. One night, I saw where someone had managed to discover one of them and I had a way to get in and see what they were doing. It was you." She hastened to say, "I didn't know anything about you or what you were trying to do at first, but I knew of an easier way to use his program so I sent that first message. When you answered and were not a jackass about it, I found that I wanted to keep helping you. And by then, I had you located so I could see what you were working on."

Shaking his head, Luke said, "Hell, Charlie, I hope no one else can!"

Smiling, she shook her head. "Nope, not from Eli's programs. Only me."

"You helped us on the case we had a couple of months ago, where we were investigating terrorists," Jack stated, staring at her pointedly.

Sucking in her lips, she nodded. "I had been contacted by what I knew was a bogus company, so I played along in an attempt to find out what they were doing. I had no idea they were terrorists or I would have never tried to interfere." Ducking her head for a moment, she added, "That was the one time I tried to rent an apartment...and of course, a couple of you showed up."

Cam jerked back, his eyes darting between Blaise

and Luke's. "You used the name Lester Wyant...I remember that! I was there!" His expression turned to one of admiration. "You had us fooled. How did you know we were coming?"

"Uh...it was all Eli's programs that allowed me to be able to see what you were working on. That's how I knew. By that time, I was following what Luke was doing fairly regularly...I just wanted to help."

"Fucking hell," Cam said, leaning back in his chair, wonder in his eyes.

Looking up at the frustration pouring off Luke, she said, "Maybe when this is all over, I can show you Eli's programs. It would make some of your work easier."

"We'll talk about that later," Jack interrupted curtly.

Luke shot his boss a quick-look, knowing Jack was not about to have someone get into their business unless he had vetted them.

Jack continued, "Ms. Trivett, we need to continue this interview to find out what you have learned about Eli's fears and findings, but," he paused and looked toward the kitchen, "it's after twelve and we know you're exhausted. Bethany and a few friends have prepared some lunch and I suggest we table the conversation until we've eaten."

Grateful for the reprieve, she nodded. As she stood, she said, "Please call me Charlie, if you will."

"All right, Charlie," Jack said, smiling at her. "Let's eat."

Luke stood and once more linked fingers with Charlie, earning a shy smile and sending her one in return. The electricity jolted straight to his heart once more and a fierce protective urge engulfed him. Walking to the kitchen, he hoped he did not stumble again. Rounding the counter corner, he felt her slam into the back of him instead, hearing her gasp.

Charlie bounced off Luke, staring at the people who had joined Bethany. Standing in the kitchen were three other women, all as beautiful as Bethany. Bart walked over to the one with long dark hair and bent to place a sweet kiss on her lips.

Luke felt Charlie stiffen beside him and knew she felt overwhelmed as the crowd of strangers grew larger. He shot Bethany a worried look over Charlie's head. *Hell, this scene is so familiar; it happens every time one of the Saints shows up with a woman.* His breath caught in his throat as his fingers flexed against hers. *Mine? Oh, hell, who knows? I just know I want to protect her.* "These are just a few friends. They're good people," he assured her.

His words washed warm against her ear as she took a deep breath. Everyone was filling their plates with sandwiches, chips, potato salad, and an open box of the most delectable cupcakes covered in pink, purple, and teal icing.

"Hi, I'm Angel," a stunning blonde whose hair was streaked with pink, purple, and teal stripes greeted, her smile matching the twinkle in her eyes. "I'm Monty's wife."

"And she's the owner of Angel's Cupcake Heaven," Bethany added with a nod toward the dessert on the counter.

"They look delicious," Charlie acknowledged, remembering Luke's comment about the cupcakes when she had met him at the diner. Just then her stomach growled loudly. It had been hours since the toast she had eaten at Luke's house.

The dark-haired beauty left Bart's arms and walked over, greeting Charlie with a shy smile. "Hi. I'm Faith, Bart's wife."

The last woman of the newcomers walked over, wearing nursing scrubs, her smile wide. "I'm Miriam, Cam's wife." Seeing Charlie glancing at her scrubs, she added, "I work part time at a nursing home. We've got a baby so I leave at lunchtime. My mom's got her right now, so when Bethany called, I wanted to come over."

Luke had walked away to get his plate as soon as he saw that Charlie was in good hands. Offering her a wink, he grabbed some food before moving over to where the Saints were congregating in the dining room. Walking up, he heard Jack ask Bart, "Do you think Faith can help?"

Nodding, while chewing, Bart finally swallowed. "It can't hurt."

Luke knew what Jack was implying. Faith worked part time as an artist for the Charlestown Police Department, as well as having special skills. She never claimed to be a seer, but would at times have visions that assisted with a few cases.

"If you want, Miriam can check her out as well, considering she's been living on the run for months," Cam offered.

Luke's mouth paused as he was about to take a bite of one of Angel's confections when he realized all the Saint's eyes were on him. Clearing his throat, he said, "Uh…you asking for my permission?" Seeing the grins, he chuckled. With a glance into the kitchen to see that Charlie was safely ensconced with the other women, he felt the jolt to his heart again. *I've been in her presence for only twelve hours and yet…I've known her for a lot longer. Mine?* Grinning, he watched as she smiled while chatting, her hands nervously fluttering about her sides. *Yeah, if she'll have me.*

CHAPTER 10

WITH LUNCH OVER, the Saints and Charlie settled back onto the sofas after Miriam and Angel left. Luke noticed that if Charlie wondered why Faith stayed in the kitchen with Bethany, she said nothing. He also noted the dark circles underneath her eyes, showcasing her fatigue. Leaning over, he whispered, "You okay?"

She twisted her head around and offered a tight nod.

Jack, taking charge as usual, said, "Charlie, we need to understand how the past five months have gone for you. Where you've traveled or, I should say, where you've hidden. What you've done...in particular with the information Eli sent to you."

Revived, with food in her belly, she plunged ahead. "I can tell you what I know and what I have discerned, but I'll warn you that the data is very incomplete. Almost as soon as I began to try to check on things, the information was immediately changed and scrambled. New encryption was placed and I haven't been able to determine what was going on. Plus," she offered a little shrug, "I had to be extra vigilant so whoever killed Eli couldn't find me."

Realizing she was somewhat nestled in the crook of Luke's arm, she allowed herself the brief fantasy of wanting to stay there, her breath hitching as she felt his fingers caress her shoulder.

"All I can tell you is that the client was a Chinese based medical company and it appeared they were taking orders for organs. What Eli told me is that he discovered there was a clinic here in the United States that was supplying them…and not legally." Twisting her head around, she watched the expressions change as the Saints began processing what she was saying.

She held up a thumb drive and said, "This is what Eli sent to me, but I'll let you know the information in here doesn't definitively prove anything. I know because I've tried. It lists the first name of the contact he was working with and spreadsheets of information but that's all."

"And that name?" Jude asked.

"Jun," she replied. For a moment, the silence in the room unnerved her as the Saints continued to type into their tablets. Shifting her gaze toward Luke, she noticed his eyes were still on hers. Offering him a little smile, she leaned over and whispered, "I'm okay."

Returning the smile, he said, "How did you know what I was thinking?"

"I'm not sure…we've only been in each other's presence less than a day, but I just knew you were wondering how I was holding up."

Nodding, he agreed. "That's exactly what I was thinking."

Jack interrupted, "You mentioned a camper van. Is it at Luke's house?"

Shaking her head, she said, "No. I didn't want there to be any evidence of it where he lived just in case someone was following it. I registered it with a fake name but I was always terrified that I'd be discovered. It's parked about two miles from his house."

Realizing she must have walked to his house in the middle of the night from her parked van, Luke startled. Jerking around, he accused, "You didn't tell me how far you walked last night!"

Blinking rapidly, she replied, "You never asked!"

"I was too busy trying to figure out how you got into my house," he retorted.

Leaning away from him, pulling out from underneath his arm, she glared back. "What? You think little ol' me can't walk a few blocks in the dark to get somewhere? I've been taking care of myself for months now! That was why I ended up at your house to begin with after the two men came."

The silence thundered in the room as Luke's face turned red. "What men?"

Sighing heavily, her shoulders slumped. "I never got around to telling you what happened before I ran again last night." Seeing all eyes on her once more, she said, "I was awakened by two men who were prowling around my van."

"How'd you get away?" Bart asked.

"I slipped outside and eliminated the threat."

No one spoke. No one moved...until Luke growled, "Eliminated the threat?"

"I've been taught a little karate, or rather a combination of karate and self-defense." she explained. "I took out the one in the back, knocking him unconscious before doing the same with the one in the front. Then I duct-taped their hands together and left them under a tree." Pinching her lips together in defiance, she added, "So you see, I can take care of myself."

Jack, ignoring the growing irritation coming from Luke and Charlie, looked over at Bart and Cam. "I want her van taken somewhere safe. Completely hidden. Get rid of tags and anything identifiable."

Charlie's eyes narrowed as her attention swung back to Jack. "Excuse me? That's my home!"

"Not anymore," Jack declared. "It may be bugged or have a tracking device. Either way, it's no longer considered safe."

Charlie opened her mouth to protest again when she felt Luke's fingers flex on her shoulder.

Luke leaned over and whispered, "That old VW van is too recognizable and someone has already found you once. You want help, so now you need to give us some trust."

Refusing to look at him, she let his words move over her for a few minutes while several of the Saints were discussing her van. The realization slid over her that Luke was right. *I am tired of doing this alone.* But the knowledge that she would need to find a new apartment or hotel was overwhelming. Her shoulders sagged in resolution as she nodded slightly, keeping quiet as Bart and Cam left the room.

Glancing out the windows, she could see the sun had moved lower over the mountains in the background. Exhaustion threatened to drown her as she once more slumped back into the deep cushions of the sofa.

"Jack," Luke called out softly, gaining the attention of his boss. He cut his eyes down to Charlie's head and Jack understood the silent message.

"Charlie," Jack said. "We've done all we can today and realize you're very tired. I'm going to move my men to our conference room and ask that you stay with Bethany and Faith for a little while. Then Luke'll take you home."

"I…" she sighed, "I'll need to find a place to stay."

"You're staying with me," Luke stated, ignoring the grins from his fellow Saints. Seeing Charlie about to protest, he added quickly, "I've got room and the ability to go over your computer programs with you. It will be easier than you traveling from a hotel where we'd have to assign security."

Not knowing how to answer, she simply twisted to look into his face. His dark eyes were warm, melting her. The need for control began to slide away as she desired to turn it all over to him. *All control...everything.* Jerking as she realized her thoughts were turning sexual, her face blushed with a hot glow. Giving a slight nod, she looked away, hoping he did not notice.

Luke grinned, watching the heat rise from the top of her shirt to her hairline. Giving her shoulder a squeeze, he whispered, "I'll take care of you." With that promise, he rose and followed the other Saints downstairs, leaving her in the capable hands of Bethany and Faith.

THIRTY MINUTES LATER, Charlie laughed at another Saints' antic, told by Bethany. "I can't believe that he trapped you, thinking you were an intruder to his super-secret lair!"

Tossing her long braid over her shoulder, Bethany laughed. "Oh, at the time I was furious! And then I was intrigued but, by the time we got back to my place with Gram, I looked in the mirror. Tangled hair, my shirt had a rip from the brambles I ran through, my jeans were dirty, and I had leaves stuck to me. Yeah, I was a real prize catch!"

The women laughed for a few more minutes and Charlie reveled in the newfound feeling of female camaraderie.

Faith leaned forward, her voice soft and hesitant. "Charlie, I want to be honest with you. I never want you to feel as though I took advantage of you."

Knitting her brow, Charlie looked at the petite woman with delicate features and wondered how she could ever take advantage of someone.

"I work part-time for the local police department as an artist. I assist people remembering things and then I draw it for them."

"Like a sketch artist?"

Nodding, Faith smiled. "Essentially, yes. But I also...get...uh...feelings, if you will. Intuitions about people and situations. Sometimes that comes through in my drawings and will often be very realistic."

"Intuitions?" Charlie pondered that word for a moment before cocking her head to the side. "Like a seer?"

Sucking in a breath, Faith replied, "No. I'm not a seer, nor am I psychic. But...I feel things very intensely and can sometimes help with memories. But only if you're willing."

Charlie's mind jumped back to the scene of Eli's murder and she grimaced. She had spent so many months trying to not see it in her mind that she occasionally wondered if she had dreamed the entire thing. Licking her bottom lip slowly, she nodded. "Eli was...well, sometimes a pain in my ass, but he was a good friend. And, I think I was his only friend, in the end. So, yes," she said, with more determination in her voice. "Yes, I'll work with you. Just let me know when."

The sweet smile on Faith's face shot to Charlie's heart and she wondered what prejudices Faith must have had to face in her life with her gift. *I guess I'm not alone in always feeling different. I've hidden myself away for so long that I forgot what it's like to really get to know people.*

THE INTENSITY OF the meeting downstairs was in vast contrast with the women's conversations upstairs. The other Saints noticed Luke prowling the length of the room after firing up his coffee maker and downing a cup of his former high-octane brew. The normally data-focused Saint was ignoring his computer, settling on pacing and ranting at the same time.

"A cop...or a fucking Fed...murder. Damn," he growled, slurping another sip.

Monty's face was stone as he cracked his knuckles. "I don't want to believe it could have been someone from the FBI." He shook his head adding, "But I'd be a lousy investigator if I didn't consider all possibilities."

"What possibility is crossing your mind?" Patrick asked, watching his brother-in-law's face morph into a grimace.

"To assume the female murderer is Lin Wang is irresponsible," Monty replied. "She's only one Asian female agent in the Bureau. There are others and there will be more than one in the Baltimore police force as well."

"But...coincidental?" Jack asked.

"Fuckin' hell," Monty spit out. "I hate coincidence!"

"As a witness to a murder, possibly by someone in law enforcement, Charlie's going to need protection," Marc stated. "Do you want us to take turns?"

Luke whirled around, sloshing out a bit of coffee. "No, I've got her," he said vehemently. Suddenly, the idea of his co-workers spending more time with Charlie than he sent a bolt of unfamiliar jealousy through him. *They're all married,* he chastised himself. *I can trust them. Well, all but Marc—*

"Hey, watch it, speed-demon," Blaise cried out, wiping some of the spilled liquid off the table next to his tablet.

"Sorry," Luke mumbled. "Look, we need to dig into Lin Wang, the Bureau files on Eli's meeting, and everything we can about someone named Jun in the medical field. I'm the most qualified, but I could use some help." His eyes shot to Jude, who had assisted on the computer aspect of investigations before. "I'll farm some of it to Jude, but I need more." Piercing Jack with his stare, he said, "I want Charlie protected so she needs to be with us anyway, but Jack? She's the most qualified to assist with the intelligence gathering in this case. Are you willing to use her talents?"

The room grew silent as all eyes moved to Jack. He pressed his lips tightly for a moment, focused sharply on Luke. Finally, he said, "I vetted every one of you before I hired you. She's still an unknown to us." Throwing his hand up before Luke could interject, he added, "But, I know she's helped us before." The room continued in silence as Jack pondered the situation.

Slowly nodding, he said, "Luke, I agree that she needs to be in on this with us. Not just as a witness. She has the background, knowledge, and skills to assist. But..." capturing Luke's undivided attention before continuing, "she works this case only. I'm not willing to give her access to anything else of ours until we have this investigation solved and know more about the resourceful and elusive Charlotte Trivett."

Quickly agreeing, Luke grinned. "Honest to God, boss, I think she and I together can make great things happen in our investigations."

"Is that all you plan on doing to make great things happen?" Blaise joked.

The other Saints chuckled, all pleased to see Luke interested in something besides his keyboard for once.

Blushing, he shrugged. "Guess I'll find out."

He was saved from more embarrassing revelations by Cam and Bart entering the room from the back stairwell, coming from the garage.

"We found the van and swept it," Bart reported. "No bugs or tracking devices, but we began disassembling it nonetheless."

"Where is it?" Luke asked.

"Got it in a safe place, off Jack's property and into the woods," Cam answered. He set a duffle bag on the floor near Luke and said, "I packed all of her personal items here. Thought she'd like to have it at your place."

"Thanks man." Looking at Jack, he said, "I'd like to get her home. She's functioning on little sleep, nerves, and adrenaline. I know she's strong and survived this long on her own, but I'd...well, I'd like to make sure she's okay."

He gratefully met the understanding smiles of the others in the room. Jack nodded and said, "Okay, we've got our assignments to begin working on. Marc leaves in a couple of weeks for his protection duty and the rest of us will work this case. Luke, take a day and then have her back here to meet with Faith again."

Nodding, Luke snagged the duffle off the floor and proceeded up the stairs, anxious to take care of Charlie.

CHAPTER 11

B Y THE TIME Luke and Charlie left the Saints' compound, he saw the exhaustion plainly written on her face. Her smile drooped as much as her eyelids. Swinging into a hamburger drive-thru, he ordered burgers and fries before heading back to his home.

The scent emanating from the bag sitting on the console between them almost drove Charlie crazy. "Mmmm," she moaned. "I know Bethany fed us, but I was too nervous to eat much. Now, I'm ravenous."

Luke glanced to the side, staring at her profile before jerking his eyes back to the road, his heart pounding. The sound of her moans shot straight to his cock, making him shift uncomfortably in the seat. *Get a grip, man. She's here for protection, not me making a move on her.* A sigh slipped out as he realized that for the first time, he was meeting a woman that interested him on all levels—intellectual as well as physical—and, for now, he needed to consider her off limits since she needed protection by the Saints.

Charlie heard his sigh and grimaced. *God, he probably hates this. Having to babysit me...in his home. Why is*

*it that I've wanted to meet him for months...secretly
fantasized about him for years...and, now that I'm here,
I'm foisted upon him and it's making him uncomfortable?*

"Luke, I really hate to make you stay with me.
Honestly, if you can just show me back to my van, I'll
be fine." She caught the surprised lifting of his eyebrows and asked, "What?"

"Your van is gone, Charlie. Bart and Cam have it
well hidden."

"But my stuff is in—"

"They emptied the van and all your things are
packed in that duffle in the backseat."

Luke pulled into his driveway and into the garage.
As the door was lowering behind them, he twisted to
her and saw the wide-eyed shock on her face. "That
VW van is like a beacon saying 'Here I am!' We didn't
discover any bugs or tracking devices, but it's not a
typical automobile on the road. Too easy to follow, too
easy to identify with you. Honest to God, Charlie, you
couldn't have gotten worse hide-out transportation."
He grabbed the burger bag and opened his door.
"Come on, let's eat while we talk."

Huffing, she followed him into the house, determined to continue their discussion. "Do not treat me as
though I'm dumb," she blurted. As her gaze landed on
the burgers and fries now on plates, she had to admit
her hunger was taking the starch out of her argument.
She noticed he stood in the kitchen with the two plates
in his hands and her eyes lifted to his face. He was

smiling at her, with one eyebrow arched.

"I know this is all new to you and your life has once again taken a strange turn. But I want to get you fed first. Think we can table your complaints until after we've eaten?"

Wanting to fight back, she glanced down at the food and her stomach loudly protested its hunger. A grin slipped onto her face as she nodded. "Yeah, it seems as though my belly agrees with you."

"Good, I'll start with your belly," he joked, "and then we'll move to getting the rest of you on board."

Thirty minutes later, she pushed back the almost-empty plate and leaned back in her chair. Rolling her head to the side, she stared at Luke as he polished off the last of her fries. "That's not fair," she grumbled.

Looking over, a french-fry drenched in ketchup hanging out of his mouth, his brows drew down in question. "What's not fair?"

"You. I was all ready to complain about my van, my belongings, my being brought here where I know you don't want me even though I want to be here, and now I'm so full and pooped all the fight has gone out of me."

Swallowing the last fry, he said, "Don't want you?"

Blushing, she realized her full tummy had numbed her brain and she had blurted out more than she meant to. "I…uh…I…"

She found her body moving as he grabbed her chair and twisted it around so that it faced him. He settled his long legs on either side of hers, effectively trapping her, before leaning his body into her space. Her eyes grew wide as she dropped her gaze to his mouth, wondering if and wishing he would kiss her.

Instead, he said, "We need to get something straight right now. I've been interested in meeting you ever since you first messaged me. My intentions were purely friendship all that time…had no idea if you were young, old, male, female. But I can't deny that there was a part of me that hoped you were young and female. Maybe that was just my fantasy, but there it is."

Eyes wide, she listened as her heart began to beat faster. His gaze bore into hers and she was incapable of staring at anything other than his beautiful eyes as he continued to speak.

"We officially met about twenty hours ago and, in that time, I've learned you've been on the run for months, the witness to a murder, and trying to investigate a crime of such proportions that you are at serious risk."

Moving closer to her, he settled his hands on her shoulders, making sure she was listening to every word before continuing. "Yes, the Saints are still working with the Bureau on Eli's life, his work, and what got him killed. But, Charlie, you are also now our mission. Your safety. Sure, we want your help in the investigation, but we are now more interested in taking care of you."

Hearing his words, she could only stare at the lips

so close to hers. *He has no idea that I've spent months looking at his picture on the internet. Wondering what it would be like to have him staring back at me. Holding me. Kissing me.* Pulled, as if by a magnet, she leaned the few inches forward to meet his lips, when he suddenly jerked back. Mortification rushed over her as she tried to hop up, but her legs were still trapped between his knees and his hands were still on her shoulders.

"Please let me up," she whispered, her eyes downcast, feeling the fiery flames of a blush heating her cheeks.

"Not happening," he said, watching her expression morph to anger, but before she could speak, he quickly added, "Not until you hear everything I've got to say."

Her eyes snapped up to his, her mouth in a tight line.

His warm eyes held hers as he confessed, "You're still my fantasy."

His words slowly seeped into her. Cocking her head in confusion, she opened and closed her mouth several times but nothing came out.

Letting out a sigh, his eyes roamed over her face, memorizing every detail. The little crease above her brow as she tried to puzzle something out. Her rich brunette hair spilling over her shoulders, the silky strands still begging for his hands. Her hazel eyes held his as the green flecks seemed to wink at him. Her smooth complexion, with a slight blush on her cheeks, and her lips were plump and pink from her biting nervously on them.

Swallowing hard, he said, "Charlie, you need to stay here because that is the easiest way for me to keep you safe. Tomorrow, you're going to tell me how you broke in. In fact, at some point, Jack will probably want you to look over everyone's security." With a wry grin, he added, "Gotta admit, I'm good at what I do, but there's obviously things you can teach me. I've wanted to meet you ever since you first contacted me months ago."

"Why do I feel that there's a *but* coming?" she asked, steeling herself for disappointment.

"There's no way I can take advantage of you," he answered, his voice rough with anguish. Lifting one hand from her shoulder, he cupped her cheek. "I can't do casual, Charlie. And I can't play on your fears or need. I'm just not wired that way."

"I...I don't do casual either," she confessed. "But, you...you don't seem casual to me. I already feel...I don't know...somehow connected." She leaned her face into his warm hand, closing her eyes for a moment, afraid to watch his reaction to her words.

"Charlie..." he moaned, barely hanging on to his restraint. Sucking in a huge breath, he let it out slowly. "You need to rest...in a real bed...safe and warm." Bending her head forward with his hand, he placed his lips on her forehead, holding them there for a long kiss. Watching as she opened her eyes, seeing them full of doubt, he added, "This isn't no. This is just me wanting to take care of you. You're right, we're already connected, but I want to do this right."

The sting of rejection gone, she smiled as she nodded. "Okay," her soft voice agreed, as she allowed him to pull her up. Glancing down at their hands as he linked fingers with hers, she smiled.

Stopping at one of the open doors in the hall, he turned and said, "This is my guest room. I know it's small, but—"

"Oh, please," she interrupted. "I've been in my tiny camper for a long time. This seems huge." She viewed the double bed with an inviting red comforter, matching dresser and comfy rocking chair in the corner.

Chuckling, he watched as she peered into the room, her eyes bright as she looked around. "The rocker was my mom's. Even when she was buried deep in her studies, she would rock while telling me stories of long ago heroes as I went to sleep."

"It's lovely," she admitted, warmed by his personal admission.

"There's a bathroom at the end of the hall," he indicated, "and I'll be across the hall." Startling, he dropped her hand and moved quickly back toward the kitchen. Returning a moment later, he had the large duffle bag in his hand. Setting it down on the floor, he said, "Is there anything else you need?"

She wanted to scream that the only thing missing was him holding her tight all during the night, but a quick shake of her head was the only answer she gave.

"Okay, then. I'll say goodnight." With another kiss on her forehead, he turned and headed into his room, then hesitated at the door. Twisting back, he gazed deeply into her eyes. "Charlie?"

Mesmerized, she cocked her head to the side, waiting.

"I...well, just know that I'm glad you're here. I'm glad you came to me. I promise we'll discover what we need to keep you safe."

Her tongue darted out to wet her dry lips as they curved into a gentle smile. "Me too, Luke. There's nowhere else I'd rather be."

With that, they each moved into their separate rooms.

Two hours later, Luke lay awake, mentally kicking himself. *I had a gorgeous woman, obviously into me and one that interests me as well, practically begging to be kissed. And I let a sense of honor keep me from going with the flow.*

The faint illumination from the security light in the hall grew larger as his door swung open, Charlie's body outlined in the darkness.

"Charlie? Everything all right?" he asked, sitting up quickly, ready to jump from the bed.

"I..."

Without waiting, he swung his legs over the edge of the bed and quickly stalked to the doorway, his hands automatically going to her shoulders as he peered into her face. Cocking his head to the side, he waited to see what she needed.

"I'm sorry," she whispered. "I know…I know what you said earlier, and I agree," she rushed. "There's a lot going on and I…I do appreciate you're…um…hesitant to jump into…um…something physical, but it's just that…" Her voice trailed off as her eyes cast downward.

Lifting her chin with his fingers, he said, "What? What do you need? I'll give you anything I can."

Slipping her arms around his waist, she slowly moved into his body, hugging him tightly. Resting her face on his chest, she heard his steady heartbeat against her ear. "I've been alone for a really long time," she confessed. "I wanted to feel someone hold me."

Closing his eyes as he rested his chin on the top of her head, he pulled her in tighter. Without a word, he moved them backward until the backs of his knees hit his bed. Twisting, he gently pushed her down and, as her eyes widened, he said, "Sleep with me in here. Just sleep."

Seeing her smile, he crawled over her body, trying to ignore the way her curves felt underneath him as he settled on the other side. Slipping under the covers, he wrapped his arms around her, pulling her in tight. With her back pressed into his front, he tucked her in. Neither spoke for a few minutes as he felt his heartbeat synchronize with hers.

Finally, in the dark, he heard her whisper, "Thank

you, Luke," before her breathing deepened in slumber.

Lying with the enigmatic woman at his side, he smiled. That night as he dreamed, the woman from the bar and from the diner and his cyber-friend, all melded into one...the beauty in his arms.

CHAPTER 12

THE EARLY MORNING light gave little comfort to the two teenagers huddled together underneath the overhang of a thick grove of trees in the park across from the World Bank. Penny Owens blinked a few times before nudging closer to David, hoping to give him some of her meager warmth. His cough had gotten worse during the night and Penny was worried about him.

A thin blanket was draped over their bodies and she pulled it up tighter to their chins while making sure to tuck it closer around their feet. The air was not cold...not yet, but the hint of the coming winter gave her pause. *What then? How will we survive then?* She glanced over to David, still sleeping, his chest rattling with each breath. They had been together through the spring and summer, since meeting at a soup kitchen. A lifetime for a homeless person who lives day by day. And with every painful rasping, her heart hurt a little more.

Pushing his dark hair back away from his forehead, she noticed how long it had become. *Maybe I can find some scissors and give him a haircut.* At that thought, she grimaced, thinking of her own overly long, dirty braid.

The sound of footsteps nearby had her instantly on alert and she shook David awake. "Someone's coming," she whispered, glad that he woke quickly, attempting to move in front of her. The two looked up as a woman walked by before stopping to smile down at the two huddled under the tree.

"Hello," she said, her voice warm and friendly. Reaching into her bag, she pulled out packs of peanut butter crackers and water bottles. "Please don't be afraid, but I'm in the area offering some snacks and water to some of the homeless in the area."

They eyed the proffered treats suspiciously, but both of their bellies growled at the same time. David doubled over with his fierce cough and the woman's eyes immediately grew concerned. Reaching into her pocket, she pulled out a card. Setting it on the ground next to the water bottles, she said, "I am leaving the name of a clinic where I work. It's not too far from here and they would be glad to see you about your cough."

"Thank you, but we have no money," Penny said, eyeing the pretty Asian woman with a mixture of suspicion and overpowering need.

The genuine smile did not leave the woman's face as she said, "Part of the clinic is for assisting those who are unable to pay." Her gaze dropped to David's pale face. "Please come in today. Be sure to bring the card with you and they'll make sure you are taken care of."

"They can make me well?" he asked, hope in his voice as his chest racked with another cough.

"They will certainly make sure you are no longer in pain," she said gently. With that, she stood and continued down the path.

As soon as she was gone, Penny jumped up and grabbed the snacks along with the woman's card. "Dr. Cheung's Medical Clinic," she read, handing one of the water bottles to David. He took a long drink, the refreshing liquid cooling his dry throat. They both tore into the crackers, relishing the early morning treat.

"What do you think?" he asked.

"We might as well go check out the clinic. You're getting sicker and we've got nothing to lose."

As the two teens finished their snack while the early morning mist slowly rose over the park, both smiled at the possibility that luck had finally come their way.

AS THE SUNLIGHT filtered through the blinds, creating slatted patterns on the bed, Charlie struggled to analyze her surrounding as her eyes blinked open. Uncertainty filled her as she jerked up, the room swimming for a moment until recognition slammed into her. *Luke's room. Oh, my God. I came in here last night.* One quick glance to the side revealed the empty space beside her and she dropped her chin to her chest. *I wonder what he thinks of me? He's certainly not here so—*

"Good morning," his warm voice came from the

doorway, causing her to whip her head around. From his tousled, dark hair down to his full lips surrounded by his stubbled jaw, to his dimple peeking deliciously. He looked even yummier in the morning than he did last night, something Charlie did not think could have been possible. Leaning against the doorframe with one muscular, jean-clad leg crossed in front of the other, her eyes drifted back to his strong arms, crossed, one hand holding a cup of coffee.

As much of a god as he appeared with the morning light illuminating his body, it was the scent of strong coffee that had her leaping from the bed. "Is that coffee for me?"

Luke laughed at the beautiful woman, her feet kicking out to untangle from the sheets in an attempt to rush to his side for the coffee. Her eyes peered into his cup as she sniffed the steam rising from the brew. He watched as her eyes closed and a soft, dreamy expression crossed her face. "So you like coffee?"

Her eyes jerked open as she lifted her hands to the cup and then gazed up at him. "Doesn't everyone?" Taking a sip of the bold brew, she moaned. "Oh, that's so good. I'm nobody to mess with in the morning until I've had this in me!"

Smiling broadly now, he handed the cup to her. *A woman after my own heart.* "Well then, you should have it," he laughed. "Go ahead and get dressed and I'll have some breakfast for you. We've got some talking to do."

His words pulled her back to the here and now,

forcing her to step back, the warm cup still in her hands. A light blush crept over her as she wondered about last night, unable to keep from checking the messy bed behind her.

"Hey," he said, pulling her head back toward him, kissing the top of her forehead. "No regrets, okay? At least not for me. I slept better than ever last night with you in my arms."

Lifting her face, she felt his words slide over her as comforting as the warm coffee. Nodding, she met his grin as she stepped back. "Okay. No regrets." Hearing a noise from the front of the house, she looked up.

"Jack's here," Luke explained.

Sighing heavily, she said, "I'll be right out."

With a wink, Luke turned and left the room leaving her staring in his wake. Sucking in a deep breath and letting it out slowly, she headed to the bathroom, coffee in hand. *Looks like I'll need this brew today.*

Later, sitting at Luke's kitchen table, the three enjoyed the breakfast sandwiches Luke cooked and served.

Tossing his napkin down, Luke leaned his tall body back from the table and turned to Charlie. "Okay, time for some info. How did you break into my place two nights ago?"

Sucking in her lips for a moment, she glanced nervously around the table, focus jumping between the two men before finally landing on Luke's smiling face. He leaned over and took her hand in his much larger one.

"It's okay, Charlie. We need to know so that we can secure the rest of our homes and facilities."

Nodding, she said, "Honestly, I don't know much about security systems, but Eli was always getting jobs where he had to create codes for security companies. He shifted some of the work to me." Twisting her fingers, she glanced over at Jack. "You...well, the Saints...contracted for some preliminary work to be done and he passed it off to me."

"You worked on Jack's system?" Luke asked, his voice hard as Jack looked at her askance.

Letting out a deep sigh, she dropped her attention to her hands. *I'm losing his trust...before I had a chance to discover if there was a real connection.* Grimacing, she lifted her head and forced the words out, staring at Jack's hard face, "Yes. I helped set up the security for your company. It was just the preliminary work...nothing that would tell me anything. But later," she shifted her eyes to Luke, "when I stumbled across someone seeking information using another one of my program creations, I knew it was you. Again. So, using the preliminary work I had done, I was able to...uh...hack your security codes."

"Our security codes?" Jack prodded. "All of them?"

"No! I never tried anything, honest." Lifting her shoulders in a small shrug, she said, "I could see what Luke was working on and was able to help since I wrote the first part of his program anyway."

"And my house?" Luke asked.

"I determined the code for getting in. Only your place...nowhere else. Only here."

The silence sat heavily in the room as they watched her carefully. Just as she felt the need to flee, Jack spoke. "I'm not normally a trusting man, but so far I have no reason not to trust you, Charlie. We want to keep you safe, but to do that, you'll have to work with us on this case. At the same time, I want you to work with Luke to review our security programs."

Nodding quickly while wiping her sweating palms on her yoga pants, she said, "Yes, yes, I can do that. I promise, I only want to help."

With a nod and short smile, Jack stood walking toward the front door, leaving Luke and Charlie alone at the table.

"He's kind of intense, isn't he?" she asked, already knowing the answer.

Chuckling, Luke agreed. "Yeah, but he has to be." After another moment, he added, "I actually think that Jack is glad to finally know who's been helping us all along. He hates unanswered questions...hates the unknown. And now, he knows who you are and what you can do."

"But he doesn't trust me, does he?"

"He will." Luke watched as her eyes widened in response to his declaration. "I do...and therefore he will too."

Taking the plates to the sink, Charlie began to clean the kitchen, but Luke grabbed her hand and pulled, saying, "Come on. I want to show you something."

He led her through the laundry room to the door leading to the garage. Smiling at her curious expression, he continued to lead her past his truck to another door. "I think you'll like this," he said, opening the door.

Peeking inside, her eyes opened wide as she took in the room. Mats covered the floor and mirrors lined one of the walls. A weighted bag hung from the ceiling on one side. He had turned the back part of the garage into an exercise room. But not just any exercise room—*a room perfect for karate practice!*

Giving a very un-karate-like squeal, she dashed into the room and turned around several times taking it all in. "I can't believe you have this here."

Luke grinned at the first sign of enthusiasm she had displayed since meeting her. "I remembered that you had some moves that worked well at Chuck's that night." Moving onto the mat he began with warm up exercises, quickly joined by her.

After several minutes they faced each other, bowing first before circling. Knowing he had a huge height and weight advantage, he jabbed and kicked carefully, but was impressed with her skill.

Charlie, heart pumping, felt her body on fire as she watched the play of muscles in Luke's arms, abs, and legs. *Keep your mind on the task,* she chastised herself, but quickly realized that was easier said than done. Seeing an in, she kicked out, connecting with the back of his knee.

Luke felt the force of her kick but managed to whirl around, taking her legs out from under her. With a quick movement, she landed on her back on the mat and he moved over her. With a grin, he subdued her easily.

Her eyes widened as she sputtered, "That's not karate!"

"I use MCMAP," he said, his body lying on top of hers, his hands securing hers to the sides of her head. Seeing her confusion, he explained, "Marine Corps Martial Arts Program. Bart taught me the moves. I already knew karate, but he showed me what the Marines use."

Her eyes twinkled as she acknowledged the benefits of the fighting techniques. "Will you teach me?"

Luke saw her mouth move and knew she spoke words but, at the moment, had no idea what she was saying. Her breath came in pants, her breasts pressing against his chest. Her eyes no longer just hazel but flecked with bits of green. All the blood in his body rushed south and his erection lay nestled at the apex of her legs. Her mouth, moist and plump. Just waiting to be—

Before he had a chance to back away, Charlie leaned the scant distance upward and molded her lips to his. Not needing any more encouragement, Luke took over the kiss. Her lips were soft and pliant, opening slightly as he angled his face to the side for better access. Slipping his tongue inside her warmth, he explored leisurely at first and then, with only the touch of her tongue against his, the kiss exploded into a tangle.

A sliver of reason crept into his consciousness and he pulled back slightly. She felt the millimeter of distance and refused to allow him to let his honor keep them apart. Bucking her hips, she caught him off guard and dislodged his body enough to heave him to the side, rolling them so that she was on top.

"You're pulling away," she accused. "Why?"

Her hair hung around him like a silken curtain, the scent filling his nostrils. Closing his eyes for a moment, he willed himself not to give in to the urges coursing through his veins. "I told you last night that I wouldn't take advantage of you."

Her eyes narrowed in frustration as she leaned down further into his space, her hands gripping his shoulders. "You listen to me, Luke Costas. Do not dare treat me as though I'm some fragile woman who can't be responsible for making her own decisions. Don't treat me as though I don't know exactly what I'm doing. I've wanted you for months, until it was the only thing I could think about. And now...now I have you right where I want you and I'll be damned if you push me away because of a misplaced sense of honor."

Straddling his hips, she felt his thick cock against her aching core. With her hands still in his, she now pressed him down and lowered her head again. "Not letting you stop," she muttered as her mouth slammed back onto his.

The kiss flamed white-hot once more and she let go of his hands to grasp his face, feeling the rough stubble underneath her fingertips.

Luke, tired of fighting the desire to claim her as his own, circled her body with his arms, pulling her tighter against him. One hand slid down to cup her ass, his fingers molding the firm flesh while he pressed upward against her heated core. The other hand moved up from her waist to the side under her arm, his thumb caressing the underside of her breast.

With a quick, unexpected roll, lips still attached, she was once more underneath him. She grabbed the bottom of his shirt at the same time he reached for hers. Grinning, he moved up to now straddle her hips and pulled his sweat-damp t-shirt off in one fluid movement, tossing it to the side. He slid his hands underneath the bottom of hers and began working it upward until it caught on her breasts.

Watching her carefully, he asked her permission with just her name. "Charlie?"

"Yes," she panted, helping him to pull her t-shirt over her head.

He looked down at her white bra, simple and unadorned, and yet her breasts spilled over the tops creating a scene worthy of a Victoria Secret model. His breath caught in his throat as he watched her unsnap the front closure and the cups separated enough to expose her pretty breasts crowned with dusty pink nipples, hard and ripe.

His swollen cock was raring to play, but he wanted to savor every moment. Shifting back on her legs, he hooked his fingers into the elastic top of her black yoga pants and shimmied them down her legs, catching her panties along the way. In a few seconds, she was completely naked, spread out on his exercise mat, her body illuminated from every angle with the bright lights.

He skimmed his hands over her, from her shoulders to her breasts, kneading the flesh before rolling her nipples between his fingers. She arched her back, pressing her breasts further into his hands, as well as her core against his erection.

Bending down, he sucked one nipple deep into his mouth, eliciting a moan from her parted lips. Moving between breasts, he made sure to give equal attention. His beard scraped her tender skin, leaving a trail of pink as his mouth made its way down over her stomach. Circling around her belly button, he eyed her as she jerked and gasped.

"I'm ticklish," she protested, trying to push his head away from her sensitive tummy.

"Then I'll have to find somewhere else to kiss," he murmured against her flesh as he moved down between her legs. Carefully sliding down her body, he kissed her stomach again before continuing his trail of kisses down to her slick folds. Licking her wetness, he pulled her folds apart to allow his tongue deeper access. *God, I love the taste of her.*

As his tongue plunged in and out of her sex, he reached up with one hand to fondle her breasts. Her hips rotated upwards, pushing into his face.

She could feel the delicious pressure building in her core, smell the scent of sex in the air, desperately needing her release. Turning her head to the side, she watched their lovemaking in the wall of mirrors. Instead of feeling embarrassed, she was turned on…more than she could have ever imagined.

He moved his mouth up towards her swollen clit, sucking it into his mouth, allowing his tongue to swirl around it. At the same time, he pinched her nipple and felt her convulse against his face.

Her hips bucked as she begged for more. He added a finger deep into her channel and she exploded as waves of bliss pounded over and over. Throwing her head back against the floor, she allowed the sensations to carry her away. Away to a place where there was no running, no fear, no worry.

Luke watched her face carefully as the pleasure washed over, grateful to have been able to take her there.

Charlie slowly opened her eyes, smiling down at him. Raising her hands, she beckoned him, needing to feel his body on hers.

He moved back up her body and carefully lowered his hips between her legs, positioning his dick at her opening after grabbing a condom from his wallet. *God, I hope this condom isn't too old.* Sliding his hand between them he guided himself in and with one thrust was fully seated. "Charlie, I want you to feel every inch," he whispered.

She felt stretched as his cock pushed all the way up into her. He began a slow thrusting, pulling almost all of the way out before pushing back in again. Kneeling on the mats between her legs, he pulled her hips upwards toward his dick. Gently pushing her legs apart as wide as she was comfortable, he began his slow thrusting again. This angle produced a new sensation for her, and she began to moan as the friction deep in her channel caused sparks to spread throughout her core.

Feeling his own release coming soon, he leaned down to grasp her nipple in his mouth. Sucking it deeply, he nipped at the hardened bud with his teeth.

"Sweetheart, come for me," he begged.

Right on cue, she felt herself lost once again in her release. The walls of her sex grabbed his cock tightly as wave after wave of pleasure crashed through her. Luke, losing control, pounded the last few thrusts deep inside, allowing her contracting muscles to milk him. Leaning up with her hips tightly held in his firm grip, he threw his head back, neck straining as his release poured deeply inside. Continuing to pump until the last drop was gone, he slowly pulled out.

They lay together on the mats, sated, as he pushed her hair from her face. Staring down into her eyes that were filled with trust, he kissed her lips with the soft promise of being exactly what she needed.

CHAPTER 13

L UKE, HIS BODY laying half on Charlie and half on the mat, lifted his head and looked around. He had used this room for several years, honing his martial arts skills and relieving stress from some of the Saints' missions, as well as staying in shape after sitting in front of his computer for hours. *Never. I'll never look at this room the same again.* It was now filled with the scent of their sex and vision of Charlie's naked beauty writing underneath him as he had loved her.

Her eyes opened slowly and he observed as the re-laxed expression on her face morphed into a smile, her lips curving upward.

"Hey," he whispered, brushing the damp hair from her forehead.

"Hey, back," she replied.

"You okay?"

Nodding, her smile grew wider. "Yeah. Oh, yeah." She watched as a crease developed on his brow and she lifted her hand to smooth it out. "No, Luke. Don't regret this. Please," she begged.

His gaze jerked down to her eyes, now filled with

the beginnings of anguish. "No, no. I don't regret one moment," he said, glad to see her face relax again under his reassurance. "I never expected this."

"Me either," she whispered. "I...haven't...well, let's just say, this isn't normal for me...but then, nothing in the past five months has been very normal."

Leaning forward to kiss her once more, this time allowing the soft touch of lips to convey his feelings, he said, "Let's shower. Then we can get ready for Faith to come over."

Standing, he pulled her forward and grabbed their clothes off the floor before leading her through the house, into his bedroom and into the bathroom. Fully intending for her to shower alone, he could not resist her invitation and discovered shower sex was exactly what he hoped it would be.

"I DON'T THINK I'm going to be able to be much help," Charlie said, sitting in the corner of Luke's comfortable sofa, her legs tucked up under her. She eyed the pretty, dark-haired woman sitting in one of the chairs facing her and could not help but notice the huge, blond man standing next to Luke. *Faith's husband. Bart...that was his name. And he looks worried.*

Faith noticed Charlie's position and smiled gently. "Ignore the men...and especially Bart. He gets nervous when I do this. Sometimes when I get...feelings, about things, it wipes me out, so he's overprotective." Faith ignored the growl she heard from the kitchen and focused all her attention on Charlie. "Let's talk a little and just see what comes out." She arranged an art pad on her lap as she said, "Tell me, in your own words, what you saw. I know you told the Saints yesterday and I heard part of that. But I want you to close your eyes and go back to when you first came upon the window."

Licking her lips, Charlie leaned her head back on one of the pillows, closed her eyes and took a deep breath. Letting the air out slowly she began.

"I walked around the side of Eli's old condo. There's an alley that runs along the back, between his building and the building directly behind, so they have a little patio; that's where the garbage cans are kept. He was neat, but I'd seen a couple of river rats back there, so it always gave me the creeps, but he spent all his time in the back room, with everything spread out. If the doorbell rang, he usually ignored it, so I got in the habit of going to the back door. He could look out and see me as I passed by the window and he'd let me in. The first floor was slightly elevated so I would stand on my tiptoes to see in.

"I got to the edge of the window and, as usual, I lifted on my toes, but heard loud voices. It sounded like a man was angry and I wondered what was going on. I wasn't frightened…just confused. A man was at the table of computers Eli worked at and I remember thinking how pissed Eli was going to be."

"Describe what you see of the man," Faith prodded

softly.

"He was tall. Taller than Eli would have been if he was standing in the kitchen. I know because he towered over Eli's bookcase that was next to him. Dark hair. Cut very short. Not shaved, but almost military short. Wearing dark pants and a dark windbreaker jacket. Then he moved out of the way and I could see Eli, sitting in a chair, with a man holding his hands behind his back. That man was not as tall, but had dark hair as well. The same cut...very black. He had the same dark clothing, but I could see a white dress shirt underneath his dark windbreaker. He had glasses."

"Good. Just keep your eyes closed and walk me through everything," Faith said, as her fingers flew over the paper.

"I saw the side of Eli's head. I could see that he was scared. His mouth was open but he wasn't saying anything. I remember gasping and immediately hoping the sound had not been loud. I reached into my purse to pull out my phone to call 911.

"Then the tall man moved to the other side of the room and I saw a shorter woman. I couldn't see what she was wearing on her legs. I mean, I don't know if it was pants or a skirt, but she had a white blouse and the same dark windbreaker. She had a gun."

By now, Charlie's voice was shaking and Luke moved forward, wanting to provide comfort. Faith shook her head at him, causing him to step back reluctantly.

"Okay, good. Now don't focus on the gun," Faith said. "Look at the woman. Tell me what you see."

Her breath now coming in shorter pants, Charlie's arms wrapped around her knees as she pulled them up protectively in front of her while keeping her eyes tightly shut. She tried to pull the woman's features to the forefront of her mind, but struggled as the image of the weapon overtook all other thoughts.

"I got a glimpse of the side of her face. She was Asian. Her black hair was cut in a bob, just above her shoulders, and hanging straight. No glasses. She...she held the gun in her...right hand, pointing at Eli. She was not really shouting, but I could clearly hear her ask 'who knows?' which is a phrase I heard our Chinese friend use. Eli shook his head.

"I had my hand on my phone and was ready to dial when the woman put her left hand on her hip and that pulled her jacket back a little. And there it was. A badge. Clipped to her waistband."

"And then?" Faith queried, her eyes darting between Charlie and the art pad in her lap.

"I hesitated. It was a badge. A badge! I suddenly didn't know what to do. I hesitated. But before I could even think, the woman fired—"

An animalistic scream pierced the room causing Charlie's eyes to jerk open as she wildly looked around, gasping as she realized the sound had come from her.

Luke rushed forward, dropping to the floor as his arms swept her up into his embrace. He whirled around, sitting down on the sofa with her in his lap. Her sobs filled the room as she clutched to his shirt. Sitting was not providing the comfort he wanted to offer, so he flipped them around so that she was lying on the sofa with half of his body on hers.

Surrounded by all that was Luke, his warmth, his soothing words, his gentle hands moving up and down her back, she began to relax. Her sobs slowed to hiccups before she finally pulled back to stare at his face through watery eyes.

He wiped her wet cheeks with the pads of his thumbs. "I'm so sorry you had to go through this, sweetheart," he whispered.

Her breath hitched a couple of times, but she finally said, "No, it's all right. It's just that, with my eyes closed and talking through the scene, it was as though I was right there under that window once more." Taking one more shuddering breath, she peered over his shoulder, seeing Bart kneeling with his arms around Faith.

"Oh, Faith, are you all right?" Charlie asked, sitting up with Luke's assistance.

Faith smiled and nodded. "I'm fine." Patting her large husband with her small hand, she assured, "Absolutely fine." She glanced down at her art pad and then back up to Charlie. "Are you ready to see what I have?"

Sucking in a deep breath, she nodded. Luke stood and offered his hand to her. Allowing him to pull her up, he wrapped his arm around her waist to assure she was steady. As they stepped over to the other side of the room, Faith lay the pad on the coffee table.

Charlie looked down at the pad filled with several smaller pictures around the edges. *The man at the computers with the bookcase in the background. The man bending over as he held Eli's hands. The woman as her back was to the group.* And in the center was the main description. *It was the woman with the gun. The same dark, sleek bob. The dark windbreaker pushed back at her hip. And the badge.*

Luke and Bart stared at the drawings also, both focused on the woman in the center of the page. There was no way to determine if the woman was Lin Wang, but the illustration bore a striking resemblance to her.

Charlie continued to stare wordlessly at the drawings, her eyes searching for anything that was not right. But there was nothing to correct except maybe the badge. Lifting her eyes to Faith, she said, "It's perfect. It's as though I'm looking into the window again." Her breath hitched again, and she felt Luke's arm pulling her around so that her front was plastered to his side. She looked up and added, "Except the badge. It doesn't look quite right."

Before Luke could respond, Bart explained, "Different law enforcement agencies have different badges. Jack wondered if you might be able to recognize it." He shifted his attention to Luke and said, "Can you pull some up for her to look at? If she can identify the right one, I'll contact Jack and we'll know better how to proceed."

Kissing the top of her head, Luke stepped away from Charlie, reluctantly, just long enough to grab his laptop. Efficiently pulling up various badges, she quickly dismissed any oblong or with five stars. Staring at the myriad of others, she slapped her hand down on the table in frustration. "Good grief, how many badges are there?"

Luke slid his hand around her jaw, gently pulling her face toward his, bending to get in her line of vision. "Charlie...it's okay. We're a helluva lot further in this case than we were."

She focused on his eyes, mesmerized by the milk chocolate color. Jumping when Bart cleared his throat behind them, she blushed, ducking her head.

"Sorry, guys," Bart said. "I'm taking Faith home and then heading to Jack's."

Standing to let them out, Luke kissed Faith on the cheek, thanking her before clasping hands with Bart. "I'm staying here today and working with Charlie from home. Tell Jack I'll check in with him when you all are there."

Nodding, Bart looked over Luke's shoulder to the pale beauty standing in Luke's living room. A slow grin formed on his face as he said, "Hits you at the damndest times." His gaze shifted back to Luke's and he continued, "Take care of her."

Luke watched as Bart smiled down at his wife and they walked arm in arm toward their SUV. Twisting to look over his shoulder at Charlie standing nervously in his house, he vowed, *I plan on doing just that.*

THAT NIGHT, FAITH woke from a dream, her body jerking. Her hands flew to her large, pregnant stomach, breathing a sigh of relief as she felt the strong movement of her baby. Slipping from bed, she padded to the bathroom. Finishing, she was about to turn off the light when an image passed through her mind...*a dragon.* No other image followed as she stopped and waited to see if something else would come. Nothing. Shaking her head, she moved back to the bed, sliding underneath the covers and into Bart's waiting embrace.

"You okay, babe?" he mumbled, his hands instinctively cupping her stomach.

"Yeah, the baby is just moving a lot," she replied, snuggling into her large husband's arms. Closing her eyes, she drifted off, the image of the dragon fading away.

PENNY OWENS AND David Ellis walked to the address listed on the card. The building was unassuming and upon pushing open the door and walking into the lobby, they were greeted by a waiting room filled with people sitting in plastic chairs. Some holding bandages, some with coughs, others sniffling.

Penny grimaced, hoping she and David did not

catch something worse than what he already had while waiting. A pretty Asian woman sitting behind the reception desk looked at the two of them. Xia Wu was on her name tag but Penny did not know how to pronounce the name so she nodded at the friendly woman.

"Do you need to see the doctor?" Xia asked.

"Um...my friend has a cough," Penny began but was interrupted when the receptionist shoved a clipboard filled with papers toward her.

"Fill these out, bring them back up here and we'll see you as soon as we can."

Penny took the clipboard, glancing back at the crowd, and wondered how long they would have to wait.

"Oh, I forgot," David said between coughs, reaching into his jeans pocket, pulling out the business card. "A lady gave me this card and said for me to give it to you when I came in."

The receptionist's eyes widened as a smile creased her face. "Oh, I didn't realize," she said, reaching for the card. With a quick glance at it, she reached over the desk and took the clipboard out of Penny's hands. "You won't need to fill this out."

"Hey," Penny protested. "What are you doing? Can't he be seen?"

"Oh yes, but you don't have to wait out here. You can be brought on back." Standing, she indicated for them to follow her as she walked through the door behind her desk.

Sharing a wide-eyed expression, the two fell in step behind the young woman.

She looked over her shoulder and explained, "We actually have a separate clinic area for special patients."

"Special?" Penny asked.

Hesitating, with her hand resting on a pair of double doors, she said, "We understand that there are some people who have needs that go beyond medical care and this clinic is run by a doctor who wants to help."

"Because we're homeless?" Penny pursued.

The woman nodded but said nothing else as she pushed through the doors. Curiosity leading them forward, they followed her into an elevator and then down a rather long, dark hall. Just as Penny was about to protest their direction, they went back up a staircase and into a small, but sparkling clean, waiting room that had no one else there. She passed them off to another receptionist, who greeted them with a friendly smile. Welcoming them, she moved to sit with them as they filled out the forms together.

Penny stiffened when she saw the questions pertaining to family and addresses. "Are you turning us in?"

"No, no," the woman rushed to say. "We understand that many young people don't have any family, but want to know who to contact in case of an emergency."

"There's no one looking for us," she replied as David nodded his agreement.

"Well, then, we'll be sure to take good care of you," she assured. Turning to David, she continued, "With your cough, we'll want to get you a room so that you can be evaluated and the doctor will offer a full physical." Looking at Penny, she added, "And one for you as well."

"I'm only here with him," Penny confirmed. "I don't need anything."

"But my dear, you've been on the streets for a while, right? And the night's lodging and medical evaluation are free to you. Why would you not want to take advantage of it?"

"Free? Absolutely free?" David asked, catching Penny's eyes. "Come on, Penny. I don't want you back out on the street without me. Stay for the night."

Chewing the inside of her lip, Penny nodded. "Okay. It sounds good to me."

"Wonderful," the woman purred. "Well, I'll have someone show you to the female ward and we'll get David in to see the doctor now and then he'll be in the male ward unless the doctor feels that he needs a room."

Feeling as though their luck was surely turning, Penny and David followed the woman even further into the clinic.

CHAPTER 14

THE GREY CLOUDS, heavy with rain, cast the bedroom in a dark gloom, but the two inhabitants were oblivious to the outside world.

Luke's body was curled around Charlie's as he slid his thick cock into her wet sex from behind. One arm under her neck allowed his hand to tease her breasts while the other hand gripped her hip firmly. The position ramped the friction up several notches and if the sounds coming from her throat were any indication, she was as turned on as he.

Heat poured off of him so she kicked the covers down, allowing the ceiling fan to help cool their bodies. Keeping her top leg lifted slightly, she slid her hand down, finding her clit slick with their combined moisture. Circling the swollen bud, her insides coiled tightly.

She barely heard the grunts coming from Luke in time with the pumping of his hips. Pushing back against his thrusts, his cock slid in deeper and deeper until she felt stretched as far as she could go.

"Come on, babe," he panted. "You close?"

Not trusting her voice, she just nodded. The fingers gripping her hips moved forward until he was able to pinch her clit at the same time the other hand tweaked her nipples with a hard tug.

Suddenly the tight coils sprung loose and she felt electric jolts firing from her core outward, sending tingling to her extremities. As waves of pleasure washed over her, she heard him shout out a long groaning "fuuuuuuck" as he emptied himself inside, pumping until he was still.

Luke's heartbeat pounded in an erratic pattern as sweat poured from him. His fingers eased their rough grip and gently smoothed over the skin of her breasts and hips. Concern flew over him as he leaned around to peer into her face. "Are you okay? Was that too rough?"

Her languorous smile greeted his worried face. "Mmmm," was her response. He plopped his head back on the pillow behind her allowing his heartbeat to steady and his thoughts to wander.

After the karate practice ending so passionately the day before, there had been no question about which bed she would sleep in. As she had come out of the bathroom in one of his t-shirts, her eyes had hesitantly sought his. His grin had met her as he reached out his hand and jerked the covers back, beckoning her to join him.

Now, in the afterglow of their morning coupling, he rubbed circles on her shoulder while planning the day. "We need to go to Jack's today to work," he said hesitantly, wondering about her response.

Charlie twisted up to look into his eyes. "How do you feel about that? Do you think Jack will start trusting me?"

Sighing, Luke admitted, "For me? It's good. It's not like you're new to this or to what we've worked on some. Jack? I don't know. But don't take his non-trust personally. He vetted each of us before we even interviewed with him." Shifting his body so that he faced her, he continued, "I'm gonna admit that he was probably vetting you yesterday."

Without blinking, she smiled slightly. "I expected as much. I know how important trust is." Glancing down at their bodies, still tangled and flushed with sweat, she said, "You hit the shower first while I make coffee."

Pulling her forward, he kissed her, first gently and then with passion overtaking. "Um mm," he moaned. "Let me take care of this condom and we'll both take a shower and then the coffee."

Grinning under the onslaught of his mouth on hers, she agreed.

HOURS LATER, LUKE looked over as Charlie sat at a small desk next to his bank of computers in the Saints' compound. "You get anything?" he asked.

Shaking her head in frustration, she said, "No. I

only know someone named Jun was the original client of Eli's and his encryption was such that I can't figure it out. How can we know who might be doing what Eli thought?" She turned to face him, her mouth turned down into a frown. "Luke, how can we even be sure that he was on the right trail?"

He lifted his hand to rub her shoulder and said, "We don't. But he was on to something that got him killed and it is too much of a coincidence that it happened after talking to someone at the FBI."

"Do you really think that his killer was someone from the FBI?"

He turned his chair so that she was directly in front of him, capturing her knees between his. Taking her cold fingers in his hands, he said, "I don't know. But this is how we investigate, Charlie. One step at a time, following a trail until we discover what we're looking for."

They looked up suddenly as Monty walked into the room, his eyes darting between them. It was not lost on Luke that Charlie was the first outsider allowed into the compound work area other than Mitch Evans, their former FBI contact.

"'Morning," Monty greeted before stepping over to his tablet as the other Saints filtered in. "Charlie, I've got several photographs of some women that I'd like you to look at to see if they are possibilities for Eli's murderer." He shifted his gaze to Luke's in question.

Luke met Monty's gaze with a tight-lipped grimace,

but knew it needed to happen. With a short nod, he stood and walked Charlie over to the table to sit with the other Saints.

She clutched his hand tightly, fingers laced, steadying her breath. Once settled with Luke plastered to her side, she nodded and Monty began his presentation.

First he flashed different types of FBI badges on the screen to see if she could identify any of them. By process of elimination, she was able to dismiss some of them but was unable to discern the exact badge.

Blowing out a frustrated breath, she pursed her lips, as Monty said, "Okay, next I have several pictures of Asian women. Some in uniforms of various kinds, some in plain clothes, and some in outfits similar to what you saw."

Luke felt his fingers loose circulation as Charlie gripped his hand tighter. "Relax, sweetie," he whispered, immediately feeling her fingers loosen. "Take your time and focus on eliminating who you can instead of trying to pick out the exact person right now."

Nodding, she sucked in a deep breath, letting it out slowly, aware of the stares from the other Saints. Monty began the slide show and she quickly realized she was going to be able to dismiss some possibilities.

"No, not her," she said, looking at a thin, pinched face woman who was much older than Eli's murderer. "No," she said again, as a round-cheeked woman appeared. She quickly got into the rhythm of giving a "yes" or "no" answer to each picture.

Pleased with her progress, Jack commented, "You're doing good, Charlie. It may not seem like it, but you are definitely identifying a body and face type and you're consistent."

"You're also consistent with the description you gave to Faith," Bart noted, with an encouraging smile.

Monty had specifically held back a photograph of Lin Wang, wanting to see if Charlie was narrowing down the search to someone similar to the FBI agent. "Ready?"

Nodding, they began the next round of pictures, this time the women were much more similar. Charlie's responses became slower and slower as she gave close attention to each one. Several more she was able to eliminate, but there were still several on her possibility list. When the photograph of Lin Wang was flashed up on the screen, Charlie hesitated, her head cocked to the side, unaware of the others in the room holding their breaths.

She squinted, sucking in her lips, as her eyes devoured the features of the pretty Asian woman wearing a dark jacket over a white blouse. Finally turning her anguished face to Luke, she said, "It could be. I can't be sure. I can't mess up someone's life if I'm not completely sure."

Luke wrapped his arm around her shoulders and pulled her in. Tucking her head under his chin, he caught the silent communication from Jack and, after a moment, when she pushed away, he stood. "Come on, let's get you upstairs for a while and we're going to keep working."

Looking over at Jack, she said, "Thank you for allowing me to assist...down here. I know you probably don't trust me—"

"Charlie, if I didn't trust you," Jack stated, holding her attention, "you wouldn't be down here."

She pondered his words for a moment, realizing it was a compliment. Nodding toward him, she said, "Thank you. I want to help any way I can."

"I'm not dismissing you," Jack said, noting with a smile, Luke's possessive arm around her. "I want you to keep looking at pictures upstairs while we discuss a few other cases as well as the one you're assisting with."

Nodding, she smiled before allowing Luke to lead her up the stairs to the large living room she had been ensconced in previously.

"Make notes on any who seem like possibilities," Luke instructed. "I'll be back up when we're finished."

Charlie watched him walk away before beginning the task of staring numbly at photograph after photograph.

As Luke rejoined the group downstairs, Monty had him set up the secure video-conference with Lin Wang. Jack glanced at Luke. "You okay?"

"Yeah, I know it's not the right time for Charlie to see Lin in a live conference now. Especially if she might recognize her voice. We don't want to give Charlie away."

In a few minutes, Lin's unsmiling face appeared on their screen. "Gentlemen," she greeted harshly. "I'm not used to secure conferences where I cannot see the whole group."

"For our own security purposes, you will be able to see only me," Monty explained.

Barking out a rude snort, Lin said, "And the security of the Bureau is less important?"

Not willing to begin a debate, Monty moved on to the information that they needed. "Ms. Wang, we have not been provided a copy of the initial consultation notes with Eli. Can you tell us when that came in?"

A crease knit her brow as she replied, "I thought you had been given everything you needed." She looked down at her papers and answered his questions.

Several points were looked at and the Saints noted that she replied to each one succinctly and without hesitation.

Glancing down at her watch, Lin said, "Gentlemen, if that's all, then I have another meeting to attend."

"Just one more thing," Monty said. "Can you tell us which agent first spoke to Eli? Which agent was his point of contact?"

Looking surprised for a second, she stared straight into the video camera and replied, "Yes. That was me. I was his contact."

Disconnecting the video-conference, Luke looked around the table. "Fuckin' hell," he said, gaining nods from the others.

"So, Lin Wang was Eli's first contact. She was the one who set up the meeting. She would have known where he lived and the exact time of the meeting," Monty agreed.

"And knowing Eli like we now do," Jude added, "she would have known he would be at home waiting since he rarely went out."

"What could her motive be? It would only make sense if she were part of the medical scheme Eli told Charlie about," Cam said. "I talked to Miriam last night and asked her about organ transplants. She never worked in that area of medicine, but said that there are databases for who needs organs. And she said that once an organ is taken from a body, there's only so many hours before it must be transplanted or it's no good."

Luke, back at his computers, twisted around in his chair to face the others. "One of the largest groups that deal in illegally harvested human organs is the Chinese mafia."

Those words hung over the group, each Saint considering the possibilities.

"Is there any way to see where their ties are in the US?" Jack asked, his gaze moving between Monty and Luke.

"I can begin searching," Luke said. "It'll be general, at first, and then I'll see what I can determine is in the DC and Baltimore area."

"Just because Eli lived in Baltimore doesn't mean

the hit was local," Blaise surmised. "Could have come from anywhere."

The eyes of the group landed back on Monty, who was rubbing his hand over his face. "Okay, look, I know what you're thinking. We need a contact in the Bureau and can't use Lin Wang right now. Not as long as she is possibly involved. I've got some former friends still there, but they are going to be very reticent to work against a fellow agent."

"So don't tell them right away," Bart said. "Problem solved."

Luke looked over at Monty, knowing that of all the Saints, Monty was the most by-the-book. "Man, I know you hate this, but if we can get any inside info at all, it will help my search. But I promise to start digging immediately."

Jack sat quietly for a moment, pondering the situation. Finally he shifted his gaze around the table landing on Luke. "I've been vetting Charlie. You know that. So far, she's as clean as they come. She's already involved, so does anyone have an objection if she begins working with Luke…for us?"

The other Saints were quiet for a moment until finally Cam spoke up. "Boss, you never wanted to involve our women before." He nodded over to Bart and said, "Even when Faith could assist."

"Faith has continued to help, but in a very limited capacity," Jack agreed. "We have no need for an involved police artist but, depending on what Luke says, we could use another skilled computer analyst." He pinned the others with his stare before adding, "The final decision will be mine, but I want to know everyone's thoughts."

Marc shifted uncomfortably before responding, "I've never objected using whoever could assist us in a case, but does this put her in more danger? I want to know what Luke thinks. It's his woman, after all."

Jerking his eyes to his friend, he sat silent. *My woman. That sounds so caveman...and yet...* "Charlie is already involved." Sighing heavily, he added, "About as involved as she can get. She's a witness to a murder and is the only one who could positively identify that person. She's got Eli's information and past experience with working on whatever he discovered. I hate like hell to put her at risk, but if she's working with us then we can protect her more easily." Twirling his pen in his hand he added, "She's smart. Tenacious. Driven." With a final nod, he said, "I'm good with it."

"That's good enough for me," Bart and Jude said simultaneously, with the others nodding in agreement.

"All right, Luke, call her back down," Jack said. "You two get to work on the Chinese mafia link and finding someone named Jun in the medical field, and Monty, dig more into Lin Wang."

CHAPTER 15

A S THE MOON moved across the night sky, Charlie lay nestled in the warmth of Luke's embrace. She was amazed at how quickly he fell asleep after they made love. But sleep was elusive for her as her mind played over and over the information they uncovered earlier in the day.

Having always worked on computer coding, she was unused to the elements of a criminal investigation that would haunt her dreams. *Dreams...if only. I can't even sleep enough to have my dreams haunted!*

The pictures she had looked at during the afternoon were burned into her brain. Since 2006, the Chinese government had been under investigation for using prisoners as unwilling organ donors. A human rights lawyer, who had since been nominated for the Nobel Peace prize, was a central figure in uncovering the horrors. *And it's a billion dollar a year industry!*

Knowing sleep was not coming she slid quietly from Luke's arms and padded barefoot down the hall to the kitchen. She searched but knew that he would not have any herbal tea in his kitchen. *No problem...wine will do.* Grabbing a bottle, she poured a large glass, taking a sip of the excellent vintage, before slamming down a large swallow.

She looked at her laptop still sitting on the table and wavered in her desire to open it up again. Deciding she had had enough for one day, she moved to the living room, settling on the sofa.

Has it only been a few days since I broke into Luke's house? As she admired the room, illuminated by the moonlight streaming in through the window behind her, she felt oddly at home. Taking another large sip of the wine, she leaned her head back, closing her eyes.

"Hey," Luke's sleepy voice came from the living room entrance and she turned her head toward the sound.

He stepped into the room, his eyes never wavering from the beauty basking in the moonlight on his sofa. Her long hair was flowing across her shoulders. Her legs were tucked up under her body in a way he recognized as her comfortable position. Her eyes had been closed peacefully but he was already able to recognize the tension in her face. "Can't sleep?"

"How do you do this?" she asked.

Cocking his head to the side, he strode over, so close she had to lean back to keep her eyes on him. Sitting down on the coffee table facing her so that she would be more comfortable, he asked, "Do what?"

"Deal with the things you find out."

Her voice was barely above a whisper, her anguish

written clearly on her face, he leaned forward and took the half-empty wine glass from her hands and set it down on the end table. Taking her cold fingers in his hands, he massaged them gently.

"I don't know," he answered honestly. "I've been investigating a long time. I suppose, somewhere along the way, I became a bit immune."

"What did you do before the Saints?" she asked. "You know almost everything there is to know about me and I hardly know you at all."

Giving her a little tug forward, he kissed her softly. "Oh, I think you know me pretty well after the last couple of days."

Rolling her eyes at him as he moved back, she said, "Such a typical man. Just because we've had sex doesn't mean I know you." Huffing, she leaned back and said, "Tell me. Tell me who Luke Costas is." She watched the hesitation on his face and said, "Please. I really want to know."

Dropping his chin to his chest, he pondered her request before lifting his head back to hold her gaze. "Okay," he agreed, but nodded to her wine glass. "Give me a minute 'cause I think I'll join you in that."

She smiled as he walked into the kitchen to pour a glass of wine for himself. Admiring the way his draw-string pajama bottoms hung on his tight ass, she was startled as he headed back to her, his naked chest and abs creating just as stunning a view.

Lifting an eyebrow, he said, "What on earth are you

thinking?"

"Just admiring the view," she said with a grin. Patting the sofa next to her, she offered the silent invitation to join her.

After an appreciative sip of the wine, he said, "I don't think there's much to tell, to be honest. My parents were scholars. Loving, but a bit absent-minded. I was the typical nerd boy, picked on in school until I finally hit a growth spurt in middle school, and that helped."

"Helped?" she queried.

"It's hard...for a boy," Luke explained. "If you're big, you have a better chance of being more popular...or at least not being picked on. But if you're not, and especially if you are different in any way, then you're much more likely to be bullied."

Her heart automatically ached for the bullied child he had been, understanding in her eyes. "What happened?"

"I was lucky. We had these great neighbors—he's the one I told you taught me about karate. With his help, I learned to defend myself and work out. With my pre-adolescent growth spurt, I was more confident."

"I heard about you when I went to MIT," she confessed.

"What'd you hear?"

"You were kind of a legend in the Engineering program. You had just graduated and were super smart...even by MIT standards. I used to look at your picture on the wall as the past Engineering Society president and have to admit...I was smitten."

"Smitten?" he laughed.

Giving his arm a playful slap, she admonished, "Don't make fun of me." Hesitating for a moment, she added, "We met...once."

His brows lowered as his mouth opened slightly, surprise on his face. "When?"

"When you came back after you graduated to give the speech. I was the girl who tripped going into the building."

A flash of memory flew through Luke as his confusion melted into a smile. "That was you? I was so nervous thinking about giving a speech to an auditorium full of people that I rushed away too quickly."

"I was just a dorky freshman and you had been such a campus hottie."

Leaning over to place a soft kiss on her wine-flavored lips, he whispered, "I like being your hottie."

Licking her lips, she stared at him, not believing that the man she used to drool over years before was now kissing her. Blinking rapidly to keep from being overwhelmed by his presence, she ordered, "Keep going. Tell me all about you."

Offering a self-deprecating shrug, he said, "I took a job with the CIA out of college."

At that, her eyes bugged. "Really. The CIA?"

"You don't have to be impressed," he added. "I thought it would be exciting and, while I turned down some very lucrative private offers, working for the government seemed the right thing to do. But I was stuck in a cubicle writing security code all day."

"Why did you leave?"

"Just when I thought I would make a difference the bureaucracy would get in the way. Security didn't want to clear a new program that I wanted to use. The higher ups said they wanted cutting edge programs but then the security nixed everything. I felt like I was always hitting a brick wall."

"Then what?"

"I met Marc on an assignment. He was a pilot for Homeland Security and then for the CIA. I was actually given a field assignment and he was the pilot. We became friends and he was just in the process of interviewing with Jack, having served with him over-seas." Chuckling, he said, "We couldn't have been more different, but we bonded."

Cocking her head to the side, she asked, "Different? How? All of you Saints seem sort-of alike."

Eyes wide, he shook his head, incredulously. "Alike?"

Giggling, she said, "You know. Tall. Big. Muscular. Kind of larger-than-life. And definitely alpha."

Hearing her giggle, Luke decided it was the sound he loved the best. And knowing she was now relaxed enough to actually find something amusing was an even better reward.

"Luke, do you remember the night at the

bar…when the fight broke out?" Gaining his nod, she continued, "Well, as soon as the first punch was thrown, all the Saints jumped up and immediately created a wall of muscle in front of the women."

"Oh, no," he protested. "Are you going to tell me that we shouldn't have done that? Or that the move was too alpha?"

"No, no," she assured. "Quite the contrary. I thought it was…nice. Every one of those women I have met so far has been smart and strong. And yet, you all created a safe haven for them in the middle of that chaos. I…guess I felt envious."

"I never told you that I saw what you did to the man in the suit that night. Gotta admit, it was the sexiest thing I've ever seen." He smiled as she laughed out loud again. "I've been telling you about me, but you've got to tell me about the karate."

"A couple of years ago, I took a self-defense class at a local YMCA." Her face scrunched at the memory. "It was actually Eli that suggested I take lessons."

"Eli?" Luke asked, unable to hide his surprise.

"Yeah. He knew I wasn't living in the best apartment building at the time and he said he wanted me safe." Her eyes searched Luke's as she added, "As odd as Eli could be, he really was a friend." Heaving a sigh, she said, "I discovered I was good at it and the instructor gave me private lessons after that."

A strange bolt of jealousy shot through Luke at the thought of Charlie's private lessons and what all that might have entailed. A punch on his shoulder jerked his attention back to her.

"What was that look for?" she asked, her eyebrows drawn together.

"Nothing. Well…actually I wondered how *private* these lessons were?" He cringed at how possessive he sounded, the unfamiliar emotion rocking him.

"Hmmm, would it make you feel better to know that the lessons included his teenage daughter and wife?"

Releasing a held breath, Luke dropped his head. "Okay…busted. Yes, it would make me feel better."

"I'd never done anything like it before," Charlie admitted. "I was the proverbial nose-in-a-book girl. I know you said it was hard for guys, but being the dorky nerd girl wasn't a piece of cake either. And college was no better. I dated rarely, just enjoying friends. And then working for myself, I really found out what lonely can be."

The two sat in silence for a few minutes, sipping their wine as the shadows passed over the room.

"You know what's crazy?" she finally asked. Seeing his curious face turn back toward her, she said, "Being on the run for the past five months has been lonely. Scary. And the nightmares of remembering his murder have been horrifying." Running her finger around the rim of her glass, she paused, sucking in her lips.

"Go on," he whispered.

"It forced me to get out of my rut and learn how to

do some things that I would have never done. I…I got stronger." She looked up quickly and added, "Please don't misunderstand me. I'm not saying that I'm glad for what happened to Eli. I'm just saying that I'm glad I didn't fall apart and not work to survive."

Luke set his empty glass on the coffee table, twisting his body around, clasping her face in his hands. "No apologies, Charlie. That just means you're resilient. You're a survivor. And I know what you mean…because if this had never happened, I'd probably not be sitting here with you right now. And I can't think of a better place I'd rather be."

Her eyes melted as he leaned in further, his lips strong and warm against hers. He tasted of wine and something that was intrinsically Luke. Sinking into his embrace, she scooted over so that she was perched on his lap, her hands clutching his shoulders.

He stood easily and she wrapped her legs around his waist. With one arm under her ass for support and the other enveloping her middle, he stalked back into the bedroom. The fears of the day gave way once more to the passion of the night. By the time they lay once more entwined in each other, Charlie fell into a deep sleep.

PENNY LOOKED AROUND the room at the few beds in the hospital dormitory. Uncertain as to the situations of the other women now fast asleep, she noted that they did not appear to be sick. All young. All hungry. All like her. They had been warned that one of the rules of the clinic was not to discuss their situations, but to simply heal. *But heal from what?*

Desperate to find David, she slipped quietly from her bed and to the door. Peeking out, the hall appeared empty. Moving stealthily down the hall, she realized she had no idea where she was going. After a few minutes of wandering around several winding halls with no luck, she came upon one with smaller, individual rooms. Looking into each one, she finally saw David lying in bed. He startled when she entered but, seeing her finger on her lips, he kept quiet.

Sitting on the edge of his bed, she said, "How's your cough?"

"Not as bad," he replied. "They gave me some medicine and said it would help me heal. The doctor that came by and checked me out said that I looked to be in good health, except for the cough."

Glancing around at the small, but private room, she wondered aloud, "Why do you suppose they give us homeless people special treatment?"

"Who knows?" he replied. "But I'm not complaining. Some lady came around to ask me questions about where I'd been living and how long I'd been on my own."

"What'd you tell her?"

Giving a rude snort, David said, "The truth. That my folks were dead and as soon as I could I got away from the foster system. She seemed to want to know if there was anyone who'd be looking for me, but I told her no. Well, with the exception of you, that is."

His words should have made Penny feel warm inside, but something about the clinic chilled her. Giving herself a mental shake, she offered him a smile. "Well, I'd better get back. I'll come see you tomorrow."

With that, she slipped unnoticed back to her bed.

LIN WANG SAT at her computer, the room illuminated by the streetlight coming from outside her condo. Her fingers hesitated over the keyboard as she pondered her next move. Tucking her sleek hair behind her ear, she thought carefully about the situation.

How much do they know? What all can they find out? She hated the partnership the FBI had with the Saints. *Everything could come crashing down. Everything I've been working for. I cannot let them find out what's going on!*

Sucking in a deep breath, her slender fingers began typing the message to her contact, Xia Wu, at the clinic.

Anything new for me?
A few new ones came in. Could be real possibilities.
Medical or other? Lin typed.
Both. One medical – excellent candidate. The other – perfect. Should be lucrative. Expect things to move forward. Came the reply.
How soon?

Medical – needs time to heal. Other – with him. Together for now. That will be the bait used.

Lin sucked in a deep breath, a smile playing about her lips as her fingers rested on the table. Standing, she walked over to pour another glass of wine. Taking it to her balcony, she stepped out into the cool breeze of the evening. Her sleek bob blew back from her shoulders as she lifted her face upwards, watching the full moon high in the sky. Taking a long sip of wine, she closed her eyes for a moment, knowing what she needed to do.

CHAPTER 16

WITH CHARLIE SAFELY ensconced in the Saints' compound, Luke traveled with Monty and Patrick to Washington D.C. to meet with Monty's new contact.

"We're old friends," Monty explained. "We never worked together as closely as I did with Mitch, but Nick's a good guy."

Arriving at the restaurant in Old Town Alexandria, the three walked inside the quaint interior and were pleased to see the lunch crowd diminished. Monty bypassed the hostess, seeing his friend already in a back corner booth. Luke observed the dark haired, square jawed man with the slight smile stand to greet Monty. Wearing khaki pants with a white shirt, his herringbone jacket gave him a professorial appearance.

"Nick," Monty greeted with a handshake-hug and made the introductions. "This is Nick Stone. Nick, meet a few of my co-workers, Luke Costas and Patrick Cartwright."

The four men sat down, making small talk until their order arrived. As the food was consumed, Monty got down to business. "I've already filled Nick in on what we need from him."

Nick ran his hand over his jaw, his eyes focusing on each of them. "Well, I might as well get this out in the open to begin with. When Monty approached me about being a contact, I was intrigued. I know Mitch and have always had the highest respect for both him and you," he said, nodding to Monty. "But, I've got to tell you, the idea of working with you to possibly take down a dirty FBI agent...hell..." Letting out another deep breath, he pinned the Saints with his stare.

Nick rested his forearms on the table next to his plate and sighed. "But the honest to God truth is that I've got no love for any agent that may be crooked. So, my answer is yes. I'll help."

Luke let out a breath he did not realize he was holding and smiled. Glancing to the side, he observed Monty and Patrick's responses to be the same.

"I wanted to have your agreement first," Monty said, sliding a file over to Nick. "Here's what we have so far. After you look this over give me a call. Luke, our computer expert, will get in touch with you to set up a secure way to have a video-conference."

Nick skimmed through the information in the file, his jaw ticking as his eyes moved down the pages. Sucking in a quick breath, he looked over at the Saints. "And this witness...they're somewhere safe?"

Luke, immediately prickling, nodded and answered with a curt, "Yes." Not willing to give the agent any more information, he sat tight-lipped.

The meeting ended as the meal was finished, and the group said their goodbyes. In the SUV on the way home, Luke asked, "You trust him?"

Monty twisted to peer at Luke. "I know what you're thinking but, yeah…I trust him."

Luke was quiet for a moment, pondering Monty's response. Finally he said, "Then that's good enough for me."

CHARLIE SPENT THE day in the compound underneath Jack and Bethany's house. Looking around she smiled, knowing this was where Luke devoted much of his time. She even noticed his coffee machine on the counter. Standing, she lifted her hands over her head, stretching her back before fixing a cup of the strong brew.

Jude and Cam entered the area from one of the back rooms and grinned at her. "You look at home there where Luke normally sits," Jude joked.

Returning their smiles, she sipped the coffee, allowing the caffeine to kick in. Turning back to her computer, she continued to pour over the data Eli had given her. *Incomplete…why can't I figure out the missing information?* From her previous investigating, she knew the client, Jun, was in the Washington D.C. area. There were hundreds of doctors in the entire northern Virginia and eastern Maryland area surrounding D.C., and she had no way of knowing if she were looking for one with a Chinese last name. Just searching Jun had not produced any positive leads. Uncertain how to narrow the field, her own work had come to a halt. But, having listened to the Saints working the problem, she now focused on anyone with a Chinese background. *Why had I never thought about the murderer speaking Chinese as a clue?* She grimaced, irritated at her inefficiency.

"What's causing that look?" Cam asked, observing the play of emotions crossing her face.

Blushing, she replied, "I'm embarrassed that I never thought to check any Chinese possibilities before. I've been trying to figure out Eli's information for several months."

Jude sat down next to her and said, "Before I became a Saint, I didn't know how to investigate a crime." Seeing that he had her undivided attention, he continued. "I had been trained as a SEAL, but an injury cut that career short. Sabrina's family had a problem and I asked her cousin, Bart, to help and, with the assistance of the Saints, we got the guy. Honestly, without their knowledge, I'd never have been able to do it on my own."

Smiling at the handsome, curly-headed young man, she said, "So the moral of your story is to stop beating myself up?"

Throwing his head back in laughter, he said, "That's exactly what I'm saying." He patted her shoulder as he stood. "Luke's really good at this...well, in fact, each of us brings our own strengths to the team. Don't worry about trying to put all the pieces together yourself. Just take one clue, start connecting the dots, and follow the trail." Smiling at her, he and Cam headed back to the equipment room.

With renewed vigor, she turned back to the computer. Deciding to give up the search for Jun for the moment, she focused her research on the Chinese governmental hospitals harvesting organs from unwilling prisoners and even a religious group that was not sanctioned by the ruling power.

But in the United States? Wouldn't patient's families be suspicious? Don't deaths have to be reported? Turning her thoughts over and over in her mind, she followed Jude's advice and slowly began to follow the trail.

Who would be patients that wouldn't be missed? Those with no family. She typed in her search on runaways and the homeless...particularly the young. The numbers were staggering. The latest data estimated there was over a million homeless youth. *Oh, my God.* The research also showed a tie between human trafficking and homelessness. And one of the largest groups involved in human trafficking...*the Chinese mafia.*

Allowing her mind to flow over the problem Eli had uncovered, she began to wonder if a pattern existed between human trafficking and organ trafficking. *Isn't it possible they could be related? That the same people at risk for one could be at risk for the other?*

PENNY, WEARING CLEAN jeans and a new long sleeved t-shirt, walked back into the female dorm room and looked at the other five girls sharing the room. Two of them were already new, replacing the sheets on the beds. Catching the eye of one she met yesterday, she nodded toward the other side of the room and asked, "Where did those two go?"

"I think when we've had a few days here and they check us out to make sure we're healthy, we leave," came the reply.

Penny pursed her lips together, looking around. The bed had been clean and comfortable and the food had been adequate. *I knew this was only temporary, but really wanted to stay long enough to keep an eye on David.* She had attempted to go back to his room this morning, but had been stopped. No females on the male ward, had been the reason given.

Sitting down on the edge of her bed, she chewed on the inside of her mouth as she tried to work through the feeling deep in her stomach that something was not right. *This is no homeless shelter…but it's also not like any medical clinic I've been in.* The staff was mixed, although the doctor, nurses, and the main receptionist had been Asian.

She gazed at the smiling girls in the ward. *They don't seem worried.* Heaving a sigh, she slid off the bed and walked toward the bathroom. *Maybe a shower will make everything seem better.* At least, she hoped it would wash away some of her concern as much as her cleaning her body.

THE SUN SLID behind the Blue Ridge Mountains behind Jack's property as the large gathering met and mingled on the deck that spanned the side of his house. A white picket fence surrounded the back yard, readying for children that would soon play there. The grass was still lush and green, although the fall colors were already creating a painted backdrop to the vista.

Charlie stood near the picnic table, watching the other women's easy camaraderie. She had met Bethany, Angel, Faith, and Miriam, but now the gathering included the rest of the Saints' wives and fiancés. Chad's wife, Dani, was placing her baby girl into a rocker-carrier, while Sabrina and Grace cooed over the infant. Patrick's fiancé, Evie, stood next to Angel, setting the cupcakes out for everyone. Both Miriam and Dani's babies were now asleep in rocker-carriers just inside the glass doors of the house. Even though they were in plain sight of everyone, the baby monitor sat in the middle of the group.

Sighing softly, Charlie could not help the sliver of envy that buried inside of her, always feeling like the outsider in a large group of people. The women, all beautiful in their own unique ways, appeared so accomplished and so at ease with each other.

After a moment, Blaise's fiancé, Grace, walked over

and stood next to Charlie. "It's not always easy, is it?" she asked softly.

Biting her lip, Charlie cocked her head to the side in silent question.

"Joining an established group," came the reply along with a head nod toward the women.

Ducking her head, Charlie said, "Everyone is so nice."

"Nice, yes...but I remember when I first met everyone, I felt like an outsider," Grace chuckled.

"And now?"

With a little shrug, Grace admitted, "I've only been with Blaise for a short while. So I'm still pretty new. Adding in the fact that I'm not a super sociable person, it can make me feel a little awkward."

Faith, having walked nearby, grinned at the two women. "Socially awkward? Grace you are a social butterfly compared to me," she joked.

Evie moved over as well, smiling at Charlie. "I've wanted to meet you since Patrick told me about you. I'm an Engineer as well."

"Really?" Charlie asked, surprised. "What field?"

"I majored in Geotechnical Engineering." Seeing Charlie's smile, Dani threw her head back and laughed, "Yeah, I know. It makes most people's eyes roll back in their heads. But I felt the same way when I first moved here and was thrust into the Saints' world."

Faith, turning her head toward Charlie, said, "Large groups can be overwhelming until you realize you're part of a big family."

Nodding, Charlie admitted, "That's what I was thinking. You all seem like one big family."

"That's because Bethany works so hard to make it that way. Jack's fabulous, but as the boss, he can be a bit intimidating and...removed. Once Bethany came into his life, she made sure to sort-of mother-hen the rest of the men...and then their women."

"Are my ears burning?" Bethany joked, as she patted her pregnant belly while walking over to stand next to Charlie. "I'm really glad you're here, by the way. I know this group can be...well, overwhelming."

Charlie knew that any attention focused on her usually made her cheeks burn, her stomach churn, and her palms sweat. But as the group slowly incorporated her into their conversations, she was actually enjoying herself.

Standing off to the side, Luke kept a watchful eye on Charlie as she met the rest of the Saints' women, knowing crowds made her nervous. After a moment, her eyes found his and she offered a smile, easing his concern.

"She'll be fine. The others will see to it," Chad said, the gentle giant walking up beside Luke. "Dani felt the same when she first met everyone."

Turning, Luke nodded to his friend and the two of them moved toward the grill where Jack and Bart were debating the barbecue sauce. Taking another beer from the cooler, Luke walked over to the railing and stared out into the dusk blanketed yard.

"You okay?" Marc asked, coming up beside him. His gaze slid over to the women encircling Charlie. "She's doing fine."

Silent for a moment, Luke replied, "It's weird...and great...having her here."

"Why is that?"

"I never expected to meet someone like her. Never expected to be at one of Jack's gatherings with someone."

"I'm glad for you, man," Marc said honestly.

"And you?" Luke asked. "You're now the lone wolf in this pack."

Shaking his head at the analogy, Marc said, "Don't see that changing anytime soon."

Luke started to make a quip about Marc not settling down to just one woman when he could have a bevy of beauties lined up, but the flash of uncertainty in Marc's eyes had him shutting down the comment before it even came out.

Just then the call from the grill masters rang out and the gathering made their way over to the tables now laden with food. Striding over to Charlie, Luke slid his hand around her waist. Bending, he whispered, "You doin' okay?"

Her wide smile was answer enough, but she said, "I really like your friends." Looking around, she added, "It's been years since I've enjoyed a group." Lifting her hand to cup his cheek, she held his eyes. "Thank you for letting me be a part of your world."

"Sweetheart, they're now your world too." With that, he placed a soft kiss on her lips before twirling her back toward the tables, where the sounds of laughter rang out into the night.

CHAPTER 17

L UKE TWISTED AROUND in his chair and watched Charlie as she sat, hunkered over her computer. Her hair was falling out of the bun she had haphazardly pulled up earlier and she constantly tried to tuck strands behind her ears. The occasional mutterings coming from her gave evidence to her frustrations.

Rubbing the back of his neck, it hit him that the other Saints had seen him in the same position a million times since he began working for Jack. *Is that how they saw me? Always at a computer? Practically living down here in the compound?*

He watched as she tucked her legs up under her body in the small chair and knew a change was inevitable. *And needed!*

Standing, he walked the few steps to where she sat scrunched up in the chair and pulled her hand off her keyboard. Before she could speak, he said, "Come on."

Allowing him to lead her up the back stairs, she was surprised when they passed through the door and were in part of Jack's garage. Several ATVs were parked to the side and she watched as Luke headed straight to them. Grabbing a helmet and tossing it to her, she caught it, but stared numbly at him for a moment.

"Put it on," he ordered with a grin, while strapping his own helmet on.

"But...why?"

Laughing, he answered, "I would have thought that would be obvious."

Looking dubiously at the ATV, she said, "But I've never been on one."

Stepping over to her, he took the helmet from her hands and placed it on her head. Securing the strap underneath her chin, he replied, "Then it's time we rectified that."

Her brow pinched with concern as she looked down at Luke settling himself on the vehicle. Swinging her leg over before pressing her front to his back, she said, "I'm used to my little Vespa. This won't go much faster, will it?"

With a grin, Luke decided not to answer but shouted, "Hang on," as they roared out of the garage into the bright sunlight.

The wind slapped Charlie in the face as she peeked over Luke's shoulder, causing her to gasp. Her hands, which had been resting on his hips, were now tightly wrapped around his waist as she clung on for dear life.

Her fear rescinded as she viewed the fall glory of the mountains as they climbed higher up the back of Jack's property. The vehicle bounced and jolted along a rutted path, over tree roots and across a stream. Her heart pounded but she quickly realized it was not out of fear…it was joyful.

Her hands felt the strength of his muscles as they bunched and corded beneath her fingers. Her breasts were plastered to his back and her thighs pressed tightly against his. The roar of the engine underneath her sent rumblings through her core and she wondered if he felt the same sensations.

Looking about, the yellows, oranges, and reds swirled by as Luke seemed to take a path that led them around and around the woods, slowly climbing higher.

Just when she thought they could not go further, he skidded to a stop at an overlook and shut the engine off. Taking his helmet off and hanging it on one of the handlebars, he twisted around and said, "Get off, sweetheart. It's time to see more of the world than what we find on a computer screen."

Obeying, she followed his lead and removed her helmet as well. Standing next to him, she looked out onto the valley below. Her breath caught in her throat as she walked near the edge.

Jack and Bethany's house sat in the distance, the white picket fence surrounding the backyard glistening in the sunlight. The warm rays pelted them but, with the slight breeze, she could not imagine a more perfect day.

Luke walked up behind her and placed his hands on her shoulders, pulling her back into his front. Sliding one arm around her waist and the other around her chest, he rested his chin on her head.

They stood silent for several long minutes, both allowing the vista to immerse them in tranquility. Finally taking a deep breath of fresh air, she said, "I've never seen anything like this. It's glorious. How could you not want to come up here all the time?"

She felt his chuckle as his chest moved against her shoulders and she twisted her neck to look at him. His chocolate eyes were focused on her as he lowered his head and placed a gentle kiss on her lips.

With a grin, he linked his fingers with hers and led her to a flat rock, near the edge but not dangerously close. Sitting, he pulled her down next to him and once more tucked her tightly into his side as they looked out onto the world from their perch.

They sat in silence for several minutes, the breeze gently blowing her hair about her face. With his free hand he tucked the wayward strands behind her ear.

"Tell me about you," he encouraged, his eyes never leaving her face.

She shot him a quick glance, her mouth partially opening before closing quickly. "You...you already know all about me," she replied, a slight blush warming her cheeks.

"No...not really." Seeing her gaze fall back to his in question, he said, "I spend my days at my computer, doing research, writing programs...often digging deep into information about whomever we're investigating. And I always thought that was enough."

"Enough?"

Sucking in a deep breath through his nose, he let it out slowly as he tried to explain what was just now filling his mind. Nodding, he said, "I thought that I could understand everything about someone from what I uncovered. Their bank accounts…their friends…their social media footprint." Shrugging, he added, "I never really thought about them in any other way except as a list of facts…information my faithful computers fed to me."

He twisted his body slightly so that he was facing her while still keeping their fingers linked as he continued. "But as I've fallen for you, I realize that there is so much I don't know about you. And desperately want to."

Charlie sat in silence for a moment, understanding what Luke was saying. She, too, had sought the safety of a computer over unpredictable relationships. Looking back over the valley below, the crisp fall air filling her nostrils, she leaned her face up toward the sun and, for the first time in a very long time, she felt free.

Releasing her long-held breath, she responded to his question. "Growing up was lonely," she admitted.

"Tell me," he encouraged.

"My father was in love with someone else and they had an argument. He found solace in a waitress that he met and I was the…product. It wasn't a one-night stand but, well, it wasn't planned. He did the right thing, married my mom and stayed with us until I was about four. But he wasn't around much. Mama always said he had to travel for business, but as I'm sure you can surmise, he actually saw his old flame. When they decided to make a go of it, he divorced us."

"Us?" Luke asked, his voice hard.

With a little shrug, Charlie nodded. "Yeah. He paid some child support until I was eighteen, but he never came around. Whether he wanted to be with me or not, or his new wife didn't want the reminder that he had another family…who knows? So, I grew up with just mama."

Luke allowed her to speak, knowing she was proving exactly what he had said a few minutes earlier. He thought about the early information he had pulled up on Charlotte and knew that while the facts had been learned, it was so different hearing them from the person involved.

"Were you lonely?"

"Mama worked all of the time and so I was often alone in the apartment. I had friends in my books, but few real friends."

"And school?"

Making a rude snort, she rolled her eyes. "Please, Luke. Being a bookworm in school hardly got me into the cool crowd."

She shrugged, but he wondered if the sting was still present when she thought about it. He lifted his hand again and, this time, after tucking a strand of hair behind her ear he allowed his fingers to glide along the softness of her jaw.

"I was good at math, good with computers, and because of financial need, got into MIT." Seeing him about to protest, she said, "Oh, that's not false modesty, it's the truth. I was smart, but doubt I would have gotten into MIT. But most colleges need to take a percentage of financially needy students, so I got in."

"And college?" he continued to push.

"That's when I first felt like I belonged."

"Eli and the others?"

Nodding, she said, "I never needed a lot of friends." She shifted around so that she could observe his face while she confided. "You know how some people are people-magnets? They seem to attract friends no matter where they go? Well, that was never me. And I wasn't jealous of that. I'd rather have a couple of really good friends than a whole slew of kinda-friends."

"What about after college? I'll tell you that Tim wasn't too happy that you followed in Eli's footsteps and just worked from home."

She pursed her lips tightly for a moment, her gaze shifting back to the ever-changing vista in front of her. As the sun moved across the sky, the fall colors caught the light as the breeze blew, creating a shimmery autumn glow.

Finally dropping her chin to her chest, she nodded slightly. "Mom died when I was in college and I seemed to pull inside myself, like a turtle. It was my way of dealing with the grief, I suppose."

"I'm sorry," he said, knowing his words, while heartfelt, were inadequate.

"Yeah, me too. I…I really miss her. She worked so hard, but was so proud of me. She was…," Charlie sighed heavily, blinking to hold back the emotions, "the only family I ever had."

"What about your grandparents?"

A small smile escaped as she looked off into the distance. "My mom's parents visited us a few times when I was little, before they passed away. Grandpa was the one who nicknamed me Charlie and it made my grandmother so mad. She hated that he gave me a boy's nickname. But I liked it."

She turned back to Luke and continued, "I finished college, a year after the others, too set in my ways to make new friends, and the thought of interviewing for corporate jobs made me sick to my stomach. So Eli's solution seemed…safe." She lifted her face and pinned Luke with her stare. "I guess I've always played it safe." Snorting, she shook her head, "At least until I witnessed a murder…the last five months have totally changed me."

"You're stronger," he observed, his admiration shining in his eyes.

"Or just plain ol' runnin' scared," she confessed.

Shaking his head, he cupped her cheeks with both hands. "No, you're totally stronger. You're right…I had investigated you. But knowing you as a real person makes me understand how much I needed this assignment from Jack. I needed to get out from underneath my computer and see people as they really are…not just the sum of bytes of information."

Charlie held his gaze, his dark eyes reflecting the sunlight, feeling their warmth as they seemed to peer deep inside of her. His hair, although short, was longer on top and blew slightly in the breeze. His stubbled jaw was dark with his beard. She raised her hands to his arms, caressing the strength of muscles underneath.

Luke watched her eyes roam over his face and could not believe his good fortune that this woman had come into his life. "Are you for real?" he asked, his voice as soft as the gentle wind.

Her eyes filled with confusion as she continued to stare at him.

"You're perfect for me," he explained, his voice barely above a whisper as he pulled her face gently toward his to close the minuscule gap between them. Claiming her lips with his own, he slid his tongue into her warmth, seeking out the sweet crevices. She tasted of mint and…Charlie.

Leaning back, he reached for a silver chain hanging around his neck, his fingers grasping the medallion resting underneath his shirt. Pulling it over his head, he held it up for her to see. "This is my St. Luke," he said, watching her eyes move between his face and the pendant. "When I was a kid, my parents told me how Luke was a scholar. I hated it then…why couldn't I have been named after some hero instead of an ancient nerd."

At that, Charlie giggled, her hazel eyes twinkling as she waited to see where he was going with this.

Luke lifted the chain over her head and settled the pendant on her chest as he continued. "But I've come to realize that a scholar is someone who is always learning. Always discovering. Always something new."

Her gaze held his as she whispered, "And what have you discovered now?"

"That there is more to people than just what I find out on my computer. And that there is someone for everyone, and for me...you're that someone."

She lifted the silver medallion with her fingers, holding it reverently as she looked to him for its meaning.

"I want you to wear my Saint, Charlie. The reason is two-fold, I confess. It is fitted with a tracker and if you are ever in trouble, we can find you."

She turned the pendant over, looking at it carefully, before lifting her focus back to him. "And the other reason?" she whispered.

Luke leaned in, placing a soft kiss on her lips as he breathed, "I want you with me. I want us to discover everything we can about each other. I know that for me...you're my other half. But I want to make sure that you feel the same way."

Dropping the pendant down to her chest, she clasped his cheeks in her hands as she deepened the kiss. Pushing him backward, she spread her body across his without losing his mouth on hers. Grasping his shoulders with her fingers, she shimmied to where her heat was at his crotch.

Tongues tangling as though in a war for dominance, she finally lifted her head up. An adorable grin escaped as she said, "I could say the same thing about you, so I guess I'm as real as you are."

With a roll of his body, Luke pinned her underneath him, making sure they were on the soft grass and not the rocky outcropping. His swollen erection pressed against her core, the desire to be inside overriding every other thought. His hands cupped her face as he rested his weight on his forearms making sure to not crush her.

Arching her back, she raised her hips, seeking the friction her body was crying out for. Sliding one hand to his ass, she pulled him closer.

Groaning, Luke kissed her jawline before nuzzling her neck. Nipping his way down, he pressed his mouth between her breasts, wishing the material of her shirt and bra were not in the way. Sliding his hand down to the bottom of her shirt, he inched it upward.

A flash of self-consciousness ran through her at the thought of being naked outdoors, but with a smile she decided to throw caution to the wind.

With another roll, she straddled him, replacing his hands on the hem of her t-shirt, whipping it over her head. With a grin, she placed her hands on his shoulders, her hair a silken curtain falling around them.

His fingers dug into her hips, the sight of her breasts spilling over the tops of her bra. Sliding one hand over the soft skin of her back to cup the back of her head, he pulled her down, fusing his mouth onto hers.

With the warm, evening sun filtering through the leaves in the trees, high on an overlook at the back of Jack's property, the two became lost in each other...and found what they had been missing.

CHAPTER 18

L IN STEPPED OUT of the black SUV and walked into the Chinese Embassy. Flashing her badge, she made her way down the carpeted hallway, past the paintings and porcelain. She eschewed the elevator and took the stairs instead, jogging up two at a time. Opening the door onto the third floor, she nodded curtly toward the startled guard. Her face passive, she inwardly smiled at the ease with which she had gained access.

Coming to the end of the hall, she rapped once and then entered Yeng Chow's office. He looked up and smiled before rising from his seat and extending his hand in greeting.

"Agent Wang, how nice to see you again."

With a nod of her head, she replied, "And you too." Her sharp eyes quickly assessed the room, its opulence evident in the furniture as well as the artwork on the walls. *And the walls have ears...and eyes, I'll wager.* Expecting his office was wired for sound and video, she turned back and offered him a polite, professional smile.

"What can I do for you today?" he asked.

"I've been assigned to investigate the possible connection between the embassy and a few of the clinics in the area."

Lifting his eyebrow, the small man smiled. "Connection?"

"Just a formality, I'm sure," she stated, keeping her voice as neutral as possible. Pulling out a folder from her slim, leather briefcase, she set it on his immaculate desk and pushed it over with her fingertips. "Here is a list of a few medical clinics in the area. I'd like you to look the list over and see if there are any connections between the clinics and the embassy."

"What type of connections are you looking for?"

"The Bureau has information concerning possible wrongdoings in at least one or more clinics with Chinese ties."

"And the informant?"

"No longer a…possibility for identification of the specifics."

Nodding at the information passed discreetly, he smiled. "I will be more than happy to take a look at the list for you. Of course, it is outside my normal duties, but I will certainly get to it as time allows."

Bending her head slightly toward him, she stood and walked to the door, with Yeng on her heels. Taking her hand in his, he bowed low.

Deciding to take the elevator, she walked to the end of the hall before turning to look over her shoulder.

Yeng was still in the doorway to his office, his head bent over the file she had given him. As she stepped into the elevator and turned back around, he was piercing her with his stare as the doors closed.

PENNY USED THE low security at night to slip back through the clinic to the wing where David's room was. Peeking inside to assure he was alone, she made her way to his bed. No longer coughing, she felt his forehead, pleased to find it cool to the touch.

Waking suddenly, he jumped. "Geez, you scared me," he exclaimed.

"Sorry," she mumbled.

"What are you doing here?" he asked. "I'm much better, so you don't have to keep checking on me."

Staring at him, she blanched. "What's wrong? You don't sound like you."

"Nothing, I just...nothing," he complained.

Sitting down on the edge of his bed, she stared at him. "David, come on. I know we haven't known each other that long, but I can tell something's not right."

He averted his eyes for a moment before finally looking at her. "It's just...well, I was talking to the doctor today. He asked about us...about you and me."

Rearing back, she narrowed her eyes. "Why was he asking about us?"

"Just about us not having a home...us living on the street. He wanted to know if I'd like to make some money...so I could take better care of you."

A sneaky-sick feeling began to crawl through Penny as she watched David appear to battle with something. "How, David? How did he tell you to make money?"

He lifted his gaze to her, his eyes moving over her thin face. "Penny, I'd give anything to be able to offer you a little place for us to live. Then we could get jobs and pay the rent. Actually have our own little home...even if it was just a single room."

Licking her lips, she shook her head slightly in confusion. "David, we're only sixteen. Who's gonna give us money? Who's gonna rent to us or give us jobs?"

"I'm almost seventeen," he stated, a slight pout on his face. "Don't you see, Penny, if we had the start up money to tide us over, we could have a place to live until everything else fell into place."

"You're not making sense. Tell me what he offered," she demanded.

"You know you can live with only one kidney, right?" David asked.

The silence in the room was deafening as she struggled to comprehend what he was talking about.

"One...one kidney?"

David's mouth twisted in a grimace, even as his eyes appeared hopeful. "There's a waiting list for people who need kidneys and will pay good money to get one. He said that his clinic can help with that. Instead of making people wait years to be on some list, he can match up donors with those in need. And he said that they'll pay top dollar for a kidney, especially one from a young person."

Realization slammed into Penny and she jumped up from the bed, her face a mask of horror. "You can't be serious? He's trying to get you to sell a body part?" Stumbling backward, she bumped into a chair, causing it to scrape against the floor. The noise startled them both.

"Shhh," he admonished. "Do you want to get caught in here?"

"I...I don't know what to say. You can't do this. You can't let them take a healthy organ from you. What if you need it? Or need it down the road? Or something goes wrong?"

Patting the mattress beside him, he coaxed her over. Taking her hand in his, he said, "Penny, if I could give you a place to live with me that was out of the cold and the rain, I'd sell my soul." Giving a slight chuckle, he said, "But I only have to sell a kidney."

"This is madness," she finally said, chest heaving with emotion. Moving up on the bed, she lay beside him, allowing him to curl his arms around her, pulling her tightly to his side.

"I don't have to make up my mind now," he said, "but I will soon. If I agree, then I get to stay here in the clinic while they make sure I'm healthy. They'll treat me well...feed me...give me medicine...and then I can recuperate here after the surgery. And I got his word that you can stay the whole time too."

"I don't want to live without you," she vowed, the youthful promise of love overwhelming to the young woman who had had little love in her life.

"I'll be fine," he promised. With Penny in his arms, David made up his mind. *A kidney for the chance to provide for her...it was a no-brainer. It'll be fine...nothing will go wrong.*

YENG CHOW DESCENDED the staircase, hidden discretely in an empty supply closet. At the bottom of the stairs he walked to the wall, pressing the switch that sent the wall sliding to the side. A musty smell assaulted him, but he quickly closed the door behind him as he continued forward. The dark hallway led down several twists and turns until he came to another door, this one leading to more stairs. Smiling, he utilized the old steam tunnels beneath the city that made for the perfect clandestine walkways. At the top, he entered a side door to the Cheung clinic and made his way unobstructed to the second floor, walking along the waxed, tiled floors. Stopping at the door labeled, Director Cheung, he stepped inside.

A pretty assistant sat in her seat behind her desk and smiled as he walked in. With a bow in her direction he proceeded to the door to her side. Opening it, he smiled at the incongruent surroundings.

Dark paneling lined three of the walls with heavy, built-in bookcases filling the last wall. Brocade draperies in red and gold hung along the sides of the windows, with matching valances covering the tops. A massive mahogany desk filled one side of the room, while a red sofa and upholstered chairs took up the rest of the space. Sitting behind the desk was Jian Cheung.

Staring at the powerful man running the successful clinic, he bowed before greeting him. "Good afternoon, cousin."

CHARLIE SAT AT Luke's dining room table staring at the computer screen before leaning back in a huff. Her legs were curled up under her but the seat was hard, causing her foot to fall asleep. Standing, she stretched her arms above her head and heard her back crack. The house was empty since Luke had left earlier to go to Jack's for a video-conference with someone from the FBI. He said Jack trusted her, but she had to accept that whatever was being discussed was not for her ears. He offered to take her so that she could work upstairs since Bethany would be there working on her wedding venue business, but Charlie had declined. Sometimes, it was just nice to work alone with no other distractions.

After getting a cold bottle of water from the refrigerator, she glanced back down at the notes scattered across the table in front of her. Taking a long swig of the refreshing liquid, she set the bottle to the side and sat back down to work.

She had hacked into the computer systems of over

twenty clinics in the northern Virginia area, but had been unable to determine if any of them were the clinic Eli had discovered. She considered narrowing her search to those with directors of Asian heritage, but was afraid that was too narrow.

She moved over to the notes on runaways and homeless persons being exploited for human trafficking. *So, how would a clinic make contact with these people if they wanted to use them for their nefarious gains?*

Looking out the window into Luke's back yard dotted with trees, she was filled with the desire to get out of the house. She found a hammock tied between two small trees and could not wait to try it out. Gingerly sitting down, she spread her arms out for balance as she swung her legs up. The hammock teetered precariously until she managed to wiggle into the middle. Lying back, she watched the clouds float through the sky between the tall trees.

The breeze gently blew across her body and she dropped one foot to the ground so that she could use it to push the swing. Relaxing, Charlie smiled. *Luke's right...sometimes you have to get outside and just feel.* Within a few minutes, she drifted off to sleep, dreams sliding in and out as thoughts of the investigation swirled about her mind.

Startling suddenly, Charlie bolted upright, shaking the hammock. Flinging her arms out to the side, she remembered where she was as she steadied the swinging motion. *Wow, I must have been really tired to have fallen asleep.*

Surprised that she had napped, she ungracefully stood up and walked back toward the house, her mind clear and fresh from the beautiful autumn day. Sucking in one last deep breath of crisp air, she made her way back into the kitchen. Walking into the dining room, she looked down at her notes, an idea filling her thoughts. *How would a clinic discover homeless persons or runaways? By offering them health services...for free!*

Charlie plopped back down into the chair, tucking her legs up under her, and refined her searches with renewed vigor.

CHAPTER 19

LUKE PATCHED NICK into their secure video-conference and, after greeting him, allowed the camera to pan the room, introducing the agent to the rest of the Saints. Moving the camera back to him, he immediately started questioning Nick on Eli's murder investigation.

Appearing momentarily uncomfortable, Nick began reviewing his findings. "I won't go back over what you already know, but I've been able to uncover a few more facts in the case. When Eli Frederick first contacted the FBI, his call went into a general call-center that handles the first line of communication. The Bureau gets hundreds of calls, emails, messages, texts a day. You name it, and someone calls it in. He left no name and wouldn't give much info so it ended up in a database for future reference if he contacted them again through the same number.

"The next time, he gave his first name and more information. It was passed to the next level and an agent spoke with him. Based on the information he gave, he was assigned to an agent to deal with him."

Nick stared at the camera, his hard face not moving except for the tick in his jaw. "The agent assigned to him was Lin Wang. They spoke on the phone at least three times that she recorded and then a meeting was arranged."

"What can you tell us about that arrangement?" Luke asked.

"It was to take place in Baltimore. Eli had chosen a library room in a public library. It appeared he craved privacy as well as a public place to meet."

"But he didn't give his address?"

Shaking his head, Nick said, "No, but later, with his full name given, I'm sure Ms. Wang had his address pulled up immediately."

"Who would have known about the meeting?"

"Obviously Ms. Wang, her partner, and her direct supervisor, for sure. And quite frankly, if they felt it was warranted, then a team could have known about it ahead of time. The meeting was to be with just her, but that doesn't mean she went alone. In fact, I'm sure her partner would have been close."

"So any number of people could have known about the meeting?" Luke confirmed.

"Absolutely. Just because he was dealing with Ms. Wang and then was compromised, doesn't mean she was the one who arranged to have him neutralized." He leaned back in his chair, the wood squeaking under his weight. "It just feels wrong to make the assumption she was involved."

"We have to investigate every angle," Monty reminded.

"Yeah, I know." Heaving another sigh, Nick continued. "According to the report, when he did not show at the appointed time, Agent Wang drove to his house after gaining approval from her superior. She also arranged to have her partner meet her there. There was no answer, either at the door or with his phone. She walked around the side, saw blood through a window, and called for backup."

"We've read the official report of the investigation—"

"How the hell did you get your hands on that?" Nick asked, his eyes widening before narrowing in anger.

Luke did not reply and, after a tense moment, Nick shook his head. "I guess you've got your ways. Probably not legal," he grumbled. Shifting in his seat again, he asked, "So what do you want to know?"

"Who was collecting the evidence at the crime scene?"

"The team that responded to Agent Wang's call."

Jack spoke up as Luke panned the camera around to him. "But with Agent Wang there by herself until her partner and the team showed up, she could have tampered with the evidence." He quickly added, "I'm not saying she did...just that she could have."

Pressing his lips together, Nick nodded. "Yeah, it's possible."

"Do we know her movements two hours before the meeting?" Monty asked. Seeing Nick's hesitation, he added, "You've seen what we've got. We've got a witness who was at the scene two hours before the meeting was to take place. The witness saw three people, including one Asian woman who was wearing a white blouse and a dark jacket. She was the one who killed Eli. On top of that, she was wearing a badge!"

"I know, I know," Nick growled. "Look, I don't know Agent Wang personally, so I've got no preconceived ideas of her innocence or guilt, but I'll be damned before I turn against a fellow Agent unless I know she's guilty."

Luke's quiet voice broke through the deafening silence. "And how will you know her guilt until you try to prove her innocence?"

"That's not the way it works," Nick bit out. "Innocent until proven guilty, remember?"

"I've got a woman who has been on the run for the past five months because of someone's guilt!" Luke shouted. "Her life has been turned upside down and she is still being chased because of what she saw. So I don't give a fuck if you hate checking into a fellow agent...are you going to help us or not?"

"Luke," Marc said softly, gaining his friend's attention. "Hold your shit together."

Sucking in a deep breath through his nose before exhaling loudly, Luke nodded. Once more the silence in the room settled on everyone as the Saints watched carefully to see what Nick would say; he appeared to be wrestling with a decision.

A long minute ticked by before Nick finally nodded. "Okay. I'll check to see what her daily log included the day of the murder. I'll also check to see what was on the books for any of her team members."

"Thank you," Luke responded, his heart rate slowly returning to normal.

HOURS LATER LUKE returned to his house and, as he drove into the driveway, he smiled knowing Charlie was inside. Rubbing his hand over his chest, he realized the house had always been a safe place...a comfortable place...even a refuge. But never more than a house. Now, with her inside waiting, it felt like he was coming home.

Opening the door, he noticed the dining room table was covered in papers, two laptops, and an empty cup of coffee with only the coffee dregs in the bottom.

"Charlie?" he called out. Walking through the kitchen, he heard music coming from the garage. Smiling, he headed through the hall and threw open the door to the workout room.

Leaning against the doorframe, he watched as Charlie, dressed only in tight yoga pants and a t-shirt, sweat glistening off her body, ran through her exercises. Her lean body, muscular and strong, made his mouth water.

As she shouted with her jabs and kicks, she never noticed him as he approached. As his fingertips touched her, she startled with a scream, swirling around with her hand flying toward his head. Ducking her hand, he caught her as she tumbled backward. Twisting so he would hit the mats first, she landed on his chest with an "umph".

"Jesus, woman," Luke ground out, his hands now trying to still her wiggling. He had wanted her on him, but in difference circumstances.

"Luke!" she managed to say, as the adrenaline rushed through her body. "What the hell are you doing, sneaking up on me like that?" She scrambled as she rolled to the side before attempting to sit up. "I could have hurt you!"

"Babe, I was in more fear of you getting hurt than anything else," he retorted. "You never heard me approach."

"Why would I be cautious in here?" She took his offered hand, allowing him to pull her up.

He took her hand and pulled her over to him, tucking her gently, chest to chest. "Because you need to be cautious everywhere," he warned. Leaning back as she was about to protest, he added, "You may be good at sneaking up on someone to take them out when they are unaware, but you haven't had enough training in handling someone who comes up silently from behind."

Pouting slightly, she looked into his concerned eyes

and asked, "So, what do we do about it?" Her eyes began to twinkle as she said, "You want to train me some more?"

Holding her close, he chuckled. "That'll never work because every time we get in the workout room, we end up having sex!" As she giggled, he said, "What you need is a training partner...one that I trust." Her brow creased, but he continued, "And I know just who to call in."

Loving the way her body was molded to his, Luke twisted around so that her back was pressed against the wall, pinning her there with his larger body, covering her mouth with his own. Deep, wet and hard. An unrestrained kiss that spoke volumes as their arms entwined. Lifting her up, she wrapped her legs around his waist as her arms clutched his shoulders. Their heads moved from side to side, noses banging, as their tongues dueled in a frenzy for dominance. She sucked his tongue into her mouth, swallowing the groan emanating from deep in his chest.

Thrusting his tongue deeply into the warmth of her mouth, he tasted the heady combination of mint and her. Distinctly her. Her breasts pressed into his chest, as one arm held her ass and the other cupped her delicate jaw.

He pushed her more firmly against the wall, supporting her so that he had both hands free. She immediately began to grind herself on his torso, desperate for the friction to ease the ache that was deep inside.

Grabbing the bottom of her shirt, he jerked it upward until it caught on her breasts. She reached out to assist and whipped it up over her head, allowing their kiss to break only long enough for the material to pass their lips.

He glanced down, consternation replacing the rush of lust as he realized she was wearing a tight sports bra and it did not appear to have a closure. "Babe?" he moaned, now dodging her lips as he tried to see how to remove the now offending garment. "What the hell do I do with this?"

The lust-filled fog lifted momentarily as Charlie glanced down to see what he was referring to. "Oh," she grunted as she leaned away from the wall and grabbed the bottom edges of the bra. Struggling as she wiggled it over her breasts, finally allowing them to bounce free, she continued to writhe as she shimmied the tight spandex over her shoulders and head before dropping it to the floor.

Lifting her gaze back to his, she saw the concern in his eyes. "What's wrong?"

As he glanced down to her breasts, now full, rosy tips budding, he shook his head. "That thing doesn't hurt?"

Giggling as she grabbed his firm jaw with her hands, "Believe me, having them bounce around when I'm working out would be much more painful."

Taking her word for it, he allowed her to pull his

mouth back in, the bra long forgotten as her nipples poked into his chest. He moved his thumbs over the peaks, alternating between pinching and gently rubbing.

Throwing her head back against the wall, she felt his lips leave a wet trail of kisses from her throat, down her neck, to the tops of her breasts. She thrust them forward as an unconscious offering, and one that he was more than willing to take. Sucking a nipple deep into his mouth, he licked, nipped, bit, and sucked until she was writhing wildly. Moving over to give the other nipple the same attention, his hand slipped down her yoga pants and found her panties soaked. Pulling the pants and panties over her hips, he jerked them off her legs then picked her back up.

Lips locked once more, he hefted her up in his arms long enough to unbutton and unzip his jeans, freeing his swollen cock. Having lost all control, he held her over the tip, finding her slick folds ready for him. His mind, filled with the pounding need that roared through him, was barely conscious of her small hands holding him closely. Needing to be inside of her was more important than his next breath.

"Sweetheart," he mumbled against her mouth. "Are you on the pill?"

Leaning her head back, she held his gaze. "Yeah," she whispered with a smile. "And I'm clean."

"Me too," he promised. "We have to get physicals working for Jack—"

"I trust you," she interrupted. "Please." Her mind was equally filled with desire and longing that drowned out all the worries she had faced. She only felt. Experienced. Every fiber of her being tingled with the need for him deep inside. *I've waited forever for someone like you. No, not like you. Just you.*

With one swift plunge he seated her firmly and completely on his cock, barely hearing her head bang on the wall behind her. *Jesus, she's perfect.*

She moved on his cock, trying to ease the ache from deep within her core. With one hand on the wall beside her head to maintain his balance, he thrust up and down.

Her short fingernails raked his back as she felt the tingles that had tempted her as she rubbed herself on his jeans now intensified as her entire sex clutched at him. Strung tight as a bow, she was aware of every movement of his thick cock stretching her tighter.

Luke could not remember the last time he had felt like this. Barely aware of anything other than the roaring in his ears, he pressed his pelvis against her clit as he continued to thrust deeply.

Finally, with his name screaming from her lips, she felt her sex clench and electric jolts moved from her core, spreading outward in all directions.

As her incredibly tight inner walls milked his cock, he found himself pouring his seed deep into her. Continuing to stroke the inside of her until every last drop was emptied, he rested all of his weight on the arm against the wall, holding him up, unsure his legs were up to the task.

Sweating and panting together, her head was resting next to his arm, eyes tightly closed as the sensations flowed over her. *I've wanted him for so long.* Opening her eyes to see his face, she saw that he was looking down as he pulled out of her, their fluids mingled.

He lifted his warm gaze, his chest still heaving with exertion. "That's the most beautiful thing I've ever seen," he said as his lips curved into a smile. "You. Me. The evidence of us together...beautiful."

Kissing her lightly, he gently lowered her legs to the floor, making sure to hold her until her tingling legs were steady. "You okay?" he asked, tucking her silken hair behind her ear.

She peered up, smiling as she touched his dimple, and nodded. "Yeah. I'm perfect." Deciding to take a chance with her heart, she added, "With you, I'm perfect."

His wide smile was the answer to her unspoken question. *He feels the same. Thank God...he feels the same.*

CHAPTER 20

L UKE STOOD IN the kitchen, stirring the ground beef, the scent of spices in the air. Deciding on simple tacos, he moved to the counter to chop lettuce and tomatoes while Charlie took a shower.

Her laptop lay open on the dining room table and the constant dinging of messages had him curious. Walking over, he scanned her message board before leaning closer to see exactly what he was looking at.

He was still in the same position a few minutes later when she walked into the room, her hair still wet and streaming down her back.

"Hey, sweetie, what smells so good?" Instead of answering her, she watched as Luke turned toward her, his face tight with anger.

"You want to tell me what the hell this is?"

Her eyes dropped to her laptop, but without her glasses or contacts she could not see the page he was on. Walking over, she squinted at the screen, seeing the numerous messages popping up and hearing the annoying ding of each one.

"Oh, my goodness! I had no idea I'd get so many

hits!" Turning her smiling face toward him, her smile drooped slightly as he continued to glower. Cocking her head to the side, she asked, "What's wrong?"

"I want to know what you're doing. I left you here to do some research and now see that you've reached out to try to get more information from...from...from whoever the hell these people are!"

Placing her palm on his chest, she said, "Luke, it's okay. I just had a brainstorm idea and followed through, trying to see if I'm right."

"Oh, hell no!" he shouted. "I'm trying to keep you safe and out of the light and here you are putting yourself right into the middle of the investigation. That was never your role."

Dropping her hand as she stepped back a foot, she pressed her lips together tightly, her eyes narrowed. "My role? My role? Who are you to decide what my role is? I've been trying to find things out for the past five months while making sure to stay out of the light. I was only discovered once and took care of that situation on my own, I might remind you."

Dragging his hand over his head, his glower still firmly in place, he began to speak but Charlie cut him off.

"No, you don't get to tell me how this is going to work, Luke. You said yourself that I'm not officially employed by Jack even though I'm working on this case. So I get to make my own rules."

"Goddamnit, Charlie," Luke cursed, holding her

stare, quickly realizing she was not planning to yield.

"You don't even know what I'm working on so how can you be so against it?" she asked.

Scrubbing his hand over his stubble, he closed his eyes for a moment, the fear of something happening to her crawling over his skin. Feeling her soft touch against his chest again, he opened his eyes to see she had moved closer. Roaming his eyes over her face, he reached up to cup her jaw, his thumb scraping gently over her cheek. Sucking in a deep breath, he nodded slowly.

"Okay. You show me what you're working on and why the hell all these people are sending you messages. And...what you're doing to keep them from knowing you and where you are."

The corners of her mouth turned up slowly as the anger slid from her eyes. "Thank you," she said, lifting up on her toes to kiss his lips. "Turn off the stove and I'll show you."

A minute later, the two sat at the dining room table as she began to explain her theory. "The information I got from Eli before he...well, before...wasn't enough to tell me exactly what was going on and where. He never gave me the clinic name, but did indicate that they were local. He only sent some partial databases and, while I've narrowed them down, I'm not getting anywhere definitive. Or at least not fast enough."

Tucking her legs underneath her, she continued, "And there are too many clinics in the northern

Virginia, Washington D.C., and Baltimore area for me to try to comb through. So I tried a different tactic. I began researching illegal organ harvesting and the one thing I kept coming up with was the Chinese government killing prisoners and taking their organs to sell on the black market."

At this pronouncement, Luke's eyebrows lifted. "I've looked into—"

"I know, I know," she gushed, "that's over there, but the Chinese mafia has a big presence in the United States, so I wondered if that was something to consider."

Shaking his head slowly, he said, "Sweetheart, just because—"

"Please hear me out," she begged, waiting until she gained his slow nod. "Okay, so then I started doing some research into the Chinese mafia, but what I found was that they were big in human trafficking." Satisfied that he was no longer interrupting or arguing, she continued. "So then my research led me to who were the likely victims of trafficking. The young. Runaways. Homeless youth. And then it hit me!"

Luke watched her face become animated as she explained her process of her investigating. Her hands waved in front of her as her voice rose an octave. As much as he hated the reason for her energy, he loved seeing her joy at her accomplishments.

"What hit you, babe?"

Charlie almost stumbled over her words and was

sure that if she had been standing, her legs would have gone out from under her. *Babe. I've never been anyone's babe. And with some guys, it's such a throwaway. But with Luke...it's so real.*

Smiling, she kept going with her explanation. "I realized that the same group of people who are at risk for human trafficking in this country are at risk for someone dealing in illegal organ harvesting. The poor. The youth. Runaways. Homeless."

Luke's mind began quickly sifting through her words and he was unable to find fault with her logic. "Okay...so what did you do?"

"I sent a message to every homeless and rescue shelter that I could find within the area that we're looking at and said that I was interested in speaking to anyone who had used a free clinic. I also pulled up a preliminary list of free clinics in the area, so I can start to comb through their information to see what I might find." Shrugging a little, she said, "It was Jude that gave me the idea."

"Jude?"

"He told me that when he first became a Saint, his SEAL training was good, but he really didn't know anything about investigating a crime. So he said he learned that you can't always try to find the big picture. Just take a piece of the puzzle and begin connecting it to other pieces."

Nodding, Luke had to agree. "To be honest, only Cam, with his background as a detective, and Monty, as an FBI agent, really have the investigative instincts down. The rest of us learn as we bring our skills to the group."

"So what do you think?"

Luke sat still for a long moment, unable to find fault with her logic, but wanting to make sure she understood the long shot it was. "I get what you were doing, and your reasoning is sound as far as the investigating goes." He glanced over to her laptop and then pierced her with his stare again. "I don't want to insult you, but you did encrypt your messages?" Seeing the roll of her eyes, he added, "I just wanted to be sure. So what's been coming in?"

"I only checked a few before I went to work out and then you came home." At the mention of his homecoming celebration in the garage gym, she blushed to her roots.

Chuckling, he reached out and tucked a still-damp strand of hair behind her ear. "Yeah, I guess that took precedence over the investigation."

Pretending to slap his hand away, she grinned while turning back to the laptop. "Wow, I've got quite a few comments." Scrolling through them, she said, it looks like many people are just telling which clinics they went to and how nice they were...or, well, here's a few that are complaining about the free services."

The two spent the next fifteen minutes scanning the messages, until Charlie's stomach growled loudly. Slapping her hand on her tummy, she tried to silence it.

"Come on, sweetheart, we can do this later. Let's get you fed." Luke walked back over to the stove to reheat the seasoned meat while Charlie gathered the salsa, cheese, and taco shells.

Stuffing themselves, they left the topic of the investigation alone while they ate. Once the kitchen was cleaned, they retired to the living room, where she settled on the sofa with her laptop, snuggled up to Luke while he turned on a football game.

He kept glancing to the side, observing her brow crinkled and her bottom lip worried between her teeth. Finally, after about fifteen minutes, his fingers twitched on her shoulder and he said, "You gettin' anywhere?"

She twisted around to look into his face. "Yeah, but I guess I hoped I would find easier clues."

Chuckling, he nodded. "Can't tell you how many times I had that very thought while on a case." As he sobered, he said, "Let me help, okay?"

She closed her computer, shifting it off her legs. "Let's just chill for tonight and let more messages come in. Tomorrow we can work together on collating what we have with what we know."

Grinning, he pulled her across his lap while turning the TV off. "That sounds good. Got anything in particular you'd like to do while we're chillin', sweetheart?"

Eyes sparkling, she dropped her eyes to his mouth as she ran her tongue over her lips. "Yeah, I can think of one or two things to occupy ourselves."

With a whoop, he stood with her easily in his strong embrace and headed toward the bedroom.

PENNY SAT IN the small lounge of the clinic, knowing this would be her last night to stay there. Two nights were all they would offer since she was not sick, unless David agreed to the surgery. Her heart ached over David's decision to consider donating a kidney. Rubbing her hand over her face, she fought back the tears. Knowing she had no one to talk to about the decision since she was not supposed to know made it worse.

Tucking the wayward blond strands behind her ears, she moved to one of the computers for their use, pulling up a list of shelters in the area. *Maybe I can find something for us.* Clicking on several sites, she noticed that a few of them had a post referencing someone wanting to speak to anyone who had used a free clinic. Curious, she clicked on the pop-up.

Biting her lip, she sent a message about the clinic she was currently in. Her fingers hesitated, wondering how much she should say, but she finally decided that maybe if the person asking really cared they might give her some advice. Hitting send, she leaned back and clicked the computer off as the night nurse called for lights out. She walked swiftly to the dorm room, not wanting to give the night staff any reason to distrust her. Lying in bed, waiting until it was late enough to sneak another visit with David, she prayed someone would actually read her message before he had to make his decision about the surgery.

JIAN CHEUNG SAT in his opulent office, his email open to the latest missive from his superiors. Rubbing his hand over his face, he grimaced at the tone they had taken with him. *Do they not realize who I am? That I am doing the best I can?*

Irritated at the notification to increase the number of organs to transplant, he sat back heavily in his chair. His nostrils flared in anger at the impotence of his situation. He was torn between the different factions—some wanting more discretion and others wanting more organs. Slapping his hand down on his mahogany desk in frustration as he stood, he stalked over to the credenza. Pouring a drink, he walked over to the large window overlooking a nearby park. The street lamps provided an illuminated pathway that meandered through the area.

Heaving a sigh, he walked back to his desk and sent a cryptic email to his associate asking for more *products to sell.*

Finishing the rest of his drink, he wrote another email—this one to Yeng, demanding a meeting. His fingers hovered over the send button, twitching with indecision. Changing his mind, he altered the wording—instead of *demanding*, he wrote *requesting*. Afterall, Yeng was powerful, having the ear of the ambassador. And the ever-present threat toward his sons back in China. Pinching his lips together once more, he hit send.

CHAPTER 21

"U MPH," CHARLIE GRUNTED, landing on her back on the mat. The wind was only slightly knocked out of her, but the early morning workout was rigorous. She had lost count of the number of times she had landed on her back.

A large hand came down toward her, palm up, and she eyed the huge man extending the invitation to assist her up. She considered refusing his offer, but as she stared into his twinkling eyes, she decided to take him up on it.

As he pulled her upward, she grabbed his wrist, quickly twisting around, and managed to kick the back of his knees, throwing him off balance.

As Marc's laughter rang out, he tumbled forward onto the mat. Rolling over, his smile was even bigger than before. "Good job, Charlie."

Grinning down at him, she allowed herself a little happy dance at finally besting him. *Maybe it was a cheating maneuver, but he's been telling me that in a real fight, use everything I have.* Flinging her arms over her head as she jumped around, she shouted, "Got him!"

Marc stood up, taking in Charlie's goofy dancing before glancing over to the door of the Saint's workout room, noting Luke leaning against the doorframe. The two men shared a grin, before Luke stepped into the room.

Seeing him, Charlie took a flying leap, jumping into his arms. "Did you see me? I finally knocked him down! Well, not really knocked down...but I surprised him!"

Kissing her swiftly, he lifted his gaze to Marc. "She doin' okay?"

Marc nodded, ruffling her hair as he walked past the couple. "Oh, yeah. Her teacher was good and I'm just showing her more street fighting moves." He stopped and turned back to watch the couple as they kissed once more. Grinning at his friends, he turned and headed to the showers.

Later, Jack stepped into the conference room, not surprised to find Luke bent over his keyboard, but Charlie as well.

"You two are at it early today," he said, carrying his cup of coffee over to his desk.

Luke looked up and explained, "Charlie's been here practicing with Marc already," pride evident in his voice. "Plus she had an idea yesterday and we're following up on it." He eyed his boss and added, "I hope it's okay that she's here."

At that, Charlie's head shot up, a slight blush creeping on her face as she stared at Jack as well. "I'm sorry if

I shouldn't be here."

"You're fine, Charlie," Jack said, his voice warm. Settling down in his chair, he looked at the couple whose fingers appeared to be itching to continue their work. Chuckling, he continued, "I've got no problem with you working down here, Charlie. In fact, I suppose we need to talk about compensation."

"Jack, I'm not doing this for money," Charlie said quickly.

He lifted his hand in protest before continuing. "I know you're invested in this case for personal reasons, and it's safer for you to be here while you're working...but essentially you are investigating for the Saints now on this case."

Smiling, she replied, "I'm just glad to have your trust."

The discussion was interrupted with the noise of others coming down the stairs, soon filling the room. Charlie threw a nervous glance toward Luke, who placed his hand on her shoulder as he leaned over.

"You're fine, sweetheart. They all accept you down here."

Sucking in a deep breath, she nodded and turned back to her computer to continue to sift through the messages that had come in while Luke shifted his seat over to the table.

After working alone for so many years, she was surprised to discover how easy it was to ignore the talk and banter at the table as she focused on her task at hand.

She continued to create a database of the clinics that some of the homeless had visited, including their comments, thoughts, complaints, and even praises. It did not take long to see a pattern of the clinics in the area that offered some free services, from the ones that appeared to be used more often to the ones that had the greatest concerns.

After sorting through most of the messages, she turned her attention to the database and began investigating the clinics individually. Tuning out the Saints' meeting, she tucked her legs up under her in the small chair, only breaking to sip her coffee.

After another hour, she rubbed her eyes, blinking several times. Leaning back in the chair, she felt her back pop as she shifted her stiff muscles. She glanced toward the table as she heard chairs scraping on the floor, not realizing Jack's meeting had ended.

Luke walked over as her hands were raised over her head in a stretch. Placing his hands on her shoulders, he leaned over placing a kiss on her forehead. "You need to move around," he advised, his fingers digging into the deep muscle tissue, eliciting a moan from her lips. The sound jolted straight to his cock and he shot a glance out in the room to ensure no one else was paying attention to them.

Whispering in her ear, he said, "Keep moaning like that and we'll need to finish our work at home."

Sitting up straight, her face flaming, Charlie sent him a reproving glare, although she was unable to keep her lips from curving in a smile.

"Okay, sweetheart," he said, sliding into the chair next to her, "what have you found?"

"So far, there are only about six clinics in the D.C. and Baltimore area that advertise as having free services, but there are a lot more that are run on a sliding scale, which for some patients would mean free or almost free. I'm pulling up the info on those now, then I'll start looking for any consistencies."

"Well, let me know when you are finished, 'cause I've got a surprise for you."

Twisting around, eyes wide, she repeated, "Surprise?"

His smile was the only answer, so she looked back at her computer screen. "The screen is blurry and I forgot my eye drops at your place."

Sliding his hand down her arm, he linked fingers with hers and gently pulled her from the chair. As her knees buckled from having been tucked for so long, he grabbed her waist and supported her tightly until she held her own weight.

Glancing down, he asked, "Why do you always tuck your legs up under you when you sit?" Her brow crinkled adorably and he chuckled. "You don't even realize you're doing it, do you?"

Shaking her head, she smiled. "I guess I don't."

"Come on, let's get out of here. Your eyes and your legs need a break."

Thirty minutes later, they were on the road. Two

hours later they pulled into the driveway of a neat, small Colonial in an older neighborhood. Charlie turned to see the smile on Luke's face as he viewed the home in front of him before glancing to the house next door.

Eyes wide, she gasped, "Did you bring me to your parents' house? Without preparing me?"

"Yep," he said, getting out and walking around to the passenger side. As soon as he opened the door, she was already fussing.

"But why?"

Leaning in to place a soft kiss on her lips, he said, "Sweetheart, if I had told you where we were going you would have made yourself sick with worry. Now, you can relax."

She knew his explanation sounded reasonable to him as she wiped her sweaty palms on her jeans before taking his proffered hand. *Oh God, I'm in jeans. Shouldn't I be wearing a dress or something fancier?*

Before she could protest further, he was guiding her to the front door. Opening it, he ushered her in with his hand on the small of her back.

"Mom? Dad? I've got someone I want you to meet," he called out.

Her eyes bugged out further as she twisted around. "You didn't tell them we were coming?" she hissed.

Continuing to guide her forward, he said, "They would have probably forgotten...believe me, this is better."

Uncertainty flashed through her eyes as they rounded the corner from the living room and walked into a study. At least Charlie thought it was a study. Two walls were lined with floor to ceiling bookcases, filled to capacity. Another wall sported two long, narrow wooden tables, covered in yellowed pieces of paper. The floor contained an equal amount of open books and papers as it did exposed wood. A tall, silver-haired man was standing at a desk, bent from the waist, peering at an old parchment through a magnifying glass. A delicate looking woman sat at an opposing desk, tapping energetically on a laptop. Her hair was still dark with only hints of silver threads running through it. Both looked up, their faces blank for a few seconds until they suddenly morphed into huge smiles.

"Luke!" they both cried out at the same time, moving faster than the clutter would allow. His father tripped over a book but quickly righted himself. By the time he made it to his son's embrace, Luke's mother was already wrapped around her son.

Luke kissed his mother's smooth cheek before moving to hug his father. "Mom, dad, this is my girlfriend, Charlotte Trivett. Charlie, these are my parents, Corban and Phoebe Costas."

Phoebe's eye widened at Luke's introduction and she immediately wrapped Charlie in a hug. "Oh, my dear, how nice to meet you!" Looking back at Luke, she wrinkled her brow as she asked, "Had you already told me about her?"

Chuckling, he shook his head. "No, mom. This is the first you're hearing about it."

Her pretty face smoothed out the concern as she smiled back at Charlie. "Oh, thank goodness. Sometimes I get a little forgetful, but I hoped that I had not forgotten something as important as this."

"Trivett? A Saxon name, I believe. Originally from the—"

"Dad," Luke interrupted. "I don't think that Charlie needs a genealogy lesson at the moment."

"Oh, it's fine," Charlie rushed to say, hoping to spare Luke's father any embarrassment. He did not seem fazed though, as he pushed his glasses up on his nose and smiled at her.

"I wish you had told us you were coming," Phoebe said. "I would have lunch prepared."

Luke grinned, knowing his mother would have forgotten all about trying to fix lunch anyway. "It's all good, mom. I talked to Chris and Tina the other day and they invited us over so that you didn't have to worry about fixing anything."

"Oh, that's perfect," Phoebe said, clapping her hands. "If you two want to run on over, we'll be there in just a few minutes."

"I'll come back over and get you," Luke promised, his hand now resting on Charlie's back again as he maneuvered out of the room.

Walking through the rather bland kitchen, Charlie's gaze shot sideways toward Luke, her eyes full of questions. "Luke," she hissed in a whisper. "Wasn't that rude to tell your neighbors and not your parents?"

As they stepped out onto the neglected back deck, their senses were assaulted with the smell of grilled steaks. Looking over, Charlie saw a handsome man at the grill with a beautiful woman next to him holding a platter.

Stepping down into the yard, Luke explained. "Sweetheart, my parents are wonderful people, but they are so into their books and studies that everything else gets forgotten. I love them, but believe me, if it wasn't for Chris and Tina...my upbringing would have been very different. Come on, come meet them."

Without giving her a choice, he linked fingers with her and they walked over to the neighbors' yard. The man at the grill was just as handsome up close as he was from a distance. Charlie could see the beginnings of crow's feet coming from his eyes and a few silver hairs amongst the sandy blond, but his muscles were well defined on his arms, tattoos peeking out from his t-shirt. The pretty woman set the plate down and rushed over, throwing her arms around Luke.

"Oh, honey, we were so glad to get your call." Stepping back, she grabbed Charlie's hands in her own and smiled warmly. "And you must be Charlie. We're so excited to meet you."

Returning the warm greeting, Charlie was introduced to Chris and Tina. "Come on," Tina said, "you can help me in the kitchen. I'm almost finished, but you can help carry things out."

As Charlie left Chris and Luke out by the grill to catch up, she found herself in a delightfully decorated kitchen. "Your house is lovely," she said, looking around and realizing it was a carbon copy of Luke's parents' house. *Well, a decorated version of their house.*

"Thank you," Tina smiled, carefully observing Charlie. "I can't tell you how excited we were to find out that Luke had someone special in his life."

"He's told me how good you and your husband were to him when he was growing up," Charlie said.

Shrugging, Tina responded, "He was always such a good kid." Her eyes glazed for a moment, lost in memories. "I have to tell you that when we first moved in, I was ready to call social services, thinking his parents neglected him. But they didn't. They were loving, but honest to God, I've never met two more absent-minded people in my life. So Luke hung out at our house all the time and we loved having him. He and Chris really bonded."

Outside, Chris smiled at his friend and protégé. "She's beautiful, man."

Luke grinned, nodding. "Smart, tenacious, resilient, hell...she even knows karate. Can't figure out what she's doing with me."

Chuckling, Chris was visibly impressed. "Damn, then you really did hook a good one. But, gotta say, she's one lucky woman to have you. Tina always said that when you settled down, it would be with someone worthy. Glad to see she was right."

Inside the house, Tina moved over to the stove while Charlie turned her head to look into the back yard, seeing the two men laughing and talking as only old friends can do. *Old friends.* A sudden longing pang shot through her as she realized that with Hai out of the country, Eli deceased, and Tim with his family in Boston, she had no old friends to hang with.

A touch on her arm brought her back to the present and she startled. "Oh, I'm sorry," she apologized. "Lost in thought."

Laughing, Tina handed her a platter of vegetables and the two walked out to the picnic table. A few minutes later, after Luke had gone to retrieve his parents, the six sat down to a friendly lunch.

It did not take long for Charlie to see that Luke's parents were very proud of their son, if a bit forgetful as to who he worked for. And the friendship with his former neighbors had made all the difference in the world to what he had once described as the childhood of a very nerdy little boy.

On the drive back home, Luke looked over at the thoughtful expression on Charlie's face. Nervously he asked, "You okay, sweetheart? Was this too much?"

Still leaning on the headrest, she rolled around to smile at him. "No, it was great. I was nervous at first, but it was a small group and they were all delightful. You have sweet parents and really nice friends."

Luke was pleased she liked them but heard the wistful note in her voice. "You're thinking about your friends aren't you?"

Nodding slowly, she rolled her head back to face the windshield. "Yeah. I look back and understand how much I kept to myself and how, now that those friends are gone, I have been very alone."

The reflective silence blanketed the two for a few minutes, each to their own thoughts. Luke realized with the Saints and their women, he now had a large group of friends to work with and rely on, even though most of his work was sitting at a computer. His focus shot down as her hand squeeze his leg, before looking back at her.

"I can tell your mind is working overtime," she accused lightly. "I don't want you to feel sorry for me. I'm learning to step outside of myself…slowly but surely."

His fingers laced with hers before he lifted her hand to place a kiss on the back. "Sweetheart, you're part of the Saints now. You're part of my family. You're part of me."

With a smile, she accepted his promise.

CHAPTER 22

NICK STONE HATED what he was about to do. His face matched his surname as he threw open the door to the bar harder than he intended, but he never flinched as it bounced on its hinges. Looking around in the dim light, he saw a man sitting alone at one of the back booths. Catching the eye of the waitress chatting with the bartender, he jerked his head toward the back. By the time he slid into the opposite seat of the booth, she appeared at his side, her gaze eagerly roaming over his body.

"What can I getcha?"

"Beer. Whatever's on tap," he replied, not looking at her.

As she sauntered away, Nick studied the man sitting in front of him as much as he knew he was being evaluated. His tablemate was medium build with fair hair that was beginning to show a little more white than blond. He also gave off the appearance of being an agent that was near retirement and less likely to be a go-getter. Sighing, Nick finally broke the silence. "Don, I'm gonna be upfront. I hate what I'm about to ask."

The other man took a long swig from his beer and said nothing as the waitress brought Nick's drink over to him. Waving her away, Nick said, "But I appreciate you coming to meet me like this."

"You've got a good reputation, Nick," Don said, "so I've gotta admit, you've got my curiosity up."

"I need to ask a couple of questions about a murder investigation and, I can let you know, I've been sanctioned by my superiors to ask, but it's being handled...carefully."

Don's eyebrows raised, but he said nothing.

"The case was Eli Frederick. You were on a team that was working the case and he ended up dead."

Nodding, Don agreed. "Yeah, and I heard his body was fished out recently. I'm not on that case now though, if you're asking about that."

"No, no. I'm seeking information on the original meeting. I know that once Eli's complaint was finally assigned to an agent, it went to Lin Wang. What I need from you is your info on how the meeting was to take place and what happened leading up to discovering him missing in his home."

"You gonna give me a reason for this *unofficial-official* inquiry?" Don asked as his fingers made air quotes.

Shaking his head, Nick replied, "Nope. At least, not until I've heard more from you."

Pinching his lips together, Don finally nodded. "Okay, fine by me. I've got nothing to hide and it's all in the report." He thought for a moment and said, "I was serving as a partner with Agent Wang when she came to see me about Eli. Said he had been in contact with her over something he had discovered. It had been already assigned to her, but she was arranging a meeting with him and would need backup." Shrugging, he added, "She set the meeting up and made the arrangements. When he didn't show up, she called me to say she was at his home and told me to meet her there. She said that when she got there, he didn't open the door. She walked around to the back and could see inside a window leading into the kitchen. There was blood on the floor and that's when she called me. By the time the Baltimore Police got there, we had ascertained that Eli was not in the house. We had the Baltimore office of the FBI do the investigation."

"Since he lived in Baltimore, why weren't they given the assignment to meet with him to begin with?"

"I assumed it was because Agent Wang was the one he first talked with. I got the feeling the man was real suspicious and non-trusting." Don shifted uncomfortably before adding, "I didn't really get into it too much. Nick, I've got less than a year to retirement and, honestly, it was Lin's case so I was just along for the ride."

"Speaking of that, tell me about the ride." Seeing Don's confusion, Nick asked, "Did the two of you go together?"

"No, not in the same vehicle. We didn't leave from

headquarters."

"Why was that?"

"She said she had an appointment on the east side of town and it would be easier if she didn't have to come all the way back to get me. So we drove separately to Baltimore."

"How long have you worked with Lin?"

Rearing back, Don responded, "Lin? You're asking about Lin?" Seeing Nick's hard face, Don sighed and continued, "About two years. She was transferred here. She's smart, driven, and a real ball-buster when she wants to be." As soon as those words left his mouth, he immediately tried to backpedal. "I don't mean that in a sexist way—"

"Forget about it." Nick waved his hand dismissively as he digested the information for a moment, leaving Don to sip his beer in silence.

The older man eyed Nick before asking, "Now you gonna tell me what you're after?"

Nick debated how much to tell Don, but decided to give him a hint to see if it would prod any more memories from him. "There was a witness to the murder."

Those words hung like a weight over the two men as it sunk into Don what Nick was saying.

"A...a witness? A witness? Where the hell have they been?"

"Not important. What is important is that they saw someone with a badge."

"Holy shit," Don cursed under his breath. "I can't believe Lin isn't all over this case then."

"She doesn't know."

"Huh?" Don replied, confusion on his face. "Why the hell not?"

"Because the person doing the killing was an Asian woman with a badge."

The news knocked Don back where he sat, slack-mouthed, his breath coming in pants.

"This is being investigated covertly," Nick said, giving the only explanation he was going to.

Understanding what Nick meant, Don nodded his head emphatically, making his slight jowls shake. "No, no, I won't say a word. I promise, I won't say a word."

"Good," Nick stated, throwing some cash down on the table as he stood. Stalking out into the evening sun, his mood was even blacker than when he went into the bar. Looking at his watch, he called Monty as soon as he got in his SUV. *Might as well set up a meeting and get this new information out there. Fuck...sometimes I hate my job.*

"DO YOU BELIEVE him?" Luke asked, facing the screen where Nick's scowling face was projected.

"I've got no reason not to," Nick responded. He had relayed the conversation to the Saints and knew the shit would hit the fan if an FBI agent was implicated in the murder of Eli Frederick. "Don's close to retirement and I can't imagine he would want to be involved in a problem that would prolong his ability to leave the Bureau. He didn't overtly implicate Lin, but what he told me gave her no alibi. But," he said, pinning the camera with a glare, "that does not mean that she's guilty of anything."

"We understand," Jack acknowledged, "but it places her on the list of persons of interest."

"I'll start digging into her," Luke said.

"My superiors know about this," Nick stated, "but if this blows up in our faces—"

"She won't know she's being looked into," Luke promised. "I'm careful…there will be no kickback."

Nick leaned back in his chair, his face still unhappy. Finally nodding, he said, "Okay. I'll continue digging on what I can find out here. I've been given clearance to work on the murder case with her so it will give me a chance to keep an eye on what is going on."

Monty looked at the man on the screen, obviously struggling with the assignment. "You know this is the right thing to do, don't you? Hard, but the right thing."

Nick sent a scorching look his way before growling, "If I didn't know it was the right thing to do…I wouldn't be doing it." With that, the video-conference ended and the Saints looked around at each other.

The silence was broken when Bart asked, "You think he'll check into her?"

Monty nodded, "Yeah, I do. I knew him when I

was at the Bureau, and he's a good guy. Likes to do things by the book and that usually doesn't include checking into fellow agents. But he's tenacious and will do what needs to be done."

"By the book, huh?" Cam asked, a slight smirk on his face.

The others chuckled, shaking their heads.

"Well, he wouldn't fit in with us very well," Blaise added, voicing what the others were thinking.

Jack, quiet as usual, had a thoughtful expression on his face as he rubbed his chin. He looked up as the good-natured bantering continued. "Okay, back to business. Luke? What are you working on?"

"I'm going to start digging into Lin Wang and see what I can find." Cracking his knuckles in front of him, he joked, "And since I don't feel the need to do everything by the book, I'll have no problem finding anything I want!"

With the continued chuckles from around the room still ringing, he turned back to his computers and began digging.

CHARLIE CONTINUED TO sift through the messages she received concerning the free services in the area. Several homeless shelter employees and social workers had messaged her as well, giving her no more information than she already had. She even received a message from someone from Medicare who had seen her request for information.

She was almost ready to close her laptop and fix dinner, when her eyes caught the last message she had opened.

Hi. My friend and I are at a free clinic. It's nice, but I'm afraid of what to do when I have to leave. I'm only 16 years old and so is my friend, who's been sick. He's why we got in here. I don't know what information you want to know, but I'd like to talk. I don't have anyone else I can talk to. Penny

The age of the responder captured her attention. *Only 16 years old!* She quickly determined the IP address but it was not at a location she was able to triangulate. *Hmm, I wonder if she'll talk to me?*

Penny, thank you for getting back in touch with me. I am researching different clinics offering free services and will pay for information. Where are you? Charlotte

Charlie had not considered offering to pay for information but she felt as though she hit the jackpot with a teenager responding. *She and her friend probably need the money and she said she had no one else to talk to.*

Not knowing when she might hear back, she left her laptop open as she headed into the kitchen.

THE NURSE STEPPED into David's room, a clipboard in her hands. He smiled as he recognized her from the other evening shift. He caught a movement behind her and realized she was not alone. Another woman walked behind the nurse, this one unsmiling. Her dark, glossy hair was tucked behind her ears and, instead of scrubs, she wore a navy skirt and jacket with a white blouse. His eyes darted between the two until the nurse smiled at him.

"Well, David, how are you feeling?

"Much better," he replied, returning her smile, while eyeing the woman standing just inside his room.

"I'm here with the paperwork for your surgery and to answer any questions you might have for me. The actual surgeon will come by in the morning to discuss the specific procedures with you. Have you made a decision?"

"Yeah, I think I have, but I want to make sure my friend will be able to stay with me."

Sitting down in a chair next to his bed, she clicked her pen and began filling in the forms. "You're referring to Penny Owens, correct?"

"That's right. We're together." His gaze moved back to the unsmiling woman as she stepped over to the nurse and peered over her shoulder at the forms.

"Together?" the woman asked. "As in...?"

"We...we're um...well, she's my girlfriend," he stammered, unused to defining their relationship.

"How sweet," the woman said, in a voice that made him feel that she did not think it was sweet at all.

The nurse continued her questionnaire, "Family to contact in case of emergency?"

His brow crinkled in thought, but finally he shrugged and replied, "Just Penny. She's the only one who'd care anyway."

As the nurse completed the forms, she stood and smiled at him again before turning to walk out of the room, the other woman with her.

"Wait," he called out. He hesitated until both women were facing him again. "I was told that if I donate the kidney, Penny would be able to stay with me. Right?"

"Don't worry," the woman said, her face giving a slight smile. "Penny will be taken care of."

With that, the two women walked out of the room as David lay back on the bed, his mind at peace with his decision.

As they moved down the hall, the nurse handed the forms to the other woman and said, "Here you go. I know you need to match his information to the database."

The woman took the form, glancing at it. "I want to see this girl."

"She's in the other hall...in the women's dorm room, Ms. Wang."

With a quick nod, the nurse headed off to the nurse's station as the woman stalked down the hall, her steps full of purpose.

CHAPTER 23

L UKE WALKED THROUGH the front door, the sight of Charlie's luscious hips swinging in time to the music on her phone's playlist blaring through the kitchen. Her back was to him as she shimmied and stirred at the same time. Her long, dark hair swished along her shoulder blades with each movement.

Deciding to test her, he slipped in, his eyes pinned on the tight pants stretched across her ass and the soft skin of her back showing each time she lifted her arms. Just as he approached, she screamed as she whirled, the spoon in her hand becoming a weapon as it sliced down toward his head. With a quick circle of her leg, she caught him behind the knees, sending him backward onto the floor.

He gazed up at her beaming face and heaving chest, his admiration mixing with lust. She stood over him, spoon still raised as the sauce dripped onto the floor. Glancing down, he quipped, "Glad that's tomato sauce and not my blood."

Grinning, as she offered a hand, she said, "If you had been someone else, that would have been your blood."

As he stood, his long arms encircled her waist, pulling her in tightly. "I see your lessons have helped."

Giggling, she nodded. "Yes, Marc's a good teacher. I was scared at first because he's so big, but he was right—If I could learn to fight him, I would become more self-confident." Stepping out of Luke's embrace, she turned back to the stove to finish dinner. Draining the pasta, she plated it first and then poured the homemade marinara sauce over the top.

Once they were eating, she said, "You know, I think Marc needs someone special."

Lifting his eyebrow at her proclamation, Luke waited to see what would follow.

"I mean, he's now the only Saint who doesn't have a special woman in his life. And that just seems…lonely. And he's such a great guy, it makes me wish I knew someone who would be perfect for him."

Shaking his head, Luke replied, "Sweetheart, the other women have been trying, but unless you know someone who can hunt, fish, loves to camp and can cook out over an open fire, I don't think you'll find the love of Marc's life."

"It can't be that bad," she said, looking askance.

"Oh, believe me, he'll hook up with someone he meets out on a hiking trail, but won't pay much attention to someone in a bar that has the look of high maintenance written all over them. He's a simple man with simple tastes."

"Hmph," she groused. "That doesn't sound too simple to me."

Laughing, Luke added, "But the others like to joke around and say that when he least expects it, someone will knock the big man onto his ass…kind of like you did to me earlier."

The meal almost complete, Charlie leaned over to kiss a dab of tomato sauce off the corner of his mouth.

His eyes flared with lust once more and he shoved his plate back. Easily lifting her, he settled her on his lap, her legs straddling his hips. One hand grabbed her ass, pulling her tightly against his straining erection. Claiming her lips, he licked, nipped, and sucked until she was grinding her crotch against his, seeking relief.

With the other hand he moved the dishes and her laptop to the side before placing both hands on her waist and hefting her ass to the table. Hooking his fingers into the waistband of her pants, he jerked them down as she balanced her feet on his chair and lifted her hips into the air. With an awkward kick, she was able to drop her pants to the side once he slid them down her legs.

Before she processed that she was ass-naked on the dining room table, he parted her legs and dove in, licking a path along her slit.

Moaning, she threw her head back as she balanced on her arms behind her. He pulled her ass to the edge of the table while tossing her legs over his shoulders. Instead of feeling exposed and vulnerable, she felt cared for and loved.

Love? Is this love? Or just great sex? As he plunged his tongue into her slick channel, all thoughts of defining what they had flew out the window. His tongue flicked in and out before his mouth moved up to suck on her clit and she dug her heels into his back as the coils tightened inside.

Her computer dinged an incoming message, but she slapped her hand to the side, hitting the silence button to quiet the interference.

Luke lifted his gaze to watch her eyes glaze over as her orgasm slammed into her. Her sex pulsated as her channel became slicker. Her heels were almost painful on his back, but he welcomed the sensation. He knew he was taking her over the edge and was as lost in her as she was in him.

As her head flopped forward, her lazy smile was met by his still lust-filled eyes as he licked her juices off his lips. Her hand moved forward to clutch his shoulders as she brought her legs back down. Kissing his lips, she tasted herself on his tongue, moaning once more.

Capturing her moan in his mouth, his cock swelled to even larger proportions, causing him to wince at the uncomfortable tightness in his pants. Luke stood, his arms still wrapped around her, never letting her mouth go as her legs encircled his waist. Stalking to the bedroom, he set her on the side of the bed before sliding her t-shirt over her head. With a flick of his fingers, her bra was unsnapped and tossed to the side.

Scooting back on the bed so that she was at the center, she cocked her head to the side and pronounced seductively, "One of us is greatly overdressed."

Grinning, he unbuttoned his shirt, allowing it to drop behind him. He watched as her gaze roamed over his naked chest, pride swelling inside. Her eyes darkened with lust as she took him in from his face, down his abs, to his narrow waist. He watched her eyes move lower as he unzipped his jeans and let the heavy material slide to the floor before stepping out of them. He did not need to look down to know that she was focused on the massive tenting in his boxers. Hooking his thumbs in the waistband, he shucked them off quickly, then stood at the edge of the bed fisting his erection.

She licked her lips as the pre-cum pearled at the tip, about to scramble to her knees.

"Oh, no, sweetheart," he warned, halting her movements. "I want to be buried so deep in you, we can't tell where you end and I begin."

Sucking in a sharp breath at his words, she was sure her sex grew wetter just at the thought. "How do you want me?" she asked, licking her lips in anticipation.

Lifting his eyebrow while still fisting his cock, he said, "Flip. Ass up and grab a pillow to put under you."

Eyes twinkling, she quickly maneuvered into position, her ass already pushing back as he leaned over her, his cock twitching at her entrance. Spreading her legs, she moved further back, rubbing along his erection, loving the feel of his fingers tightening on her hips.

He slid his hands from her hips up to her shoulders before sliding them down the smooth expanse of petal-soft skin on her back. Palming her ass cheeks, he chuckled as he heard the sounds coming from her lips. "Now who's moaning?"

As his hands roamed around to her breasts, he tweaked her sensitive nipples. No longer moaning but full out begging, she pleaded for him to take her as she pushed her ass back even further.

Wanting to make sure she was ready, he kept one hand working her nipple as the other slid through her wet folds. Grinning as she cast a peek over her shoulder at him, "I'm just making sure you're okay first."

"Luke," Charlie pouted. "I need you now!"

Laughing, he slid the tip of his cock to her entrance, saying, "All for you, sweetheart."

Plunging in, they both gasped—her, at the delicious sensation of fullness and, him, at the exquisite torture of tightness. Thrusting in and out, slowly at first and then with more vigor, he closed his eyes in awe of the beauty that was all her. His fingers dug into the flesh at her hips, careful not to bruise but desiring to crush her to him.

Her slick channel grabbed him, causing her entire body to tingle. The electric jolts shot from her core outward as the friction increased. Her fingers clutched the edge of the mattress in an attempt to hold her body in place as his thrusts pushed her forward.

As his hands continued to roam from her breasts to her ass, she felt the coils tighten. *Close...oh, so close.* As though he heard her thoughts, he reached around and moved his fingers over her slick clit, tweaking it slightly. The coils released quickly as the orgasm hit her, the twinges flowing outward.

His balls tightened and he was close to coming. With a final thrust, he powered through his orgasm as his fingers clutched her hips, binding her body to his.

Coming together, they both screamed out their torturous pleasure. Collapsing onto her back, he held her with one hand, using the other to keep from crushing her against the bed. Barely able to think, he managed to roll to the side, pulling her along with him. Their sweaty bodies, entwined together, panted until their breathing slowed in unison.

Luke lifted his hand with effort and pushed a few damp strands of hair back from her brow before sliding his fingers along her cheek. Cupping it, he held her gaze, searching her eyes as though trying to discover the mystery of the ages within their depths.

"What are you looking at?" she whispered self-consciously, noting his intense expression.

"Just wondering how I managed to get so incredibly lucky to have found you," he whispered back before his lips grazed hers.

They lay in each other's arms until necessity called him to take care of the condom. Walking back into the bedroom, he crawled into bed, tucking her into his embrace once more.

PENNY SAT FOR a few minutes staring at the computer monitor, her lips pulled in as her thoughts swirled. Thrilled that her message had been received and answered, she hoped the person, who had given the name of Charlotte, would reply back. *We're running out of time...I wonder if David's made up his mind for sure?*

Hearing a slight noise behind her, she immediately cleared the history before hitting the power button, turning off the computer.

"Miss Owens?" came a woman's voice that, thankfully, was not directly behind her.

Twisting around, she saw a pretty, Asian woman standing just inside the room. Dark navy clothing paired with a white blouse, created a professional ensemble in Penny's eyes. "Yes, that's me."

The woman walked into the room, her dark, beady eyes focused directly on Penny with only a flicker toward the black computer monitor behind Penny's head. "Contacting someone?"

"No...no," Penny lied, instinctively wary. The nurses had seemed friendly, but this woman's serious stare made her nervous. "Just doing a little research." Seeing the woman's scrutiny, she shrugged and said, "I'm looking for cheap places to live."

"I see," the woman replied, her face impassive. "Your...friend, David, has just signed the paperwork for his surgery."

Blinking rapidly, her heart sinking, Penny pinched her lips but said nothing.

"The agreement with him is that you will be able to stay in our facility. Of course, that is an expense to us. Is there family that you can stay with? Friends?" The woman crossed her arms, exposing for a brief second the head of a dragon tattoo on her wrist. She immediately shifted her hand so her jacket covered her wrist, leaving Penny to wonder if she had imagined the image.

Shaking her head, Penny answered, "No. No one. Just David."

For the first time since entering the room, the woman's lips curved into a slight smile. So slight that Penny was not sure it was real. "Well," she said, "I guess we'll just have to take care of you then."

Swallowing deeply, Penny asked, "Will I stay here? Both of us?"

The woman took so long to answer that Penny wondered if she had heard her, but finally she said, "No. After the surgery you will both be moved somewhere else."

Nodding, Penny said nothing. With one last glance to the blank monitor behind Penny's head, the woman turned and walked out of the room. Releasing a long breath she had not realized she had been holding, Penny stood on shaky legs and made her way back to the women's dorm room. Afraid of being caught, she decided to visit David much later in the night to decrease the chance. *And to give the creepy lady a chance to leave!*

Glancing over her shoulder at the computer, she sent up a prayer that Charlotte would read her message...and respond. Hopefully before David went under the knife.

CHAPTER 24

LUKE POURED OVER the information he procured about Lin Wang. Her parents emigrated from China when they attended college and then remained, finally obtaining U.S citizenship. Her father had died seven years ago, just as Lin graduated from college, and her mother continued to live in their house in California. Luke knew that Lin's background would produce little information not already known, considering she had been investigated to become an FBI employee.

Hacking into her bank accounts, he found nothing unusual. Small savings, although it appeared she lived frugally. Her Bureau paycheck managed to pay her bills plus leave some for savings each month. Noticing regular withdrawals, he quickly traced that she sent some money every month to her mother. Not a significant amount, but enough to probably assist her mother with her living expenses.

Abandoning his seat to stalk over to his coffee machine, he looked down at Charlie bent over her computer. Jack had moved a desk into the corner of the room for her to work, against her protestations. Luke knew that she felt self-conscious when everyone was there, but he convinced her that they were more efficient when they worked together. She relented, and now seemed to enjoy having a designated space. The other Saints filtered in and out of the room throughout the morning, but with no meeting scheduled, Luke focused on Lin Wang.

Standing at the coffee maker, he hesitated. *What the hell...I need the caffeine.* Grinning at the reminder of why he was so sleepy today, he fixed half a cup. *I'd gladly deal with an ulcer if I could spend every night wrapped up in Charlie's body.*

On his way back to his computer station he set a steaming cup on her desk before he moved back to his seat to deepen his search.

Charlie smiled up at him, blushing as she noticed the flash of lust in his eyes. Turning her gaze back to her messages, she re-read the one from Penny.

Hi Charlotte, I don't have a phone and I don't think I can use one here. They watch us closely – they say it's for our protection, but I'm not sure. I'm at the Cheung Clinic in D.C. I don't now how long I can stay here. Hope to talk to you soon, Penny

Charlie pulled up the Cheung clinic, seeing the clinic's founder was a surgeon, Dr. Jian Cheung. *Jian?* Turning toward Luke, heart pounding, she called out, "Can you do some digging for me?"

Dragging his gaze from his own monitor over to her, he responded, "Sure. I'm not getting anywhere with Lin Wang anyway. Whatcha need?"

"I've been in contact with a teenager who is on her own and has been in a clinic in D.C. It's the Cheung Clinic. She's got some concerns and I can see that it's run by a Dr. Jian Cheung. J.I.A.N. Do you think that was the name that Eli meant? Not J.U.N.? He misspelled the name? Oh, my God, maybe I've been looking at the wrong name all along. I don't have your tools for hacking into their accounts. If you can get me in, then I can do the searching."

Luke immediately began working on the research for the clinic, digging into their accounts. Charlie dragged her chair over so that she could watch his screen as well. He spent the next thirty minutes showing her how he hacked accounts, before turning over some of the investigating to her.

Scooting her chair back over she said, "I'll start going through the employee records if you'll check out the clinic's finances." Not sure what she was looking for, she began the arduous task of using various search words to go through the accounts. Homeless. Indigent. Teenagers. Runaways.

"Anything?" Luke asked.

"No. So far it looks like a regular medical clinic. But I'm going to dig more into this doctor. Can you get me into their emails?"

"Yeah, give me a few minutes and I'll send it to you."

The Saints filtered in and out of the room during the day as they worked on various missions, each smiling at the couple in the corner, heads bent together pouring over their data.

Seeing a message come in from Penny, Charlie breathed easier reading that Penny sent the phone number for a public telephone at a nearby library.

Good, I will call you tomorrow at 10am. Charlie messaged back.

Thank you. I really am looking forward to talking to you before it's too late.

Too late for what? Charlie asked, but received no answer. Chewing on the inside of her mouth, she hated the sick feeling creeping into her stomach. *I've got to figure out what the hell is going on!*

PENNY TIPTOED DOWN the noiseless halls to David's room, each step causing her heart to beat faster. Afraid that the clinic would not honor David's request that they stay together, she was leery of being sent away before having a chance to see him one more time. Entering his room, she breathed a sigh of relief.

"Hey," she whispered softly, smiling as she observed him looking healthier than when they first came to the clinic.

His wide smile greeted her. Patting the mattress beside him, he said, "Hey, yourself. Come here."

Rushing to his side, she climbed up onto the bed, snuggling into his arms. "You look so much better," she assured.

"I feel a thousand times better," he agreed. "The cough is gone and they've been feeding me really well and giving me lots of vitamins and shit. The doctor says that they want me healthy for the operation."

At the mention of the word *operation*, she sucked in a quick breath. David heard the change and lowered his chin to be able to see into her eyes. "You gotta stop worrying, Penny. I've got this covered."

Leaning up, her face tight with concern, she said, "I can't help but worry. Right now, you're well. We could walk out of here together. Right now. Not waiting for anything. I just don't see why you want to put yourself at risk."

David raised his hand to cup the soft skin of her cheek. "Do you remember when we first met?"

A small smile curved the corners of her lips. "Yeah," she replied. "We were both eating at that soup kitchen over on 21st Street. I was hoping no one would notice me when suddenly you sat down in front of me."

"I was so friggin' hungry and cold and was thrilled to find that place open," he said. "I didn't want anyone messing with me, so I tried to look older than I was. Got my bowl of chili and then turned around to see where to sit, looking for a place that wasn't too crowded." His thumb caressed her cheek as he continued to hold her gaze. "I looked over and saw the most beautiful blue eyes I've ever seen. Like an angel sitting in the corner by herself. I knew then and there I wanted to meet you."

"I was scared at first," she confessed. "At least, until you spoke the first time; I thought your voice was so pretty."

"Pretty, huh?" he groused. "I should be insulted."

"No, no, don't be," she giggled. "I just mean that when you talked to me, I felt…safe."

Leaning down to place a soft kiss on her lips, he said, "You're always safe with me, Penny. And that's why I'm doing this. It's for us. I hate not being able to take care of you. I never want you to have to go back to that piece-of-shit stepfather of yours. I never want you to have to worry that someone else will try to take advantage of you." He saw her eyes darken with fear and he rushed on, "This money will set us up. I get three weeks of care after the surgery and paid well. They've assured me that you'll get to be with me during the three weeks. And then, we'll get a place to live."

It all sounded so good, Penny was tempted to let go of her worry and just enjoy having someone else carry the burden for a little while. But the memory of the unsmiling Asian woman pushed to the forefront of her mind and the worry came back. *Something's not right. But maybe talking to Charlotte can help me know what to do.* Keeping these thoughts to herself, she snuggled back into David's embrace, her head on his chest, and listened to his steady heartbeat as he held her close.

PENNY HUSTLED INTO the large public library, checking behind to make sure she was not followed. She bounced between chastising herself for the paranoia that continually crept into her consciousness and thinking that she was crazy for assuming someone cared about the comings and goings of a homeless teenager.

Feeling safe, she moved over to the neglected public phone booth, knowing it had been there since long before everyone had cell phones. Well, everyone except her and David. Glancing at the clock on the wall, she was just in time. Waiting only a few minutes, the phone rang and she grabbed it anxiously.

"Hello?" she rushed.

"Hello. Is this Penny Owens?"

"Yes, yes. Charlotte?"

"Yes, I'm Charlotte. How are you?"

Penny smiled at the calm voice of the woman on the other end of the line assuring her, hoping she would be able to advise her. "I'm fine. I'm glad you called though. I don't know what information you're looking for, but I'd like to help. And…maybe you could just listen to some of my concerns."

"Absolutely," Charlotte agreed. "And I'll pay for your time. I can drive to where you are and meet with you."

Penny hoped the woman would keep her word, but more than the money, she wanted someone to talk to. "That's fine, but I don't want to wait too long. Can we talk now?"

Agreeing, Charlotte explained, "I'm trying to find

out what services the Cheung clinic offers...besides what is listed on their website."

"They've been nice so far," Penny admitted. "They're taking good care of me and my friend."

"How did you hear about them?"

"Me and David were resting in the park," Penny stated, embarrassed to admit they had been sleeping under a tree, "and a woman came up to us. She gave us water and snacks and said she was out helping people. She heard David's cough and gave us a card with the clinic's name on it. She said they could help even if we couldn't pay."

"Penny, can you be honest with me? Are you and David homeless? Do you have any family that knows where you are?"

Hesitating for only a second, she replied, "Yeah, we are. I've been on my own for about nine months and David's been homeless for a little less than that. We met last spring at a soup kitchen."

"And family?" Charlie prodded.

"No. David's folks died and he was in a bad foster home so he left. My mom let my stepdad...uh...get a little too close, so I booked it out of there."

Charlie's heart ached to hear the admission from Penny. "Okay, honey, let's go over what happened with the clinic. Did you go right away?"

"Yeah, we went that day. It was crowded with lots of people piled in waiting to see one of the doctors, but we didn't have to wait. We got straight in."

Her curiosity piqued, Charlie asked, "How was that?"

"Oh, the lady in the park gave us a card. She said to give it to the receptionist when we got into the clinic. At first, we were given a bunch of papers to fill out and told to sit with everyone else, but when David handed her the card, we got special treatment."

"Special? How special?"

"We were taken to a different part of the clinic, where no one else was waiting. We both got physicals and we got to stay."

Knowing none of this information was on any of the marketing websites for the Cheung Clinic, Charlie began to get a sinking feeling in her stomach. "Okay, Penny, I want you to tell me everything you can about where you are staying."

For the next several minutes, Penny described the small, but private, room David had been placed in and how they had treated his cough, as well as the small dorm room she had been assigned to. "From what I can tell, they give extra care to those of us who have no money or no place to live."

"And they asked about family and contacts?"

"Yeah. David and I said we only had each other."

"So why are they letting you stay if he's better?" Charlie asked, typing all her notes into her laptop as Penny spoke. Hearing the hesitation, she prodded, "I just want to help, but need you to give me all the information."

"He's agreed to having an operation so he gets to stay and so do I."

"I thought you said he was better? He needs an operation?"

"Well, he doesn't need it, but he's agreed to it."

The airwaves were silent as Charlie processed the new information Penny gave her. Biting her bottom lip as the ill feeling in her stomach became more prominent, she could feel the young woman's reticence, but knew she needed more information. "What kind of operation?"

"He's donating a kidney," came the slow response. "They'll let me stay to take care of him."

Before Charlie could respond, Penny said hurriedly, "I've got to go. I think someone followed me. I'll contact you again." Hanging up before sliding down behind a bookshelf, she eyed the entrance to the library, watching as an Asian man walked in, looking around. She was unable to tell if he were looking for her or if he was just a random man who happened to be in the library. *Jeez, I'm suspecting anyone who looks like they may have come from the clinic!* As he moved over to the elevator, she grimaced. *Damn, I just hung up on Charlotte and didn't even get her advice.* Seeing the bank of computers on tables set up underneath a tall window, she slipped around the back bookshelves until coming to the one farthest from the front door.

Quickly logging into her email, she fired off another note to Charlotte. **Sorry, might have been a false**

alarm. I don't want to be gone too long. Call again tomorrow. Same time. I'll be here if I can.

With a last glance around, she slipped out a side door and made her way unnoticed back to the clinic.

CHAPTER 25

"GOOD MORNING," CHARLIE said, her perfectly painted lips curved in what she hoped was a gracious and sincere smile. Her red, curly wig once more partially hid her face, along with the glasses with the purple frames.

"Hello," the young woman greeted, returning her smile. "May I help you?"

Charlie noted the name badge on the woman's scrubs. Xia. *No last name...or maybe that is her last name. Damn, I can't tell.* With a quick look to the side, she observed the crowded waiting room of the Cheung Clinic, most of the plastic chairs filled with families or moms with their children. The noise level was high and Charlie leaned in a little closer so that her request could be heard.

"I hope so," she replied. "I'm working on behalf of an anonymous donor who is looking to make a donation to an organization that supplies assistance to the area's homeless."

The woman's smile widened and she said, "Wonderful. Let me give you a brochure on the clinic."

Reaching over to a plastic holder sitting on her desk, she whipped out a shiny, tri-fold brochure.

At a glance, Charlie knew it held no new information for her. "Thank you, but I have this information. I was hoping to arrange a tour or speak to someone about the special services for the homeless."

Xia's eyes narrowed instantly, but her smile remained on her face. With a spread of her arm, she said, "What you are looking at is essentially all there is to see. Of course, behind me are the examining rooms which, I'm sure you can understand, would be off limits to protect the privacy of our patients. We also have a small lab, x-ray equipment, a sonogram machine, EKG equipment, and a few other specialized rooms to assist with the families that come to us."

"How on earth do you provide all of this?" Charlie asked, her voice dripping with awe.

"We obtain funding through many sources, and the director uses his influence with the area's societies looking to assist."

"I was under the impression that you also had room for some patients to stay overnight if necessary."

"I'm sorry, but you are mistaken. We are only a walk-in clinic, not a hospital."

"Oh, so no surgeries can be performed here?" Charlie prodded.

"Certainly not. Our physicians deliver care to the people who come, regardless of their ability to pay or not."

Tapping a fake nail on her chin, Charlie wondered what her next step should be. This woman was not going to let her gain any further information. Deciding to push her luck, she added, "So, no one from this clinic solicits the homeless in the area to get them to come? No one seeks out potential patients and gives them…oh, I don't know…perhaps a card to bring in with them for access to special treatment?"

At that statement, Xia's wide-eyed, tight-lipped expression hardened her face as she glared at Charlie. "No. Certainly not. As you can see from our packed waiting room, we have no need to solicit for patients. We are stretched thin as it is."

Nodding her head toward the noisy, chaotic waiting room, she smiled. "Yes, I can see that you are. Well, I will certainly let the benefactor know what I have learned." Turning, she headed out of the clinic and walked down the street, hailing a taxi at the corner.

The driver glanced in the rear-view mirror, his eyes hidden behind his sunglasses. "Any luck?"

Charlie smiled up at Luke and said, "They're hiding something. I know they are. Did you get it on tape?"

Luke spoke into his earpiece and, after a moment, nodded his head. "Yeah, Jude's got the video and audio right now." Within a few minutes, the two alighted from the taxi and jumped into the waiting Saints' SUV.

LIN WANG'S CELL phone vibrated during a long-ass, boring staff meeting and she discreetly checked the caller. Slipping out of the room with an apologetic grimace to the man sitting next to her, she walked out of the room and down the hall.

"Wang," she answered succinctly.

"Problem."

"Immediate?"

"Maybe."

Disconnecting, her grimace was no longer fake as she pondered how best to get to her contact while in the middle of the FBI headquarters. The noise from around the corner indicated the meeting had ended and she was glad to have only missed the last minute of it, to avoid suspicion.

"Got a problem?" came a deep voice from behind.

Startling, she quickly recovered as she turned, a small smile that did not reach her eyes on her face. "Nick, I hear you've been assigned to assist with the investigation into Eli's murder."

Nodding, his typical impassive expression in place, he observed her carefully, noting she avoided his question. "Yeah. I'm reviewing the forensic evidence to see if it matches up to any of the cold cases I've worked on."

The two continued down the hall toward another group of offices, their physical differences almost comical. Lin's petite stature next to Nick's six foot, four-inch muscular frame caused her to have to twist her head while leaning back to look into his face.

"You seemed upset by your phone call," he reminded. "Everything okay?"

"Yes, absolutely," she quipped dismissively, stopping at her cubicle. "I'll forward you the file I've worked on, if you'd like."

"I've already started but see no reason not to avail myself of your work as well," he replied smoothly before watching her turn toward her desk. "Just email it to me." He watched her nod, tight lipped, as she sat down, before heading to his own office.

Once she ascertained he had left the vicinity, she used her phone to send a quick message. **Lunch. 1.**

Forty minutes later, at one p.m. exactly, Lin walked into a dingy diner on 7th Street in the small, but historical, Chinatown district. Sliding into the booth, already occupied, she quickly ordered in Chinese and waited until the waiter left. Turning to the woman sitting across, she demanded, "Talk."

Xia Wu leaned forward and said, "A woman came to the clinic today. She was nosing around for what we do for the homeless."

Lin lifted her eyebrow expecting Xia to continue.

"She wasn't just there to ask questions about the clinic...she wanted to specifically know if the homeless were sought out and given cards for special treatment."

"Tā mā de," Lin cursed, her lips twisting in anger. "Who the hell can she be?"

"I don't know. She was a red-head with big glasses.

Long fingernails. Nicely dressed. Said she worked for a benefactor who wanted to donate to the clinic."

Lin, no longer listening to Xia, her mind already problem-solving, knew she could get the clinic's reception area's security video, but anticipated not being able to identify the woman. *Unless...* "Did the woman touch anything?"

"Uh, uh...no," Xia said, her face lined with worry. "Wait a minute, I handed her a brochure and she had it in her hand, but I don't know if she kept it."

"Go back there, right now, and double check. If she left it, I want it." Seeing Xia hesitate, Lin bit out, "Now!"

The young woman immediately slid out of the booth and, with a longing glance toward the waiter just bringing out the food, hurried out of the restaurant.

"WHAT DO YOU mean we aren't going to do anything?" Charlie asked, disbelief evident in her strident voice and her gaze darting around the Saints sitting at the table.

"Charlie—" Luke began.

"Don't patronize me," she said, glaring at Luke before turning her ire toward Jack. "This girl's told me that something's going on. They blatantly lied to me when I went in and asked about their homeless services. It's got to be tied into Eli's suspicions. And we're doing nothing?"

Luke placed his hands on Charlie's shoulders, applying just enough pressure to get her attention. "You need to listen to Jack so we can figure out what to do."

Plopping back down in her seat, Charlie pinched her lips together, knowing Luke was right but struggling to maintain her composure all the same. Taking a calming breath, she nodded. "I'm sorry I'm making a spectacle of myself," she said. "I just can't sit around and not do something to help."

Jack offered her a grim smile and replied, "Charlie, what you've found out is good information. Now we need to find out more. We can't go in guns blazing someplace without due cause. I've got a license for private investigating and, while we're no usual PI business, we have protocols. Right now, you have no evidence of wrongdoing, nor any evidence that someone is in imminent danger. But," he threw up his hand to stop her from retorting, "what you do have is compelling information that we need to investigate further."

Charlie noticed the sympathetic looks thrown her way by the other Saints but instead of feeling comforted, she wanted to growl.

"What you've found out is really good," Monty praised.

She observed him closely, pleased that he was not patronizing her. Slowly letting out her held breath, she realized they were all on the same side. "I don't know how you do this," she admitted, her anger slipping away.

"It's not easy," Jude agreed, "but this just means that it's time for us all to dig deeper with what you've given us."

"Okay," she agreed, reaching out to hold Luke's hand that had been resting on her leg. "What now? I don't want to lose momentum in the case."

"Good," Jack acknowledged, "because we need you more than ever. This Penny is the first real link we've had to something that Eli might have been talking about and we don't want to lose her." Turning to Luke, he asked, "What have you found?"

"Based on Charlie's impression that the name Eli meant was possibly Jian and not Jun, we have found quite a few doctors with that name. I thought that it might be like the English name of John, something common and therefore harder to narrow down. But with the name that Penny gave her, it is too much of a coincidence that the Cheung clinic is run by Jian Cheung."

"How did you find her again?" Bart asked.

Charlie looked over to the large Saint, his blond surfer appearance belying his sharp mind. She also knew from his wife, Faith, that he doubted quickly and strived for facts to follow. Intuition was not his forte.

Jude smiled encouragingly at her, saying, "Connect the dots for him."

Feeling Luke's hand still on her leg, giving a squeeze of assurance, she chose her words carefully, so as not to be dismissed. "We know Eli discovered something to do with the possible illegal harvesting of organs. With little else to go on, I began to try to find any clinics or doctors with the name of Jun, but did not have any success. So, I did some research into who was likely to be involved in organ harvesting. The over-whelming information points to what the Chinese have been doing in their own country with prisoners or political enemies. But I knew you couldn't just do something like that here. People would question. The family would go public if they thought something was wrong."

"So what was next?" Bart continued to press.

"I thought about who would be the most likely vic-tims. Who wouldn't have a family to search for them or question for them. And I came up with the homeless and young runaways." Her eyes searched the group of men around the table, finding them listening attentive-ly. *Come on…believe in me.*

Pressing her advantage, she continued quickly. "And what I realized is that not only is this the largest possible group for something like this, they are the most likely to become victims of human traffick-ing…being sold into slavery. And do you know who is one of the largest organizations dealing in trafficking?" Having their rapt attention at this point, she said, "The Chinese mafia. The triad. The tongs. And their ties to the Chinese government is strong."

The silence around the table settled in as each Saint pondered her words. "So I placed notices at all the shelters and soup kitchens that I could in the northern Virginia and lower Maryland area, asking for contact with anyone who had used free clinic services in the past year. Sifting through them, no one gave me any real information that I had not already discerned except for Penny, the young teenager who is staying at the Cheung clinic. And she just told me that her friend has agreed to have a kidney removed."

Rubbing his hand over his beard, Jack regarded the impassioned woman sitting amongst the hardened men. Finally turning to the others, he said, "So where do we take this?"

Monty quickly responded, "I'll get hold of Nick and see what information he has on this clinic. He can let us know if there are any suspicions from the FBI or any reports."

Grinning, Bart leaned back in his seat and said, "Cam and I can do a little night time reconnaissance."

The others smiled in response, knowing the two best friends enjoyed breaking and entering as part of the investigations the Saints worked on.

Luke agreed. "I think that makes sense. I'd like to know what's going on in there that we can't divine. Charlie and I'll continue to delve into the Clinic's systems. I can tell you that on the surface, they are a walk-in clinic for the indigent and do not list any other resources. So, if they are housing patients, it's not on their books."

"If they do that only for the homeless, then they

could keep it hidden," Blaise added.

"Right," Jack agreed. "Monty, contact Nick. Jude, work with Luke and Charlie to cover more bases. Patrick, you saddle up and go out with Bart and Cam tonight. Marc, you fly them up. Chad and Blaise, help them get their equipment ready."

With everyone's assignments given, Charlie breathed a sigh of relief. *They believe me! Now to find out what the hell is going on!*

CHAPTER 26

LIN, A SMILE on her face, walked back from the lab, a file held close to her chest. It took almost three hours for her technician friend to give her the fingerprint analysis which, of course, only gave the closest matches. Lin knew Eli's house had been dusted for fingerprints and, while there were not many, she believed his former classmate and friend had been one of them—the elusive Charlotte Trivett.

Sitting down in her cubicle, she glanced around to make sure no one was watching and opened the file. Running down through the list of possible matches, she searched for just one name. And there it was. Charlotte Trivett.

Slamming the file closed, Lin rubbed her forehead, wondering how best to proceed. Uncertain of her next move, one thing was evident…the threat needed to be eliminated.

CHARLIE LAY BACK in the hammock once more, discovering it was fast becoming her new go-to place when she needed to unwind and let her mind process a problem slowly. Leaving the investigation into the accounts of the Cheung Clinic to Luke and Jude, she stayed home today, going back over the information Eli had given her before he was killed. He had rambled quite a bit, but the words came back to her.

"It's a Chinese based medical company that has a database of organ needs to match donors. On the surface it would look normal."

She rolled the words around and around in her head while the white clouds floated through the autumn blue sky. *Chinese based medical company. Chinese based medical company.*

"He may have known."

"What?" Charlie shouted out loud. "Oh my God, how did I not remember Eli saying that?"

Flinging from the hammock she tripped on her way into the house, scaring the birds at the feeders. Running to her computer, she searched for her old contacts. *There he is…Hai Zhou.* With a few more clicks, she discovered his mother still lived in California. Grabbing her phone, she placed the call, hoping Hai's mother spoke English.

An older woman answered, "Hello?"

"Mrs. Zhou?"

A pause followed and Charlie realized that her knowledge of the culture was limited. *Maybe his mom's name isn't Zhou.* Just as she was getting ready to ask again, the woman answered her question.

"Yes, this is me."

"Ma'am, I am an old college friend of your son. Hai? I know it's been several years since he went back to China but I'd love to talk to him. Do you have his contact information? Phone number or email?"

This time the pause was much longer and Charlie pulled her phone away from her ear to check the screen, wondering if the connection had been lost. Seeing that they were still connected, she prompted, "Ma'am, are you there?"

She could hear a shuffling sound and a younger woman's voice came on the line. "Hello, I am Ana Le. I am a neighbor of Mrs. Zhou. She seems upset and just handed the phone to me."

"Oh, I am sorry," Charlie apologized. "I told her I was an old college friend of her son and wanted to get his contact information. We fell out of contact when he moved back to China."

"China?"

"Yes, he told me he was quitting his job in California and moving to China."

"When was this?"

"Um...about two years ago," Charlie replied, the sick feeling that she got when she was about to find out something she did not want to know growing in her stomach. Licking her dry lips, she continued, "Did he not go back to China?"

Ana answered, "I don't know where you got your information, but Hai died two years ago."

Almost dropping the phone, Charlie repeated numbly, "Died? Two years ago?"

"Yes. He died when he fell asleep in his car and crashed."

"I…I…" Charlie stumbled over her words before pulling herself together. "Thank you, Ms. Le. This is such a shock. Can you perhaps give me the date of his death?"

"Yes, the date was October 12, two years ago."

Hanging up, her heart pounded and her hands shook as she quickly searched her email history. There it was—Hai's group email to her, Eli, and Tim. It came in response to a group email she had sent to everyone. He had said he was moving back to China to take up a position there and it had been nice knowing everyone.

Almost in a trance, Charlie's gaze moved to the date of his email. October 13. The day after he died. *Or was killed. Holy moly!*

She thought of calling Luke, but stared at the phone in her hand. Patrick told her it was a burner phone when he gave it to her, but she had been too embarrassed to let him know she had no idea what that meant. *I just used it to call Hai's mom. Is that traceable? Aughhh!*

Marc had picked him up this morning to go to the compound, so his SUV was still in the garage. A quick glance behind her revealed the keys on the peg next to the door leading from the kitchen to the garage. Grabbing her purse, she snagged her laptop and the keys and floored the vehicle down the road.

When she got to the security gates at Jack's place, she looked dumbfounded at the panel. Not knowing the code, she pushed a few buttons until a voice came on.

"Girl, what the hell are you doing?" Bethany laughed. "I saw you drive up and didn't have time to buzz you in before you started hitting the buttons."

"I'm sorry," Charlie said, feeling foolish. "I really need to get in—" The gate had already begun to swing open. "Um…do I just drive in?"

"Charlie, come on, straight to the house."

She recognized Luke's voice and scrunched her nose in irritation. *Oh, hell, they'll probably all be there waiting for me.* She was partially right. When she came to the end of the drive, Luke was the only one standing on the front porch, but as soon as she alighted and ran to him, she could see the others in the living room through the open front door.

"Babe, what's wrong?" Luke asked, his heart pounding on high alert.

Grabbing his hand, she pulled him into the house as she said, "Come on, I'll tell you all at once." Stumbling over the threshold, Luke threw his arm around her waist to steady her. Glancing around the room at the other Saints, then turning her body fully toward Luke, she blurted, "Hai Zhou never went to China. He's dead."

An instant of stunned silence was followed with

curses as her pronouncement sunk in. Jack barked out, "Back downstairs," and everyone snapped to attention. As she was hustled in front of Luke, she twisted her head around to explain, "I was afraid to use the burner phone. I thought I'd better come."

Squeezing her hand in his, he said, "No problem, sweetheart. I'd rather you be with me now anyway."

Grinning in spite of the situation, she rounded the bottom of the stairs and entered the conference room. Quickly sitting, the group looked at her expectantly and she proceeded to tell them of her discovery.

Finishing, she said, "I haven't checked out anything else, yet. As soon as I realized the date the email was sent was after he died, I knew I needed to come." She held her phone out in her palm and added, "I called from this phone, but then I didn't know what to do with it."

Patrick walked over and took it from her hand. "No problem. I'll get you another."

"Good work," Jack praised Charlie, as he looked over to Luke. "Get us what you can."

Luke left her side and immediately went to his bank of computers, quickly followed by Charlie. As she moved she could not help but notice the expressions of admiration coming from the others. Smiling to herself, she ducked her head as she turned back to stare over Luke's shoulder.

"Hai worked in California for Chow Medical In-corporation. Their site says they are world leaders in meeting the medical community's needs for better, more effective organ transplant technologies. Give me a minute to hack into the HR."

Charlie's fingers dug into his shoulders as she watched him work his magic.

"Got it," he proclaimed. "Hai's employee record is marked as inactive, reason deceased. The official date is October 12."

"Can you find out what he worked on?" Monty asked, looking at his watch. "Jack? We've got a conference with Nick in about ten minutes."

"Good," Jack responded. "We'll have a lot to go over."

Charlie sat quickly in her chair and said, "We can do this faster with two of us working." As Luke worked to determine Hai's department at Chow Medical, Charlie looked into his death report.

"Luke?" Charlie waited until he lifted his head to look at her before she said, "Remember, Hai was a software engineer. He would have been hired to work on their programs in some capacity."

"Thanks, sweetheart," he replied with a smile, looking back at his monitor.

Once more, she could not hold back the grin, feeling the energy in the room and knowing she was a part of it. As she and Luke continued to work on Hai, Jude set up the video-conference with Nick, who shortly appeared on the screen. His familiar scowl in place, he greeted the Saints.

"You got more for me?" Nick asked.

"We've got a lot," Monty replied and began to review the intelligence Charlie had uncovered about the Cheung Medical clinic. Covering her conversations with Penny and her suspicions about human trafficking as well as organ trafficking, he ended his report with the latest on Hai Zhou.

"Goddammit," Nick cursed, rubbing his hand over his short, dark hair.

"I can see Hai's old email account. It was deactivated but I've got it pulled up," Luke stated. He began scrolling through and added, "It appears someone went through and deleted some messages after October 12 of that year. Someone would only do that if they had something to hide."

"Encrypted?" Charlie asked, glancing back to his monitor.

"Nope. Looks like an amateur job of trying to hide some things." Cursing loudly, Luke shook his head. "I accepted Tim's explanation too readily about Hai and did not follow through enough!"

"I never questioned it either," Charlie said. "Neither did Eli or Tim."

"Whoever did it probably figured no one would come looking after he was dead by an apparent accident," Blaise surmised.

"Hey, guys," Charlie called out. "His accident report doesn't give me much, but an insurance claim was filed on behalf of his mom and the report from the insurance company that investigated stated that the brakes on his car did not work. They don't list why, but it was the reason they denied the claim. It appears the mom never questioned the report."

"It's rare that brakes suddenly just stop working," Cam threw out. "I've seen too many cuts in my time not to lean that way."

"Got it," Luke called out again. "He was working on the programs that list the transplant donor national database, to be used by hospitals. I've got an email here where he contacted his supervisor saying as he worked on the final program he questioned why it only went to certain private doctors and not the national center."

Luke and Charlie looked at each other, both of their minds quickly analyzing the possibilities.

Charlie looked at the group, including the screen with Nick's image staring at her, and said, "If we are considering the possibility of illegal organ transplantation, then it would make sense that someone has to have a way to connect the doctors that are harvesting the organs with doctors that don't mind getting an organ any way they can for their patients."

Cam interjected, "Remember, Miriam said that organs have to be used within a certain time frame."

"What if this company was looking into a way to extend that time? Then organs harvested anywhere in the world could be sent to the highest bidder." Charlie surmised.

The room resounded with *fuckin' hells and damns,*

even from the screen as Nick joined the others, before she continued, "And what better victims to do this to than young runaways or homeless persons; no one checks up on their whereabouts."

Taking a deep breath, Nick said, "This investigation just got a whole lot bigger and a fuckuva lot more complicated."

"I don't care," Charlie stated emphatically. "Right now, I want Penny and her friend safe."

"What about the human trafficking angle?" Chad asked, his eyes full of concern. "How does that fit in?"

Shrugging, Charlie said, "I don't know. Maybe nowhere. It's just that there seemed to be a connection between the Chinese mafia and trafficking of young people as well as organs."

Jack looked at Nick and said, "I'm sending some of my men into Cheung's clinic tonight to see what they can find."

For once Nick did not argue the legality of such a search, but had to add the throwaway caution, "Whatever they find, get it to me so I can work on this in a way that'll stand up in court."

The Saints spared a grin, remembering the number of times Mitch would say the same thing.

Bart, leaning forward, resting his arms on the table, pinned the group with a stare. "And if we find something that needs immediate attention...like Penny or someone else?"

Nick's lips thinned for only a second before answering, "Then you take care of it."

Bart's handsome face relaxed into a slight smile as he winked at Charlie. "You got it."

CHAPTER 27

PENNY SLIPPED INTO David's room, her heart skipping a beat when she saw his bed was empty. A noise from the other side of the room startled her, but her fear was replaced with a grin as David stood from the chair, his arms out wide.

Rushing in for a hug, she smiled up at him. His color was good and he appeared to be in the peak of health. Trying to push down her fears, she held on tightly as her arms squeezed around his middle.

He kissed the top of her head and said, "We need to talk."

An involuntary jerk shot through her body as the smile dropped from her face. He led her over to the bed and pulled her up in it next to him. She lay her head on his chest, hearing his strong heartbeat.

"The surgery is going to be tomorrow."

The words came out plainly with no fanfare, but they slammed into Penny as though blared with trumpets. Her fingers, which had been resting on his stomach, clenched in fear.

"Now, before you say anything," he began, "let me

tell you what I've been told. I'll be prepped tomorrow but I won't be in this building. They have a separate surgical place and that's where I'll be."

Jerking her head from his chest, she peered into his face. "What about me? I don't want to stay here without you."

"I know. I asked about that. They said that you'll be taken with me."

Releasing her held breath, she searched his face, trying to judge his emotion. "How are you with all of this, David? How do you really feel? Please be honest with me…that's all we have."

He cupped her face, running his thumb over her soft skin, but said nothing for a while. Finally, he asked, "Do you realize we've never even had sex?"

Blinking in confusion at the change in topic, she cocked her head to the side. "Well…I…yeah, of course I know."

"Have you ever wondered why?" he asked, his soft breath caressing her face.

Biting her bottom lip, she shook her head. "I just thought…uh…that maybe you didn't really want—"

Chuckling, he said, "Penny, I'm a normal sixteen, almost seventeen-year-old male. Of course I've thought of sex." Grinning at her blush, he added, "I'd be thinking about it even if you were plain and homely…but you're not. You're gorgeous and sweet and loving. And I've thought of having sex with you every day for all these months we've been together."

Blue eyes wide, she blushed as she asked, "Then why haven't you—"

"Because I made a promise to myself that I would not have you until we could be in a real bed. You were too precious to try to make love to under a tree where anyone could see…or crammed into a shelter where others around would know what we were doing. For me…I would wait until I could give you what you deserved, and that was just the two of us in a real bed."

He let the words flow over her before he continued. "And that's one of the reasons I'm doing this surgery. I want that money…I want to be able to get a small place with you and have that bed. I want our first time to be special."

Penny attempted to blink away the first tear that fell, but was unable to stem the flow. No one in her life had ever offered her a more precious gift. Not her dad that left when she was a baby. Not her stepdad who leered at her and barely waited to touch her when he could. And not her mom, who knew the monster she married but did not protect her own daughter. But this man-boy…was offering her everything he had to give.

The sobs burst forth as she buried her face in his t-shirt, her body bucking with their force. He wrapped his arms around her tightly and held on for his life, while making soft, gently shushing noises.

When her sobs finally subsided, she gazed up at him again through watery eyes and said, "If you want…we're in a bed now."

His breath caught in his throat as he realized what she was offering. The inner battle raged inside as her soft body pressed closely to his. His swollen erection pressed against her stomach, his body ready and eager.

Drawing in a ragged breath, he made up his mind as he leaned the scant distance to kiss her lips, tasting the salt of her tears. "No, babe. Not now. Not when we're scared and desperate. But soon. As soon as I recover and we have our place. Then, and only then, will we make love for the first time."

Nodding while still snuggled close to him, she whispered into the darkness, "I love you, David."

Instead of leaving his bed and heading back to her room, she continued to rest her head on his chest, and heard the words she longed to hear as he promised, "I love you too, Penny. I'll love you as long as I live."

EASILY RE-WIRING THE security on the Cheung Medical clinic, Bart and Cam slipped into the back of the building. Using the building's blueprints, they made their way from the back examining rooms and labs, checking the reception area, and then back to the staff rooms.

Following their standard operating procedures, they slipped specialized thumb drives into every computer in the clinic, including the one in reception, and notified Luke they were ready. He was in a Saints' van parked down the street and began the process of downloading everything from the computers. Charlie had come with him, fascinated to see how he worked in the field and eager to learn.

It had taken almost ten minutes before he was able to give them the signal to pull the drives out. Looking over at Charlie, he noticed her grinning. "Like this?"

"Oh, yeah," she gushed. "I never knew how you obtained all of your information, only able to see part of what you were doing. But this," she said, waving her hands around at the equipment in the van, "is amazing." Pausing to hold his gaze for a moment, she added, "Thanks for letting me come."

Leaning over, he kissed her quickly before replying, "You'll have to thank Jack. I think he's finally getting used to you working with us."

Inside the clinic, Bart and Cam stopped at the end of a hallway, staring at each other.

"What the fuck?" Bart cursed.

Cam looked around, his face a study in concentration. "What's on the blueprint of the clinic doesn't show any connection to another part of the building, but according to what the teenager told Charlie, they just walked from here to where she and her friend are staying. They've got something hidden."

"Charlie?" Bart called over his radio. "Can you get us the rest of the building? There must be something hidden that we haven't found."

Luke, still pounding away on his keyboard, said, "There could be an underground passageway that's not on the modern blueprint. These old buildings used to be connected to steam tunnels."

Charlie twisted her head back and up to look at the building. "It's all dark in the front, but the building at the back has lights on. It looks like an apartment building. There're definitely people there."

"Goddamnit," Bart fumed. "We didn't see a way to get below and there is no elevator that we could find. Not even a fuckin' staircase."

"It's got to be hidden then," Luke said. "Shit, let me pull up the old plans from when the building was first built and see what I can find."

"I really want to go in too," Charlie said, drawing an instant reaction from Luke.

"Oh, hell no!" he bit out. "You have no idea what you could be facing and Bart and Cam need to be able to do what they're trained to do without worrying about you."

She saw the wisdom in his explanation, but it stung nonetheless. Looking back at the building, all she could think about was how Penny was somewhere inside.

"Okay, I've got it," Luke declared. "I can tell there are old tunnels, but from the outside, we can see that there are lights and people moving around nearby so you can't get a clear shot to check it out. Return and we'll analyze the drives you're bringing in. We'll convene and see what's next."

Within a moment, the side panel door opened and Bart and Cam entered the van, consuming most of the space. Luke had moved to the driver's seat and Charlie twisted around to observe the irritated faces of the two Saints. She knew now was not the time to pepper them with questions so she turned back to face the front. The four drove most of the way back to Jack's in silence, the frustration of the evening pressing upon them.

LITTLE SLEEP AND large quantities of caffeine kept Luke and Charlie going through the night. Several times he looked over at her drooping eyelids and tried to insist she go to bed, but she stubbornly refused. Using their combined programs, they worked through the information taken from the computers.

So far, they contained the normal data expected from any clinic. Patients' records, company information, with no unusual searches or email detected.

Finally, in frustration, Charlie said, "They must keep the two clinics separate. This is just the front. This is the legitimate business, the one that Dr. Cheung gets accolades for his community work with, by running a free clinic." Slapping her hand down on the table, she said, "But he makes sure to keep his other affairs out of this one."

Studying the exhaustion on her face written with dark circles underneath her eyes, Luke stood and cracked his back before walking over to her. Grabbing her hands, he pulled her from the chair as he checked the time. "Sweetheart, it's almost five a.m. and you need to sleep. Come on."

Fatigue had won the day and she followed him to the bedroom, not protesting when he pulled her shirt over her head and unsnapped her pants. Kicking them off her feet, she took off her bra and allowed him to slide one of his soft, worn t-shirts over her body. Falling into bed, her eyes almost closed, she watched as he turned to leave the room. "You're not coming to bed too?"

The hall light illuminated behind him, casting his facial features in the shadows, but she knew them by heart and could tell when he offered her a smile.

"No, I've just got one more drive to check and then I'll be to bed. That way we can start fresh tomorrow."

Her eyes closed in sleep before her head hit the pillow and Luke padded back to the dining room, staring at his computer once again.

The last one to check was the drive marked as the receptionist. Quickly jotting down her name from the information, he said to the darkened room, "Okay, Xia Wu, let's see what you've got for me." Not expecting much, he was just about to close down and join Charlie in bed when he saw the name of one of her email correspondents.

L. Wang

Oh, fuck! He was unable to trace the origination of the emails but quickly scanned through their cryptic messages. Following the trail, he noted the correspondents had been in contact since Xia Wu's employment at the clinic four months earlier. Feeling the excitement of the first real step forward in the case, he shot off a message to Jack, letting him know they needed to convene a meeting ASAP, including Nick as well. With renewed vigor, he began a detailed check into the old building plans and the connecting tunnels.

By the time seven a.m. rolled around, he slipped noiselessly into the bedroom and grabbed some clean clothes. Smiling at Charlie's unmoving figure in his bed, he left as quietly as he had entered, knowing she should sleep for several more hours. Leaving her a note telling her he would be at Jack's for an early meeting, he alarmed his house and headed to his vehicle.

THE SAINTS FILED into the room, quickly settling just before Nick was patched into their secure video-conference system.

Jack spoke first, saying, "Luke's got information he's been working on all night. We need to hear it and proceed."

Nodding, Luke began, "None of the drives obtained last night from Bart and Cam—"

"Jesus," Nick growled, interrupting, as he ran his hand over his face. "Can you not leave out where the hell you get this stuff?" No one spoke for a few seconds as he pulled himself together. "Sorry...need my coffee this morning. Keep going."

With a smirk, Luke continued. "None of the computers held anything special; just what you would expect to find with a normal medical clinic. Nothing suspicious at all...until I got to the receptionist's emails."

Flashing up what he found onto the screen next to the one with Nick's image, he said, "Nick, I'm sending this to you as well. As you can see her name is Xia Wu. She's been working at the clinic for about four months and there is one contact that she has corresponded with numerous times in those four months. Someone named L. Wang."

The intake of multiple breaths was heard around the table and Nick cursed, "Goddammit."

"Now, I pulled up all her messages and you can see they are very cryptic, but put together with what we suspect, they paint a picture of this L. Wang asking about the clinic's special practices ever since Xia Wu was employed. This would indicate a relationship between the two."

"What do we know about her?" Monty asked, already typing away on his computer.

"She is twenty-six years old and has lived in the D.C. area her whole life. Her father was born in China but left as a child through Hong Kong. Her mother is American, from the Chinatown part of San Francisco. I've hacked her personal accounts and she has received payments of $500 a month since taking the receptionist job. She always deposited the cash, so I have no trace of where the money came from, except to say that I've also checked Lin Wang's bank account and she has with-drawn $500 each month from her account. The dates correspond."

"Fuck!" Nick growled again.

"I've also pulled up the old building plans from their origin and there are tunnels that run between some of the buildings. That is probably how the two clinics are connected while kept separate."

"We didn't see any way to get through," Bart com-plained. "How the hell did we miss it?"

"From looking at the old plans compared with what we have now, it appears a freight elevator is behind one of the walls. They probably leave it open during the day so it looks just like an elevator and then shut the panels at night for security."

"So we need to go back tonight and check out the building behind the clinic," Cam stated, his eyes gleaming with a chance to complete the mission.

"No fuckin' way," Nick said. "You can't go into a building without the proper procedure. You've got no authority, no warrants, no—"

"We don't play by your rules, Nick," Monty inter-jected, his voice firm but sympathetic. "I get it...seriously, I was where you are. But we play by our own rules."

"But you can't do anything with what you find. You will let them get away if the legalities are thwart-ed."

Jack cleared his throat and said, "Nick, we only

gather the information then hand it over to you. We're supposed to be working on this case with Lin Wang, but now that she is a suspect, we've been given you. We don't go in guns blazing unless it is called for...we'll get information and turn it over to you so that you know where to look; you can use the proper procedures to "discover" it yourself."

The room was quiet for a moment, the Saints' eyes pinned on the FBI agent as he wrestled with his decision. Finally, leaning back in his chair, he said, "If you get me what you have, then I'll take it to my superior and meet with Lin."

Jack, nodding, turned his gaze toward Luke. "This is still your mission, Luke. Your call as to how to play it, but I want you in the field."

Bart and Cam grinned at each other as Luke let out a breath he had not realized he had been holding. *For someone who always lived behind a computer, I could get used to running things from the field!* Grinning, he nodded toward his boss.

"Then let's plan. I want us to get up there today."

CHAPTER 28

CHARLIE WOKE HOURS later, stretching her arms above her head as she slowly came to consciousness. The sunlight coming through the blinds was bright and she rolled over to see Luke's side of the bed empty and obviously not slept in. Pursing her lips, deciding he needed a lecture on not putting her to bed if he was not going to do the same, she rolled in the other direction to swing her legs over the edge. Glancing at the clock, she realized it was after three p.m.

Stunned at how long she had slept, she jumped from the bed and stalked out to the living room. Peeking into the study she saw it was empty. Rounding the corner to the dining room, she saw her laptop still in place on the table, but his was gone. And so were the drives. And so were his notes. With her hands on her hips and her lips pursed, she glanced into the kitchen. *Gone? He left already?* Her eyes landed on a handwritten note lying on the kitchen counter next to the coffee maker. Smiling, she walked over, until she read it, and then her smile dropped.

"He went to Jack's without me?" she groused aloud.

"Hmph." Quickly fixing some coffee, and making a piece of toast, she walked back to where her laptop sat on the table. She stood in the dining room in indecision for a moment, until she noticed she had a new message. Plopping down in a chair, the toast still sticking out of her mouth, she looked at who had sent the missive. *Penny!*

Quickly chewing and swallowing, she tossed the remainder of her breakfast onto the table next to her and opened up the message.

I think I need you today. I might be moving to a new place tonight or tomorrow.

Looking at the time stamp, she realized the message had been sent earlier in the day and hoped Penny would still be able to get to a computer. *Of all the stupid times to stay up all night and sleep all day!*

Penny, I was there. I only saw a normal clinic. How do I get to where you are?

Killing time while waiting for Penny to answer, she threw a load of laundry into the washer while continuing to monitor her laptop. Finally, after an hour, her incoming message alert sounded.

We went through a door when the wall slid back. Then an elevator down. We walked down a dark hall and then up another elevator to a nicer clinic.

Excited, Charlie thought, *So Luke was right! They did go through tunnels!* Grabbing her phone from the table beside her, she dialed Luke. He picked up on the second ring.

"Hey, sweetie," he greeted. "Did you finally get

some rest?"

"Yes, yes, but that's not why I called," she rushed. "I just heard from Penny. We're messaging right now. She said she went down an elevator, through a darkened hallway and then up another elevator to the clinic she is now in. You were right."

"Thanks for the call, but we figured that out," he said. "I found something on one of the drives and we are in D.C. to meet with Nick."

"Without me?" she questioned, hating the whiny sound in her voice.

"Sorry, sweetheart," Luke said sincerely. "This just needed to be us today. I'll be late...I have Bart and Cam with me."

"Since you're going to be there, I might drive up as well. I got a message that Penny wants to meet me. She's afraid of being moved and I'd like to try to see her today."

She heard voices in the background before Luke came back on and said, "Let me know what you're doing and where you are, if you come. I've got to go. I'll talk to you later." With that, he disconnected.

Huffing, Charlie did not see any new messages coming in from Penny so she took the opportunity to jump in the shower. Thirty minutes later, showered, shampooed, and with clean clothes, she felt refreshed.

As she looked back down at her laptop on her way into the kitchen, she saw another message from Penny.

Can you come get me and my friend? I don't want

him to have the surgery and I think we need to get out of here.

Typing quickly, her heart beginning to pound, **I'm on my way. I may have some friends who get there before me, but if they do they will tell you they are from Charlie. Got that?**

Yes. Thank you.

Charlie raced up the stairs to grab her shoes and then slammed the door as she tore out of Luke's house. She tried calling his phone, but he was not picking up. Leaving a voice message, she pulled out of his driveway, her phone's GPS telling her the way.

LUKE SAT IN the small restaurant booth with Monty next to him and Nick across. Having just reviewed the plans for the evening, Nick nodded.

"I know you've gotten the okay from the higher-ups from the Bureau," Nick finally admitted, "but it's just not the way I'm used to operating."

Monty gave a rueful smile. "Regulations were drilled into us and then we find out the Bureau had others do some of the dirty investigations for them. I remember how it hit me when I found out as well."

Nick held Monty's gaze for a while, his scowl replaced by an expression of thoughtfulness as he rubbed his chin. "What did it for you? What made you get out?"

Sucking in a breath, Monty admitted, "One case too many that didn't get solved. One case too many where the right hand didn't tell the left hand what was going on. Tired of regulations that got in our way causing the criminals to get off."

Luke watched as Nick's gaze shifted down to the beer in front of him and wondered what the agent was thinking. "I was CIA," he said, noting Nick's sharp eyes back upon him. "Gotta say the same thing had me getting out."

Nick's lips were pinched together as he said, "Yeah, but if no one stays in and does it by the book, then how will we ever take the assholes down?"

"You're right," Monty said quickly. "We all have to do what we need to. I've got no problem with you being right where you are. Makes our job a helluva lot easier having someone on the inside we can trust."

"And that gets us back to the point, doesn't it?" Nick stated. "Lin Wang."

Luke continued his briefing, "We need to get back into the building now that we know where the tunnel is. We plan on having Bart and Cam back in there tonight. Depending on what we find out, we'll have you on standby."

"As soon as you find any evidence, let me know," Nick said. "I've got my supervisor on board but he's even more of a stickler for procedure than I am."

Nodding, Luke agreed, before giving the high sign to Bart and Cam to join them. Within a minute the two large Saints walked in and took a seat at the table and the evening's plans came together.

XIA WU, GLANCING around nervously, placed the phone call and prayed the recipient would pick up.

"Yes?"

Breathing a sigh of relief, Xia said, "I think you need to get here. I went to the back earlier to take someone new and I saw them talking to that Penny girl. She was crying. I think they're going to do something tonight."

"Shit," Lin cursed. "Okay, I'm on my way."

Hanging up, Xia Wu glanced around before hustling to her car and locking the doors as soon as she was seated. She did not start the car, but sat waiting in the darkness. Just waiting...and watching.

CHARLIE CURSED AT the traffic getting into D.C. An accident on the highway combined with rush-hour traffic had her moving at a snail's pace. She had not heard from Luke since sending him the message that she was coming, but assumed he was embroiled in the same type of work as they had been the previous night. *At least I got some sleep...how is he functioning on no sleep?* While sitting in traffic, she texted Luke to let him know what she was doing and sent another message out to Penny to let her know she was on her way. Finally, the flashing blue police lights and red ambulance lights could be seen to the side ahead and as she maneuvered her way around the accident, traffic eventually picking up. *Thank goodness.*

Weaving through some of the downtown roads, she passed the front of the clinic and turned the corner to go toward the building in the back. *Damnit, I hate parallel parking!* It took several attempts, backing up and pulling forward, until she was finally close enough to the curb to be relatively sure she was not sticking out into the road. Getting out, she slammed the door and walked around to peer up at the building. Dusk had settled on the city and the sidewalk was empty.

Walking to the front door, she tried to jerk it open, but it was locked. Glancing to the side, she noticed there was no bell to ring. *There has to be a service entrance somewhere.* She walked around the next corner to see what was on the back of the building, facing the alley. A noise sounded behind her and she turned to see the front clinic's pretty receptionist standing on the sidewalk behind her.

"I thought I recognized you even though you had a disguise. You were here the other day," the woman accused, although her voice was not angry.

"Yes," Charlie answered, too preoccupied to care that she was found out as her gaze assessed the dark street. "I need to get inside."

Xia's face contorted, her eyes giving away her indecision. Charlie decided to press her. "I don't know if you know what's going on, but there's a girl trapped in here who wants out. I've come to get her. I can easily call the police right now, or you can let me in to get her." Trying to lock her knees to keep them from knocking together, Charlie kept her expression impassive, hoping to bluster her way inside.

"I don't know what's going on inside," Xia said. "I only work the front reception desk."

"And take certain homeless persons to the back if they have a card, right?"

Swallowing deeply, Xia said, "Those are my instructions. They get special treatment."

"That may be true, but I'll warrant there are more sinister things going on inside. Do you want to be a part of that?"

"I...I..."

Charlie nodded to the door. "Can you get me in? If so, just get the door unlocked and I'll take it from there."

Xia looked around, her gaze indecisive. Finally, she turned back to Charlie and said, "Fine." She darted around and headed to the door. Her key fit the lock and she swung the door open. "I'm not going in...but I won't keep you out."

With that Charlie slipped by the woman and, with a nod of thanks, headed into the dark hallway.

PENNY FOLLOWED THE woman down the underground hallway, her hands clutched at her sides, fingernails biting into her palms. *Where is Charlotte? She was supposed to be here by now.* Unable to wait any longer, she had no choice but to follow the woman back into the tunnels, heading to where she would wait for David when he came out of surgery.

At a metal door, she turned and looked at the woman behind her. A man appeared and unlocked it.

"Is this where I'll wait for David?" Penny asked nervously, her eyes focused on the dragon tattoo on the woman's wrist. *Why would I wait down here?*

With a slow smile, the woman simply nodded as the door swung open. Penny's arm was grabbed by the man standing by her side and she was shoved unceremoniously inside before the door slammed shut.

"Noooo!" she screamed, her fists pounding on the door. Hearing a noise from behind her, she whirled in fright. A group of women stood huddled toward the back, staring at her with a mixture of pity and understanding. Recognizing most of them from the dorms, she stared dumbfounded. "Why are you here?"

"We...it's...," one of the women whispered, "it's where they bring us...before they send us somewhere else."

Penny's mind scrambled to make sense of what the woman was saying. "Somewhere else? Where?"

The woman who had spoken simply shrugged, her eyes slightly glazed over. "Who knows? The highest bidder probably."

The reality of the situation slowly dawned on Penny as her heart pounded in her chest. "They...they're not here to help us, are they?"

The other women in the room held her gaze sadly as one answered, "No. We're the forgotten ones."

Penny turned back to the door, her eyes prickling with tears, realizing she would never see David again.

CHAPTER 29

O PENING THE DOOR to the stairs, Charlie jogged up two flights. Not knowing where to look, she was grateful for the empty halls. With most doors closed, it appeared that everyone had retired for the evening; there was virtually no staff in sight. Curious, she peeked into one room with a window in the door and saw four beds, each empty.

Checking three other rooms, she found them all empty. Penny had indicated that there were others in the dorm-like rooms with her...*so where could they all be?*

Entering the staircase again, she went up one more flight. Rounding the corner, Charlie quickly walked to a door across the hall and opened it. This room was different. Set up like a hospital room, she stared at an empty bed, the sheets gone, leaving the mattress bare.

Charlie's breath left her in a whoosh as she took in the rest of the small, neat room containing not only the bed, but a plastic chair and a door leading to a small bathroom as well.

"Are you looking for someone?" a woman's voice

sounded behind her.

Charlie whirled around, her eyes landing on the petite Asian woman facing her with a gun in her hand. She immediately took a defensive stance, her eyes not leaving the weapon.

"Tsk, tsk. Such unfounded heroics, Ms. Trivett."

At hearing her name, Charlie's gaze moved from the gun up to the woman's face and back down again. The head of a dragon tattoo snaked along the woman's wrist. The memory slammed back into her at having seen the tattoo before. *Oh, my God, how could I have forgotten that? Eli's killer. Oh, Jesus, Eli's killer!* "You!" she panted, eyes wide as her focus dropped from the woman's face back to the gun being held.

"Ah, so you did see me?"

Licking her lips, Charlie wondered what to say, but the woman gave her little time to process the situation.

With a sly smile that did not reach her eyes, she jerked the gun. "Let's go. Walk."

Charlie, her body shaking, shuffled in front of the woman as they moved back into the hall. Reaching her hand up to the St. Luke medallion around her neck, she grasped it, hoping one of the Saints would discover her.

THEY PARKED THE van near the alley toward the back of the clinic. Nick had chosen to ride with them, deciding to take his chances not following procedures.

While he, Monty, and Luke stayed in the vehicle, keeping an eye on the monitoring equipment, Bart and Cam alighted from the van.

Luke smiled as another van pulled up in front of him, knowing Nick was in for a surprise. Jude, Patrick, and Chad exited the vehicle, all but Jude dressed similarly to Bart and Cam.

"What the hell is going on?" Nick asked, twisting his head around to stare at Luke.

"The Saints have stepped up the game. Jack got the okay to send in the full group. They go in, gather intelligence, and then come back out to report to you. Depending on what they find, you can get the necessary warrants to take these guys down. And, if Lin Wang is involved, you get her at the same time. Jack and Blaise are at the Bureau headquarters waiting to see what evidence we find."

Luke checked his phone, the last message coming from Charlie saying she was stuck in traffic. He had sent her a message telling her to keep away and that they would look for Penny, but had not received one back. Glancing up at the building, he hoped she was still in traffic and not traipsing around somewhere.

Chad and Jude jogged over and smiled at Luke. "Okay man, Jude will monitor the equipment. You get to go in on this one."

Grinning, Luke jumped in the back, quickly suiting up before joining the others as they entered the back of the building after Cam disabled the alarm system. Bart turned toward him and said, "We're following the tunnels from your diagram."

This time Bart and Cam avoided the clinic and entered from the alley where they knew from Luke's building plans they would be able to enter one of the tunnels. As the men descended into the dark and dank tunnel, they moved stealthily toward the back, looking for the way up into the area where Penny had indicated she was staying.

Hearing a loud rattling, they slipped unnoticed behind some crates, waiting to see who was coming. Luke steadied his breathing, his heart pounding with adrenaline. Used to being back in the van with the computers and monitors, he hoped he had the experience to work in the field. *Too late to have those doubts now!* As the noise of footsteps, voices, and the squeaky wheels of a cart sounded louder, he pressed back into the shadows even more. From his vantage point, he was able to see a woman pushing a large cart, escorted by a man. Both wearing scrubs, they stopped outside a large metal door.

The man opened the door with a key and the woman entered. "Here. Eat." Rattling sounds emanated and the couple retraced their steps back down the hall after the man shut and locked the door behind him.

As soon as they disappeared, the Saints looked at each other, questions in their eyes. Luke nodded toward the door and Cam moved into position in front of it with Bart and Patrick on either side, weapons ready. Cam, using a variety of instruments, quickly unlocked the door. Giving the signal, he swung it open with Bart and Patrick darting inside, their weapons now drawn and pointing in.

"Fuck," Bart breathed as Luke entered the room right behind him.

"Oh, Jesus," Luke said, as Bart and Patrick lowered their weapons.

The inhabitants of the room, all women, were huddled against the back wall, their haunted eyes wide. Luke immediately threw his hands up in front of him and said, "Easy, easy. We're here to help."

A toilet was in the corner of the room and the food remnants were near the door. Several mattresses were on the other side of the room, pushed together to form a large bed. One young woman, her dark hair matted but her eyes clear and hard, stepped forward. "Can you get us out of here?"

"Absolutely," Bart said, as Luke immediately radioed Monty.

"Get Nick in here now," he barked. "Seems like Charlie's supposed connection with human trafficking was right. There's a roomful of women imprisoned here."

"Charlie?" whispered one young girl, her eyes wide. "You're Charlie's friends?"

Luke stared at the girl, her blue eyes brighter and blonde hair cleaner than the other women inside the room. "Penny?"

"Yes!" she cried out, racing forward to slam into

him. He caught her slight weight before pushing her back gently to look into her face.

"I thought Charlie came earlier to get you," he asked, forcing his voice to steady.

"She was supposed to but they took me before she got here. Please, you've got to help me find David."

While Luke questioned Penny about Charlie's possible whereabouts, Bart and Patrick carefully attended the women, who appeared to be in good, although unkempt, shape.

"How long have you been here?" Cam asked the woman he was squatting next to.

"Three days," she said, her voice shaky. "They were going to ship us out tomorrow."

"Did they say where?"

Before she could answer, Monty and Nick entered, both men's faces tight with anger. Nick, surveying the situation, pulled out his phone and called his supervisor. Giving a terse explanation, he arranged for the FBI to get to the facility immediately.

Luke, still holding onto Penny's shoulders, asked, "David?"

"My friend. The one Charlotte was going to help me get out of here. He agreed to give up his kidney for money and they're going to do the surgery tonight."

Luke's gaze swung around to the Saints, landing on Nick's wide-eyes. "Fuckin' hell, Charlie was right. This place is a front for organ harvesting as well as human trafficking."

LEAVING SOME TO stay with the women, Luke prepared to lead the others and Nick to the stairwell. He halted his instruction as Jude spoke in his earpiece. Eyes wide, he cursed, "Shit!" Quickly looking at the others, he said, "Jude's just gotten an alarm from Charlie's medallion. She's here…in this building…right now!"

His mind racing, "She must have gone inside or was taken inside." His gaze moved back toward the horror they had just discovered and he choked out, "Find her. Priority One."

"Me too!" shouted Penny as the men left the room. They appeared to ignore her, but she followed them nonetheless.

The Saints, immediately flying into action, jogged up the stairs and out onto the first floor. Spreading out, they searched the rooms before clearing the area. Rounding the corner, heading back to the stairwell, they ran right into a petite woman, her dark bob swinging as she came to a halt, her gun held firmly in her hand.

"Agent Wang!" Luke growled, his eyes pinned on her.

Nick rounded the corner, his weapon drawn, facing her. "Put down your weapon, Agent Wang," he ordered.

Penny heard the name Wang and peeked around the large man standing in her line of vision. Fuming at the woman who had thrust her into the dungeon, she was stunned to see a different woman standing there.

"What the fuck are you doing here?" Lin bit out, her dark eyes narrowed in anger. "You're going to ruin everything!"

"I said put it down!" Nick repeated.

"Where's Charlie?" Luke interrupted.

Lin's eyes jumped from Nick's to Luke's. "Who the hell is Charlie?"

"Charlotte Trivett," he yelled. "Where do you have her? With the others you keep downstairs?"

"What others?" she asked, her voice hard.

"That's not her," Penny said, jumping back a step as the men angrily turned toward her. "There's another woman named Wang...the one who put me in the room, but it's not her. The other woman has a dragon tattoo on her wrist."

"Damnit, we've had the wrong L. Wang!" Luke swore.

Lowering her gun, Lin grimaced. "No shit. It's like Smith or Johnson...you think there's only one Chinese woman with the last name Wang?"

A side door opened and Xia Wu popped out, her face stunned as she realized she had stumbled into a guns drawn standoff. Her eyes sought Lin's, but she said nothing.

"Is he still there?" Lin asked.

Xia, nervously shaking her head, said, "No, his room is empty. They're all empty upstairs."

"What the hell is going on?" Nick asked, his eyes

never leaving the other agent's face.

"I've been investigating this clinic for almost five months," Lin answered tersely. "And you and your band of Merry Men are about to fuck my whole investigation up!"

"I don't know what your game is, but Charlie is in this building and I want to know where," Luke barked.

"I saw her," Xia answered quickly. "She came in the back, from the side door. But I haven't seen her since."

"And who the fuck are you?" Luke asked, his gaze moving between Lin and the other woman.

"She's mine," Lin stated, her voice as hard as her expression. "I've had her on the inside reporting to me."

Nick, his focus still on Lin, said, "You've been investigating? Why didn't anyone at the Bureau know about it? Why didn't anyone tell me?"

Lin pinched her lips together, lowering her weapon. "Because I was working on my own, trying to see what I'd missed."

"Missed?"

"Yes!" she shouted. "Eli Frederick was my case. He was given to me and I didn't give it enough credence. I was working other cases, stretched too thin, and thought he was one of a million other conspiracy theorists out there. I set up the meeting, but I wasn't careful and someone got to him. He's dead and I vowed to figure out who the hell set us both up!"

"Fuckin' hell, you went rogue," Nick accused.

"Miss Do-it-by-the-book went fuckin' rogue!"

While the two agents squared off, Luke listened to his earpiece and then turned to shout at Bart. "Jude's got Charlie on the move. Get back downstairs."

"Not that way!" Xia shouted. Seeing the incredulous expressions, she said, "This building has lots of secrets. I'm only supposed to be in the front clinic and not back here, but I've noticed things when I've brought people back. There's a separate staircase that leads to a different part of the building. I don't know what's there but I've seen Lisa Wang and Dr. Cheung come from there."

"Bart, you and the others head back the way we came in case they're heading that way. I'll go with this woman."

The Saints split up, Nick standing for a moment of indecision, still glaring at Lin, before turning and following Luke, Lin hard on his heels.

CHAPTER 30

C HARLIE BANGED ON the door of the room she was
in, but to no avail. Fighting the panic, she tried to
think logically. Glancing down at the St. Luke medallion around her neck she hoped the tracer worked. *But
what if it can't reach through walls? Or no one knows to
look for me?* Jerking her head, she forced those negative
thoughts from her mind. Sucking in a deep cleansing
breath, she stepped back, realizing that if someone
came into the room she needed to give them time to
enter before she tried to take them down.

Marc's instructions ran over and over in her mind.
*Keep your opponent off balance. Try to get behind them.
Go for the weapon arm if possible. Go for behind the
knees.* Hanging her head, she grimaced. Somehow
practicing with Luke and Marc when she knew they
would never hurt her was a poor substitute for the fear
she felt as the gun had been pointed at her. Looking
behind her, she saw another door, leading to what she
assumed was a closet. *Maybe, just maybe that's a way
out.*

Striding over, she pulled the door open only to find

another room similar to the one she was in. A rolling stretcher was in the middle of the room, a body covered in a bloody sheet lying there. Heart pounding, she continued in, her steady legs now rubbery. Only the top of the head was visible, short brown hair sticking out. Her eyes roamed down the entirety of the sheet, soaked with red.

Swallowing hard, she reached her hand out slowly, as though in a trance, to lift the sheet ever so slightly— just enough to make sure the person was truly dead. Her mind was unable to comprehend what her eyes saw as a bloodcurdling scream shook the room.

Dropping the sheet, she scrambled backward until she slammed into a wall. Unable to stop, she bent forward and retched, dropping to her knees with the force of her stomach emptying its contents. Gagging over and over, she finally raised herself to a standing position, her eyes still staring at the floor. Her right hand slid along the wall searching for the door as she stumbled back into the room she had come from, closing the door behind her. All of her former bravado gone, she slumped to the floor, silent tears sliding down her face.

DR. CHEUNG WIPED his brow. This was his second surgery of the night. The call earlier from Yeng Chow had forced him to take on more than what he normally did. He looked down at the young man, anesthetized on the table. Glancing at his assistant he grimaced. The surgical nurse appeared impassive, as though the last surgery had not affected her at all. He reminded himself what Yeng often said. *The homeless have no purpose in life anyway. They have no one to miss them. But the ones willing to pay top dollar for their organs, these people have families…lives worth living. What is one worthless life compared to the one of someone who have something to live for?*

Wiping his brow, he was about to begin when Lisa Wang entered the surgical room. He raised his eyes, observing her above his surgical mask, in surprise.

"I've got another one for you tonight," she pronounced.

Glaring, he growled, "No. Yeng's already got me doing three tonight. We can't handle another one."

"You've got no choice, dear doctor," she said, with a sly smile. "It's someone who needs to permanently shut up; why not make money off of her at the same time."

"Will she be missed? This is for the homeless only!" he shouted, not caring about the wide-eyed expression from his nurse. "This is not some way for you to dispose of someone who's gotten too close! Take her with the others!"

Lisa's eyes narrowed as she argued. "She's not like the others…too much of a risk to let her live. Even as a slave, she would pose a threat!"

Leaning down, Jian bit out, "That's not my problem!"

"You don't call the shots here, doctor dear," she reminded him. As short as she was, she managed to create the air of one in charge as she turned on her heels and said over her shoulder, "You'll find her in the prep room with your last...patient."

"Biǎo zi!" he cursed, staring at her back. Looking down at the young man in front of him, he battled whether to begin on him or go rescue the young woman from the hellish room she was in, waiting for him to end her life here on his table.

LUKE TOOK THE lead down a set of back stairs, glancing back at the eclectic group in tow. His focus was centered on finding Charlie, but he could not stop the thought that ran through his mind about the menagerie following. Xia Wu whispered the directions. Nick followed along with Lin, after informing her she was not to be out of his sight. Penny raced along, trying to keep up with them, not wanting to be left behind.

Rounding the corner at the bottom of the stairs, the door opened before they had a chance to get to it. Luke halted as another petite Asian woman, her glossy black hair pulled back in a ponytail, came barreling through the door. Her eyes jerked wide in surprise, but before she was able to retreat, Luke had her arm twisted behind her and her face pressed against the wall.

"That's one of the nurses that works for Dr.

Cheung," Xia rushed to explain.

The nurse began to shout in rapid-fire Chinese, but Luke did not lessen his hold. Lin stepped up, slapping handcuffs on the woman, her growling voice speaking back in Chinese. The woman, her face contorted in anger, got quiet as Blaise took her by the arm and handed her off to one of the other FBI agents who were now accompanying them.

LISA WANG HEARD the shouts and, only hesitating for a few seconds, she whirled around and raced back to the room holding Charlie. Throwing it open, she pointed the gun at her and barked, "Let's go!"

Charlie stared at the weapon, trying to think of a way to disarm the woman, but Lisa was too fast.

"Don't even consider it," Lisa said, her face contorted in rage. "If you don't come with me, I'll leave you here and go after Penny. I've got no problem silencing her."

At that threat, Charlie walked in front of Lisa and, with the gun prodding her in the back, she made her way through a door and into a tunnel of dank hallways.

Lisa quickly maneuvered them forward until halting Charlie at another door. "Open it," she ordered.

Charlie hesitantly put her hand on the knob and turned, uncertain what fate awaited her on the other side. As the door swung open, exposing a small closet, she was propelled forward with the barrel of the gun on her back. Upon command, she stepped in and opened the next door, stunned when she walked into the next hall.

A dark red, plush carpeting with gold figures covered the floor, silencing their steps. *Where are we?* Forced to hurry along, she quickly noted the Chinese characters on the nameplates on several of the doors they passed. Stopping at one of them at Lisa's order, she was startled when she noticed the sign indicated this room belonged to Ambassador Secretary Yeng Chow. Stepping through the doorway they entered an office, where the dark red carpeting continued and was now matched with cream wallpaper accented with red and gold patterns. A huge, dark desk was centered in front of a window, heavy drapes drawn for privacy. A man sitting behind the desk looked up sharply, his gaze instantly assessing the newcomers.

Charlie watched as his face contorted in rage, spitting out a slew of Chinese, none of which she understood, but she had no trouble interpreting that it must have been a cursing rampage.

Lisa immediately began replying in rapid-fire Chinese and Charlie found herself in the middle of a battle of words. Forcing her mind to focus on the room and a possible escape she still felt the barrel of the gun pressing into her back, halting her thoughts.

As the other two quieted, Charlie watched as the man rose from his desk, his eyes boring into hers.

"Ms. Trivett. It appears that Ms. Wang has decided

to seek the safety of the Chinese Embassy; she has sealed your fate."

Chinese Embassy? The embassy and the clinic are connected underground! Oh, Jesus, this is bigger than I thought!

"Take her away," he ordered, his scrutiny now on Lisa. "Then come back here. We have much to discuss."

Poked in the back, Charlie moved through the door and back into the hall. "Where are you taking me?" she asked.

"I had wanted the good doctor to take care of you, but it appears that his facility has been breached. So, you'll be here, where no one will come looking for you...at least not until I have a chance to dispose of you."

At those words, Charlie sucked in a quick breath, her eyes now categorizing her surroundings. *If I get trapped here, at the embassy, even Luke can't come in to find me!*

After several turns down different hallways and descending to a lower floor, Lisa had her stop outside of another door, this one leading into a supply closet.

"This will hold you for now. Get in," Lisa ordered.

Charlie turned to face her captor, her gaze dropping from Lisa's face to the gun still pointed at her.

CHAPTER 31

"WHERE'S DAVID?" PENNY cried, trying to push her way past the large men. Chad, who had arrived with Cam after the FBI took over with the victims, grabbed her by her shoulders, holding her carefully in place.

Lin turned and said, "Through here," pointing to the door the nurse had come from.

Luke, attempting a semblance of control, barked into his radio for Bart's group to meet them. Turning, he pinned Chad with a stare and, with a nod toward Penny, ordered, "Protect her." Receiving a head jerk in acknowledgment, he turned and headed through the doorway.

The hall revealed nothing but a pair of swinging double doors to the side and another door at the end. Cam and Blaise met them, coming through the entrance. Positioning on either side of the double door, weapons drawn, Luke gave the signal for the Saints to move in.

Rounding the entry, Luke saw a man wearing a surgical mask bending over a body lying on the operating table, a scalpel in his hand. The man and the two assistants looked up, their eyes wide as the masks sucked in with their gasps.

"Stop!" Luke shouted, his eyes dropping to the young man lying on the table. Dirty blond hair. Pale white face. Eyes closed.

The surgeon halted, his hands in the air, the scalpel still grasped in his gloved fingers.

"Nooooooo!" screamed Penny, as she tried to lunge forward, seeing David on the table. Chad managed to snag her around the waist, but she squirmed and fought his hold. Finally, he managed to wrap her in his huge embrace and turn her from the table.

Blaise rushed to the patient and immediately assessed David's condition. He was sedated but the surgery had not begun.

"Where's Charlie?" Luke shouted.

The eyes peering at him over the masks gave no evidence of understanding his question.

"The girl? Charlotte Trivett?" Luke yelled, knowing his cool composure was slipping but unable to keep the fright from his voice.

"I don't know," Jian said, tossing down the scalpel, allowing it to clatter to the floor. "I thought she was left in the next room, but if she's not there, then I have no idea where she took her."

Cam came from the adjoining room, his breath coming out in harsh pants. "Nothing in there but a male corpse...one you butchered," he bit out, his eyes dropping to the ice chest containers by the door, ready for pick up. "Jesus, man…you're a doctor!"

Face set in stone, Jian grimaced for a moment before turning, pulling the mask from his face. "You have no idea what it's like. They have my sons in their sights. As long as I do their bidding, my sons enjoy their university life in China and will be set up for life. If I don't…"

"Who's in charge of this operation? Of the trafficking?" Lin asked, bypassing a scowling Nick as he stepped up behind her.

"That can wait till later," Luke bit out. "We need to find Charlie." Stepping over to Jian, he ordered, "And I mean right fuckin' now!"

"She was to be my next…patient," he answered, "but if she's not in the next room, then Lisa must have taken her somewhere else."

"Lisa?"

"Lisa Wang," Jian replied.

Luke whirled around, about to speak when he heard Jude in his earpiece. Stunned, he pierced the others with his stare as he repeated, "Jude's traced Charlie to the Chinese Embassy, two blocks over."

"Fuck!" both Lin and Nick shouted at the same time, swinging their glares back to Jian.

He nodded slowly, and said, "The Chinese Embassy is connected to this clinic."

"I've seen Yeng Chow with Dr. Cheung," Lin offered. "I've been working to find a connection."

"I've got to get hold of my superiors," Nick stated, his voice hard with frustration. "I can't go in guns blazing to an embassy."

Stepping around him, Luke said, "But we can."

Nick grabbed his arm, but Luke jerked loose, pinning the agent with his stare. "You do what you've gotta do, man." He nodded toward Jian and said, "Take care of him, but do not get in my way. Embassy immunity means nothing to me. I'll go to hell and back to get Charlie."

With the full power of the Saints readily at his back, Luke ran out of the room, following the directions Jude shouted in his ear.

WITHIN TWO MINUTES, Luke had found the back entrance to the Chinese embassy, but hesitated at the door. Listening carefully to the instructions from the van outside, he looked back to the men behind him. "Jude's disabling their alarms now," he reported. Thirty seconds later, he threw open the door, moving forward.

As the Saints slipped into an empty, carpeted hallway of the embassy, they moved silently forward. Rounding a corner, Luke came face to face with a guard making his rounds. Before the guard was able to draw his weapon, Luke kicked his arm, sending the gun skidding noiselessly to the other side of the hall. Whirling around, with a kick, he took the man's legs out from under him, Bart securing the guard's hands behind his back as Cam taped his mouth.

Luke, hearing a slight noise behind him, twisted quickly and sliced his arm in a downward motion, knocking the gun from the next guard coming around the corner. Bart and Cam subdued him as well.

"Damn, man," Bart said, with a smirk. "You keep going and we'll have a pile of guards on the floor."

Continuing down the dark hall, Luke spied a sliver of light coming from underneath the door marked for Ambassador Secretary Yeng Chow. *Bingo...just who Lin Wang suspected.*

With a nod to the left and right at the Saints on either side, he tried the doorknob, only to find it locked. Stepping back, Cam picked the lock, his skills of breaking and entering working once more.

Rushing in, they found the secretary standing behind his desk, reaching for a weapon. His eyes narrowed at the contingency of men entering his office, his face twisting, before being replaced by a calm air of superiority.

"Gentlemen, I have no idea who you are, but you are on dangerous ground here."

Luke stepped up to the massive wooden desk, his eyes glinting in the low light of the room. "You have no immunity from me. And I don't follow your rules. But you will tell me what I want to know."

Yeng blinked at the hard, demanding voice of the man in front of him. He licked his lips nervously, before surmising, "You are looking for the girl." Seeing the flash in Luke's eyes, he continued, "You may have her...and the woman who brought her here. Neither is of any use to me."

Hearing Jude's voice giving him further directions to where Charlie was, Luke smiled long and slow. Turning quickly he barked, "Watch him," to Bart, while running out the door, followed by the others.

CHARLIE LIFTED HER gaze from the gun pointing at her to the woman holding her hostage. *I've got one chance. "That's all it takes, Charlie," Marc had said in their practices. "Use your brains and look for your one chance. Then fight as dirty as you can."* Shifting her focus over Lisa's right shoulder, she curved her lips in a slight smile, her eyes lighting.

Lisa quickly twisted her head to see what Charlie was smiling at, when a sharp pain hit her arm. "Augggh!" she screamed, turning back around.

Charlie grabbed Lisa's wrist, forcing the gun away from her body. It fired down into the floor, jolting Lisa's arm back toward Charlie. The two women grappled for a few seconds, until Charlie finally pried the gun loose from Lisa's fingers and it clattered to the floor.

"Nǐ biǎo zi!" Lisa screamed as she fought.

Charlie recognized the curse, having heard Hai use it occasionally. The thought of another one of her friends now dead at the hands of the Chinese mafia brought her full attention back to the fight. With a quick turn, she whirled around and, with a kick, knocked Lisa down to the floor. Landing on top of her, Charlie pinned Lisa's hands above her head. As Lisa fought to free herself, Charlie head butted her, wincing in pain at the contact of her forehead against Lisa's nose.

Lisa screamed in pain, her struggles ceasing. The sound of running footsteps from around the corner had Charlie's eyes darting to her escape route. Just as she lifted herself from Lisa's body, a group of men came into sight, led by...*Luke!*

Scrambling awkwardly off the squirming body on the floor, she launched herself at Luke, screaming his name.

Having heard a gunshot, his heart was in his throat as he had raced toward the location Jude directed. Rounding the corner, weapon drawn, his gaze landed on Charlie straddling an Asian woman bearing a striking resemblance to Lin Wang laying on the floor with her hands holding her bloody nose.

Before he could react, his arms were full of Charlie as she bolted into his embrace, jumping up to wrap her legs around his waist. Having to take a step back to keep from falling over, he held her close, her pounding heart matching his beat for beat.

"David! We've got to get to David!" Charlie cried out as she shifted her body so Luke could set her down.

"It's okay," he assured, then, seeing her anguished

face, he repeated, "David's okay. We got to him. He's fine."

"What about Pen—"

"Shhh, she's fine too. We've got her and the others."

Holding his cheeks in her hands, she searched his face as her mind attempted to catch up to his words. "Fine? She's fine?"

"Yeah, sweetheart, they're all fine."

Sucking in her lips, her hazel eyes crinkled as she asked, "What others?"

Allowing Charlie's body to slide down his while still clinging on tightly, he explained, "We found a room where they were holding other women. Women they were going to sell."

At this, her knees buckled, and Luke's arms were all that kept her upright as Nick and Lin came up behind them.

"We called it in," Nick explained. "With the connection between the clinic and the embassy, we got permission to take the investigation inside. The full force of the FBI will be here shortly. What have you got?"

Charlie twisted in Luke's arms and said, "This is the woman who shot Eli. I can't believe I forgot that I had seen her tattoo. But she had a badge—that I clearly remembered!"

Lin jerked Lisa up from the floor, handcuffing her arms behind her back. Lin pinned Lisa with her glare as

Lisa narrowed her eyes on the FBI agent holding her and growled words in Chinese.

"You what?" Lin yelled, jerking Lisa back around. "You wore a badge to implicate *me? ME?*" Shoving her toward Nick, she growled, "Get her the fuck away from me before I do something that'll really get me kicked out of the agency!"

"There's a man here who knows what is going on also. The name on his door said Yeng Chow...the ambassador's secretary."

"We got him," Luke said. "Bart's upstairs detaining him."

As the hall began to fill with arriving FBI agents, Nick took over, directing their investigation. Barking orders, he moved toward Lin, his glare still in place. "You're gonna have a lot of explaining to do."

Her face, pinched with irritation, nodded. "I know...but at least those women are safe."

Nick held her gaze for a moment, before offering a head jerk as he walked away with several more agents.

Luke watched the agents swarming around, then eyed the other Saints in the hall. "Let's go," he said to them, tucking Charlie safely under his arm.

CHAPTER 32

CHARLIE AND LUKE walked into the hospital room and smiled seeing the two young people there. "Hey, Penny. David," Charlie greeted.

"Charlie?" Penny darted across the room, throwing her arms around Charlie, knocking her back into Luke's strong front. His hands on her shoulders kept her steady as Penny hugged her tightly. "David, this is the woman I told you about. The one who was trying to help us."

Charlie looked over the top of Penny's head and smiled at the young man in the hospital bed. "How are you, David?"

"I'm good," he replied, his warm gaze leaving Penny just long enough to carefully look at Charlie and Luke. "They had me in here to check me out, but I had no ill effects from my experience. They checked Penny out as well."

Penny leaned away from Charlie, but grabbed her hand and pulled her over to one of the chairs in the room. Turning her large blue eyes to Charlie, she gushed, "I don't know how to ever thank you enough.

If it hadn't been for you, David would be dead and I'd be...God knows where!" She looked over at Luke and smiled shyly. "Thank you for finding me."

Luke nodded as he leaned against the wall, enjoying the sight of Charlie and Penny together.

Smiling, Charlie replied, "I'm just glad we were able to get to you in time. When I first started investigating, I had no idea what all was involved." She watched as Penny settled on the hospital bed, sitting next to David. "So...what happens next with you two? I'm here to beg you not to go back out onto the streets."

David's vehement answer satisfied her. "No! I never want Penny back on the streets." He held Penny's hand tightly. "A nice social worker has come to talk to us. They're going to work with us so that we don't have to be very separated."

Intrigued, she waited for him to explain, but Penny answered first.

"We're going into foster care, but with some conditions. David and I will be with families that are close to each other and they won't try to keep us from seeing each other. I'm going back to high school and he's going to get his GED and then start classes at a community college."

"Have you met the foster families yet?" Charlie asked.

"Yeah, and they seem real nice," Penny continued.

"Actually, they're not strangers," Luke commented,

drawing Charlie's attention over to him. "Cam and Miriam's parents each do foster work for special cases. As soon as they heard about the situation, they contacted social services. Cam's parents will have David and Miriam's parents will take care of Penny. The two families live close together in Richland and will allow Penny and David to have contact and see each other."

Charlie's hazel gaze held Luke's for a moment, her unspoken question answered by his smile. *I should have known he would have stepped in to help them.* With hugs to the teens, they left the room, walking arm in arm down the hall.

"So did you orchestrate that?" she asked, twisting her head around to peer at him.

"Let's just say that I put the feelers out to Cam, who already had the same idea. One call to his parents, and another to Miriam's, and they took it from there."

Squeezing his waist, her smile spoke volumes. "So, what's next?"

"We need to debrief at Jack's and then…we'll figure it out from there."

She wanted to ask what that meant but uncertainty held her back. *I'm safe now…so do I go back to my life before Eli's death?* Wanting to see Luke's expression as they drove back to Charlestown, she kept her gaze on the passing scenery instead. Closing her eyes for a moment, she knew that no matter what happened at Jack's debriefing, she could never return to that lonely existence. *Not after discovering what life can hold.*

THE SAINTS SAT at the conference table, their tablets in front of them and Nick on the videoconference screen. Luke's gaze continually shot sideways toward Charlie, unable to discern her thoughts. All the way back from the hospital, he wondered how she felt now that the danger had passed. *Would she want to keep working for Jack? Would she want to continue staying with him? And why the hell am I too scared to just ask?* Forcing his mind to focus on Nick, he looked up toward the screen.

"So, the investigation is just beginning but, combining Lin, Charlie, and the Saints' information, here is what we know so far. Yeng Chow is part of the Chinese mafia who have their fingers in numerous activities in the US, including the Chow Medical facility in California. The research they did there required a constant supply of organs and they had a long list of clients ready and willing to pay top dollar to be moved to the head of the organ transplant list. We have a lot to go back and check on, but my guess is Hai Zhao uncovered something and probably refused to toe the line for the Chinese mafia, so he was eliminated."

Nick hesitated momentarily, adding, "Sorry, Charlie. I know he was your friend."

She smiled gratefully toward the camera and nodded. "Thank you, but please go on. You don't have to worry about upsetting me. I think at this point I need to know the truth."

Unable to help himself, Luke reached out, taking

her hand in his and giving it a gentle squeeze.

Nick continued, "We don't know if it was coincidence or if Hai sent Eli any information. All we know right now is that Eli began working on their database software also and farmed some of it to Charlie. That's when the trail was discovered for how they were obtaining some of their organs in the U.S."

"So, pulling in runaways and homeless persons, the Chinese mafia were able to not only harvest organs when needed, but to also feed their human trafficking organization," Jack surmised.

"Like killing two birds with one stone," Bart stated, then winced as he quickly added, "No pun or disrespect intended toward the victims."

"How did Lin figure into it all?" Jude asked.

This time Nick was the one who grimaced as he shook his head. "She hated being too late to save Eli and continued to investigate on her own, even when her caseload became too much for her to handle. Not knowing who to trust in the agency, in case someone from the inside had Eli killed, she never included in her report that he mentioned Chow Medical—she didn't want to let on that she had made the connection before she was able to nail them. She found the connection between the company in California and Yeng Chow at the embassy. She also noted the relationship between the secretary and the medical director, Jian Cheung."

"And then I stumbled into it all," Charlie stated, drawing all eyes around the table to her.

"Well, before you did, Eli did," Luke interjected. "I found where, probably in his nervousness, Eli did not encrypt one of his messages to Lin when setting up the meeting. That error on his part probably cost him his life."

Eyes wide, Charlie looked a Luke, her heart aching for Eli and Hai. She felt the squeeze of Luke's fingers on her cold hands once more. Sucking in a deep breath, she let it out slowly.

"So, all I can tell you is that Yeng Chow blackmailed numerous doctors to provide the same services that Jian Cheung was. Jian's family was still in China and his sons' lives were threatened in order to coerce the doctor to do as he was bid. We've rounded up the clinic employees, as well as Yeng Chow, whose status of diplomatic immunity is immediately being revoked by the Chinese ambassador, who is quick to separate himself from the debacle."

Monty leaned back in his seat and added, "But I'm sure the surface has just been scratched as to this investigation. It will have long reaching implications for the United States and Chinese, but that's for the politicians to sort out after the FBI is finished with the case, and that won't be for a while."

The Saints looked to the screen as Nick, his ever-present scowl in place, appeared to struggle. Finally, he said, "You all did good work. I was resistant at first...there are rules in place for us to follow. Rules that make sure what we do and the evidence we obtain is legal." Heaving a sigh, he added, "But you got the job done. And if you ever need the FBI again, keep me in mind."

With that he signed off, leaving the Saints smiling in his wake.

"Here's to not following the fuckin' rules," Bart joked, grinning as the laughter from the other Saints joined in.

"And here's to our tech expert also being an expert leader in the field," Jack added, looking over at Luke.

"Here, here," came the resounding agreements from the others, as Luke smiled.

Shaking his head, he said, "Thank you for the opportunity. I discovered quite a bit about myself on this assignment."

"And here's to our newest Saint," Jack proclaimed, nodding toward Charlie, who visibly startled at his words.

Stunned by the cheers from the others, she glanced over to Luke quickly, sucking in her lips as she saw his huge smile.

"Welcome aboard, Charlie," he said, squeezing her fingers once more.

She looked around the table before her gaze landed on Jack. "I didn't know if you would want me to continue."

"The job is yours if you want it," Jack said. "Luke needs help with all of our cyber-investigating and I'd like him out in the field more anyway. Plus, it seems you have a real knack for getting into our system...I'd like to make sure you can keep others out."

"Is this okay, Luke?" she whispered.

Looking over, he realized she needed his assurance and he sure as hell could not give it to the best of his ability with an audience. Pushing his seat back, he pulled her gently from her chair and said, "Gentlemen, we'll be back."

Leading her up the stairs and into the garage, he ignored her quizzical look as he walked over to the ATVs. Fastening a helmet on her head, he nodded for her to join him. "Come on, sweetheart. Take a chance."

Swinging her leg over the vehicle, she held on tightly as they raced up the mountain, taking the same path as before. Once at the overlook, they climbed off and tossed the helmets to the ground. Luke led her to the large, flat rock overlooking Jack's property with the setting sun moving across the sky.

"Why are we here?" Charlie asked, uncertain of Luke's intentions.

Settling her down, he stretched his long legs beside hers and lifted his hand to cup her cheek. "Charlie, all the way back from D.C. I wanted to let you know how much I wanted you to stay here. With me...working for Jack. But I needed to know it was what you wanted." He placed his thumb over her lips as she was beginning to speak, adding, "But I realized that what I need to do is to let you know how I feel. I've fallen in love with you. I've discovered that you are my other half and the idea of you returning to your life, before all of this, fills me with fear."

She smiled, her hazel eyes holding his dark ones. "I don't want to go back to that life, Luke. I've discovered that I'm better with friends...stronger with people...and better with you. I love you too."

Leaning forward, he kissed her, his lips moving softly over hers. A kiss of forever.

CHAPTER 33

EPILOGUE
(SIXTEEN MONTHS LATER)

CHARLIE AND LUKE sat with David, all three clapping and whistling as Penny walked across the stage, receiving her high school diploma. She turned her bright blue eyes and wide smile to the trio sitting near the front of the parents' section.

As the graduates were finally released, she rushed over to them, receiving hugs of congratulations. David mimicked Luke's position, placing his arm around Penny just as Charlie was tucked next to Luke.

"I'm so glad you came," Penny said. "The Delaros are throwing me a party. Will you come?"

"Of course," Charlie replied, her warm smile matching the new grad's.

An hour later, Charlie stepped out of Miriam's parents' back door, surveying the scene in front of her. The backyard was filled with people. All of the Saints were there, including their wives and fiancés. Glancing down at her left hand, the beautiful diamond engagement ring sparkled in the late spring sunshine. Luke had proposed last Christmas and she could not wait to become Mrs. Luke Costas. Her job with the Saints had continued and she threw herself into the world of cyber-investigating. Smiling, she remembered laughing as Luke presented her with her own St. Charles medallion, discovering he was the patron saint of learning.

Hearing screams of laughter, she watched as some of the Saints' children ran, supervised by the adults. Cam's family was there as well, having grown fond of Penny, including seeing her relationship with David mature with time.

Penny and David, sharing smiles as they moved amongst the guests, caused Charlie's eyes to close momentarily, remembering how close they came to losing them. She jumped as hands came to settle on her waist from behind.

"Hey sweetheart," Luke whispered in her ear. "Whatcha doing?"

"Just looking around," she replied, leaning her head back against his chest. "Sometimes it's still hard for me to believe."

Wrapping his arms around her body, he pulled her tighter. "What is, babe?"

"All this," she indicated, her hand sweeping out over the crowd. Twisting her head around to look into his face, she explained, "After all those years of being a loner, it's hard to believe that I have all of this. Friends, co-workers, people I trust and love."

Dropping a kiss on her nose, he inquired, "And with all of these people, is there anyone in particular you've found to love?"

Pretending to ponder his question, she giggled when he poked her in the ribs. "Yes, of course," she admitted easily. "You. You're my greatest discovery of all."

Turning her in his arms, he kissed her lips, battling the desire to carry her away somewhere private where he could show her just how he felt about her admission. Pulling back, he said, "Too many eyes are here, but tonight sweetheart...we'll discover each other all over again."

With that promise, she smiled as they turned to walk down the path to join their friends.

The next Saints Protection & Investigation book,
Surviving Love will be released May 2017.

The spin-off series, Baytown Boys Series, has begun!
Coming Home is now available.

Other books by Maryann Jordan

(all standalone books)

All of my books are stand-alone, each with their own HEA!! You can read them in any order!

Saints Protection & Investigation

(an elite group, assigned to the cases no one else wants...or can solve)

Serial Love

Healing Love

Revealing Love

Seeing Love

Honor Love

Sacrifice Love

Protecting Love

Remember Love

Alvarez Security Series

(a group of former Special Forces brothers-in-arms now working to provide security in the southern city of Richland)

Gabe

Tony

Vinny

Jobe

Love's Series

(detectives solving crimes while protecting the women they love)

Love's Taming

Love's Tempting

Love's Trusting

The Fairfield Series

(small town detectives and the women they love)

Carol's Image

Laurie's Time

Emma's Home

Fireworks Over Fairfield

I love to hear from readers, so please email me!

Email

authormaryannjordan@gmail.com

Website

www.maryannjordanauthor.com

Facebook

facebook.com/authormaryannjordan

Twitter

@authorMAJordan

MORE ABOUT MARYANN JORDAN

As an Amazon Best Selling Author, I have always been an avid reader. I joke that I "cut my romance teeth" on the historical romance books from the 1970's. In 2013 I started a blog to showcase wonderful writers. In 2014, I finally gave in to the characters in my head pleading for their story to be told. Thus, Emma's Home was created.

My first novel, Emma's Home became an Amazon Best Seller in 3 categories within the first month of publishing. Its success was followed by the rest of the Fairfield Series and then led into the Love's Series. From there I have continued with the romantic suspense Alvarez Security Series and now the Saints Protection & Investigation Series, all bestsellers.

My books are filled with sweet romance and hot sex; mystery, suspense, real life characters and situations. My heroes are alphas, take charge men who love the strong, independent women they fall in love with.

I worked as a counselor in a high school and have been involved in education for the past 30 years. I recently retired and now can spend more time devoted to my writing.

I have been married to a wonderfully patient man for 34 years and have 2 adult very supportive daughters and 1 grandson.

When writing, my dog or one of my cats will usually be found in my lap!

Made in the USA
Middletown, DE
01 March 2020